THE PERFECT FACE

A Psychological Thriller

C.G. TWILES

Chapter One

RUBY

*M*om says when she was pregnant with me, she prayed every single day for one thing: For God to make me beautiful.

Where Mom and I come from, smarts or being talented may or may not get you anywhere. But a beautiful girl can do anything, go anywhere, and be anyone. That's what my mom says anyway. So, she wasn't too surprised when the first thing someone (a nurse at the hospital) said about me was "What a beautiful baby."

After that, it got routine. Mom said when she took me out in the stroller, she could hardly walk ten feet before someone (always a woman) would stop her and say, "That's the most beautiful baby." But Mom didn't have the money to move to a place like New York or Chicago, where beautiful babies can earn money modeling. She took pictures of me and sent them to agencies but never heard back.

She tried to save up money so we could move to a place like that but she says when she told my father her plans (he didn't have much to do with us but lived only one town away), he threatened to bring her to court if she left the state. So, she tried other ways of getting me attention.

When I was about seven, she made a social media account for me and it started to get a lot of followers but Mom couldn't figure out how to make money off it, though I did get a few free t-shirts and things. Then Dad said being online would make perverts want to kidnap me, so she took it down, because Dad could be mean and she was scared of him.

So, we were stuck here, in this dead-end town.

When I was 11, my dad died in a car accident. It was really sad because when we were together, he was nice to me, and I wish I'd gotten to know him better. But also it probably wasn't as sad as it would be for someone who saw their father more than a few times a year.

Feeling like she was finally free to get me noticed, Mom started to pray again. "God," she said, "when I asked for a beautiful baby, you were nice enough to give me my Ruby (my name is Karolina Ruby, but my mom only ever calls me Ruby, because she says I shine like a ruby). I hate to come to you again so soon. But my baby is almost grown up and these looks from heaven you gave her aren't doing much for us. I'm still bartending, serving drunks all day, fighting off scum.

Ruby gets complimented all the time, but compliments don't pay the rent. And I want to do more than pay rent. I want to buy us a nice house, a car that doesn't break down all the time, and have money so

Ruby can go to a good college one day and get out of here forever.

Please God, send us a way for Ruby to be seen by the world. Why would you make such a gorgeous piece of art no one can see? At least no one who's important?"

A couple of weeks later, Mom's friend sent her an ad she'd seen online. "Looking for The Perfect Face," it said. The winner was promised a modeling contract with an agency it didn't name.

There were categories for girls, teens, and adults. I had just turned 12, so I'd enter the 10-12 category, which was the youngest one.

My mom brought me out to a field where wild flowers were blooming because it was spring, and took a ton of photos. She made me change outfits tons of times. She put a dab of pink lip gloss on me, but that was it, because she wanted me to look natural and like my own age. Mom had done these little photoshoots before, so I kind of knew what I was doing.

I skipped in the field. I held flowers to my face. I climbed trees. I could look all girlish or I could look more adult. I could be carefree or look like I'm thinking deep thoughts. And I liked being in front of the camera. It felt like my friend.

Despite taking hundreds, maybe thousands, of pictures that day, the one Mom chose to send to the contest was the very last one of the day. It was late after-noon, and I was tired and hungry. We must have been there six hours, easy. She said, "Okay, Ruby, we got enough. Let's go get something to eat at Maxie's." I kind of looked at her and smiled a little because I was thinking of a big, juicy hamburger with lots of pickles and a side order of curly fries and a chocolate shake.

Right then, her finger hit the shutter and snapped a picture of me. I wasn't even trying to pose. It was only me thinking of food. That's the photo she picked to send into the contest.

A week later, she got a call. Out of thousands of girls my age, I'd been chosen to fly to New York. There, I was put into a room with more girls my age. All of them were so pretty. I'd always felt like the prettiest girl anywhere I went, but not now. One by one, we were called into another room, where a woman took more pictures. Me and Mom were put up at a really fancy, old-fashioned hotel for another week.

Then we got another call.

I'd won "The Perfect Face" contest for my age group!

I'd thought my mom would be so happy. This was everything she ever wanted for me. I'd probably be on the covers of all the glamor magazines. I'd wear fashionable clothes on the runways, travel to places like Paris and Milan, places I'd heard about. And Mom would get to come with me because I was too young to travel alone.

But instead of jumping up and down, she grew very quiet. For the next few days, she seemed distracted and uncertain. I kept asking her what was wrong, what was happening, where did we go next, but she wouldn't tell me anything. It was really frustrating and confusing.

"Please, Mom," I said. "I want to be a famous model. I want us to be rich. Why aren't you happy?"

"Honey, you don't understand," she said, quietly. "This isn't exactly what I thought it was."

She told me how we would be flown to a special island. A man owned the island, and he was very, very rich. Richer than we could even imagine. And this man knew everyone—movie stars, scientists, billionaires, even presidents. There, Mom would be given enough money that we wouldn't ever have to worry about money ever again. She'd also have to sign some papers saying she would never, ever say where she had been, or what she had seen or heard. And that went for me, too. If we *did* ever say anything to anyone, we'd be in a lot of trouble. *A lot* of trouble.

"Who's the man?" I asked her. "Does he own the modeling agency? Why can't we say we met him?"

Her eyes grew distant and she didn't answer me.

Later, a man and woman I'd never seen before came to the hotel. They were dressed really fancy. They ordered a huge ice cream sundae for me, which was delivered on a silver tray by another man in an outfit, and then the dressed-up man and woman brought my mom to the other room in our suite. I could hear them talking through the thick wooden door but couldn't tell what they were saying.

Soon after they left, my mom sat down next to me on the big, white, super comfy king-sized bed. She looked more relaxed than she had the past few days. More like herself.

"Ruby," she said, "this is our chance. We're going to have enough money that we can buy a nice house on the beach, like we've always wanted. And we'd have enough that I could quit the bar and look for something better. And I've been told that your education will be paid for. We could send you to a good private school, and then a good college if you get the grades."

"That's amazing!" I squealed.

But then she grew kind of—well, I don't know the word for it. It's a big word. All I can say is my mom gets that look when she comes home from work and she's bone-tired, and smells nasty like stale beer, and some dumb guy at the bar gave her a hard time. It's a look I dread seeing on her, because it makes me feel so sad. Like I would do anything to erase that look and make her smile.

"So then what's wrong, Mom?"

That's when she held my hand. She squeezed it tight and said, "If we go to the man's island, it will change our lives. But, baby,"—she sucked in her breath and looked right into my eyes—"you're going to have to be very brave."

The way she said it made my chest start to shake, like there were tears inside trying to not come out. Because I wanted that house on the beach and to go to a better school. And I really, really wanted, more than anything, for Mom to quit the bar.

"I can be brave," I said, though I didn't feel brave right then.

"And you're going to have to be quiet. Very quiet about something you might want to talk about."

I felt my lower lip start to shake, because Mom always said that I should speak up if I felt something was wrong. If she wanted me to keep some kind of big secret, then it couldn't be wrong. But my stomach felt like it was.

"But why be quiet?" I asked.

"Because this man is very powerful. He can help us. But he can also hurt us." She put her hand under my chin. "We can't tell anyone what will happen on his island."

"Will it be bad? What is it?" Mom was really starting to scare me.

"Honey," she said. "Ruby…"

She stared out the window for what seemed a long time. Then she finally looked back at me.

And she told me.

Chapter Two

$\mathcal{T}$he young girl across from Maddie made eye contact with her. She was a stunningly beautiful young lady—long colt legs, thick wheat-colored hair down to her waist, and even from across the aisle, Maddie could tell the girl had green eyes—a dark forest green. The girl looked 13, maybe 14. Maddie felt sorry for the girl. She must already be getting hassled by lecherous full-grown men, gossiped about by jealous girls.

The woman sitting next to the girl was clearly not doing well at all. Poised at the woman's mouth was one of the paper bags the ferry workers had handed out and her face was contorted and pallid. You hear about faces that turn green with nausea. Of course, that's fiction. Sort of. She *did* look green.

Maddie couldn't blame her. Her own sick bag was tight in her fist, in case she needed it. Her stomach was a strong one, she'd never been seasick before, but she'd never been in waters this relentlessly heaving before. Up, down, up, down, up, down, with barely a second between. Not side to side. Straight up and down.

Each plummet back down from the tip of a wave sent her stomach catapulting upwards, the feeling you'd get when your side of the ferris wheel drops. It's not like it was even stormy out. The skies were blue and sunny, not a drop of rain to be had. Just the way the Aegean could be. History would tell you it had swallowed up countless ships and sailors. Hopefully, today it wouldn't swallow up Maddie and all these tourists.

Suddenly, the woman next to the coltish young girl bolted forward, staggering towards the bathroom sign. But Maddie knew she wasn't going to make it. Why bother with that when everyone was puking right out here in the open? The woman crouched on her knees, the bag pressed up against her mouth.

"Mom!" the young girl cried. The woman stayed on the steel beamed floor, vomiting into the bag as the ferry swung up, down, up, down, up, down.

Maddie grasped one of the poles and managed to get closer to the woman. She didn't know if the woman spoke English, but the young girl's "Mom" had the ring of an American accent.

"Ma'am," Maddie said, thrusting out one arm. "Hold your wrist," she said, demonstrating while keeping a hold on the pole. She couldn't tell if the woman heard her. "With your thumb. Like this. Press down hard, right on the vein." She was speaking loudly because the boat was slapping so loud and hard against the waves. "It's an acupressure point. It helps."

The woman peered up from her bag, face ashen,

with an expression hanging between *Thank you* and *Go away*. She appeared somewhere in her thirties, with a scraggly, pulled-back ponytail, locks the same wheat color as the young girl's but without its sunshiny gloss.

To be honest, if the girl hadn't called the woman "Mom," Maddie would have taken her for a family friend. Other than the same hair shade, there was no resemblance. The mother was as ordinary as the girl was extraordinary.

But that was a bit unfair considering the woman was currently hugging the ferry floor, trying not to throw up again. Appearing to understand Maddie's directive, the woman grimaced, using the thumb on the hand holding the sick bag to press down on her wrist. The young girl staggered over, then fell right down by her mother.

"Woah!" Maddie called, reaching for the girl, but unable to grab hold as the boat free-fell then ricocheted up with a straight bounce off a wave. Maddie clung tighter to the pole with one arm and tried reaching out again, this time managing to grasp the girl's skinny arm. "You okay?" she said, helping her up to the plastic, bright orange bench. "You speak English?"

The girl seemed to nod but it was hard to tell with the slamming up, down, up, down motion of the boat, like it was being sling-shot between waves.

"She'll be okay," Maddie said, because the girl looked so worried. "We're almost there."

Then Maddie had to stop speaking as nausea was gathering momentum in her stomach, bile beginning to slosh around the back of her throat. She squeezed her wrist harder and stared determinedly at the pewter waves through the window on the lower deck (they'd all been ordered downstairs as the waves were slopping over the upper deck). Up, down, up, down.

She noticed most people couldn't even glance out of the windows, that seeing the waves would make them even more ill. They were desperately staring at the floor or holding their heads between their knees.

But not Maddie. If she watched the waves, it helped keep the bile at bay, because she could imagine jumping off the ferry if it began to capsize. She'd grown up around the water and was a good swimmer. Realistically, she likely couldn't survive in waves like this, but imagining she could was enough to keep her from puking.

"How much longer?" the girl asked.

"I think about half an hour."

"Oh my God!" she cried. "Mom won't survive it."

"Sure she will. She'll be fine once she's off the boat."

The girl gave a weak, distressed smile, and Maddie stopped speaking, because that was only empowering the nausea threatening to have its way with her. She took pride in being one of the few on the boat who hadn't vomited yet. In fact, it was more the sickly stench permeating the air than the bouncing of the boat that was giving her a queasy stomach.

She noticed that the ferry workers, all young, sturdy-looking Greek men, hardly seemed aware of the choppy sea. One of them was even standing at the seating area's opening, casually smoking a cigarette.

THIRTY OR SO MINUTES LATER, easily the longest thirty minutes of Maddie's life, the boat docked and its sea-battered occupants stumbled out weak-kneed. Many immediately dropped to the dock, needing to be on the unmoving earth.

Maddie didn't want to intrude on the mother and daughter, who were slightly in front of her, holding onto each other, but she kept an eye on them. They headed to a bench, and the girl sat on it but the mother, like most others who'd disembarked, lay flat on the dock. As soon as Maddie stepped off the still undulating ferry boat, she felt fine.

"You guys okay?" she asked them.

The mother lay on her stomach, saying nothing, hands clawing at the dock.

"Can I help you at all?" Maddie pressed.

"Mmmmm," the woman groaned.

Maddie decided she better sit on the bench with the girl until the mother was better. It didn't seem right to leave the girl in charge of the situation.

"I can try to get you a taxi," Maddie said to the girl. "Bring you to your hotel."

Maddie had only been on the island, Kyrie, for a few days, but had already figured out there was a drastic shortage of taxis. There was one taxi stand and the line at it was usually an hour long. There was some sort of law on the island that you couldn't call or hail a taxi. You actually had to go to the stand and wait for one. Barbaric.

"We… we don't have a hotel," the girl said.

Maddie noticed that the girl's forest green eyes had

12

gold flecks in them. Probably the prettiest eyes she'd ever seen. Mesmerizing. What people must have felt when they looked at a young Elizabeth Taylor.

"You don't?" she asked. "Where are you staying? Or are you catching a flight out today?"

God help them if they were. Given the shape the mother was in, it didn't seem likely they were getting back on a ferry any time soon.

"N-no…" the girl said, looking hesitant. "Not, umm…"

On the ground, the mother groaned again.

"Listen," Maddie said, projecting to the mother. "I'm staying at a studio right up the street. Can you walk? You can lay down there until you feel better."

"Mom?" the girl asked, hopefully.

The mother somehow managed to push herself half up from the dock, and slowly wobbled her head. Maddie stood, and motioned for the girl to do the same.

"I'm Maddie. What's your name?"

"It's, well…" The girl dangled a long finger in her mouth. Had the rough seas affected her so badly that she'd forgotten her own name? Or was she reluctant to share it with a stranger, even a female stranger?

"Doris," the mother said from the ground. "She's Doris. I'm—"

The rest cut off as a strangled retching erupted from the woman's mouth as she vomited on the dock.

"Let's help your mother, Doris," Maddie said.

Chapter Three

*M*addie and the girl—could her name really be *Doris?*—walked to the *chora*, the center of the island, veined with a cobbled labyrinth of alleyways flanked by white-washed, blue-trimmed shops and restaurants, and draped with vibrant pink bougainvillea.

Nothing could be more beautiful than a Greek island, Maddie mused. No wonder it was the land that (mythologically) produced Aphrodite and Helen of Troy. And she was ecstatic to be away from the congealed humidity of Manhattan, where she lived. She'd smartly followed her friend Athena's suggestion that Maddie take a break from her demoralizing work situation and come to Greece for her summer vacation. The temperature must be in the 90s Fahrenheit, but it didn't feel that hot thanks to a strong, steady breeze off the water. Besides, a beach was never more than a short walk away. If you started to sweat, you simply headed for the shoreline.

After leaving the dock, Maddie and the girl had managed to stumble the mother along the few blocks to the rental, called Sideratos, where the woman promptly collapsed on Maddie's bed and crimped into the fetal position.

Maddie couldn't believe the woman was still so affected by the turbulent ferry ride back from a small abandoned island that was one of the world's most intact ancient archaeological sites. Along with a couple dozen others, Maddie had spent three hours gazing in awe at the ruins of Greco-Roman houses adorned with colorful mosaics, theaters, churches, temples, art, and ancient but sophisticated aqueduct and plumbing systems. Attention consumed, she hadn't noticed the girl and her mother.

Perhaps the mother—who eventually moaned out that her name was Stella—had some travel bug.

She felt bad for the daughter, who apparently hadn't eaten since the morning, several times braying, "Mom, I'm staaaaarving." Maddie offered to take her out to get food, and to go to a pharmacy and try to get medicine to calm Stella's stomach. Granted, it was a bit uncomfortable to offer to take charge of a random young minor but sometimes you had to shove aside feelings of discomfort when help was needed. Besides, they were all female. The odds of one of them being a serial killer were virtually nil.

Virtually.

First, she and the girl walked to a food stall inside the *chora* and ordered tiropita and spanakopita with the intent of eating while walking to their next destination

—a pharmacy. But it was closed. Now Maddie remembered from past trips to Europe that retail hours could be inconvenient—often closed all afternoon, then open until late into the night.

The girl had no money—she and her mother had stored their belongings back at the ferry terminal and the mom had been too sick to go get them—so Maddie paid for her food.

Then they sat on a bench overlooking the crystal-blue Aegean and dug into their sumptuously greasy meals. Beaches were ubiquitous but not uniform. There were red sand beaches, white "sugar" sand beaches, pebbled beaches, and lava beaches, covered with black pebbles from millions of years of lava cooling and being pummeled into bite-sized pieces. Maddie and the girl currently stared out over a shore layered with multicolored pebbles.

"How old are you, Doris?" she asked the girl.

"Twelve."

"Oh! You're so tall. I thought you were a little older."

Now it definitely seemed odd to be sitting here with a random child—for despite the long legs and Katherine Hepburn cheekbones, Doris was indeed a *child*. But these were the Greek islands. Children of all ages ran around unattended. It wasn't the United States, with its kidnapping hysteria and parental micromanaging.

Even in Athens, where Maddie had stayed for two days before flying to a nearby larger island, then taking a ferry to Kyrie, she'd seen kids, looking as young as seven or eight, free-roaming all over the city.

It seemed okay to sit here with a random child, unlike at home, where Maddie would have been crawling with vague guilt, keeping one eye out for cops or Chris Hansen.

The girl steadily munched away on her food. She wasn't very talkative.

"Are you and your mother on vacation?" Maddie probed.

"Sort of," the girl said, resting her food on her lap, staring out to the gloriously sparkling sea. Hard to believe an hour ago it had almost devoured their ferry. "We're going to visit my uncle. He lives on another island."

"Lucky him. Which island?"

The girl shrugged. "I forgot the name of it."

"Does he live there year-round?"

"Yeah." She paused, took another bite of food and chewed, staring out at the electric-blue Aegean. "He's really rich."

"Even nicer."

But Maddie's tone was flat. She knew about rich men. She'd been covering them for five years for *Wealthy* magazine. One of these rich men, she felt certain, had been responsible for disrupting her career and was indirectly the reason she was even on Kyrie. Her friend Athena was on the island, restoring her great-grandparents' house. And Maddie's job was not going well. She figured she'd better use her vacation time before she was fired.

But surely the girl's uncle wasn't the kind of rich man *Wealthy* magazine wrote about? Not *billionaire* rich.

The public perception that there were billionaires on every corner was far from reality—there were only a handful of true billionaires in the world.

The girl didn't give the impression she was familiar with that kind of private plane, private island, politicians-in-your-pockets, celebrities-in-your-bed kind of rich. She seemed too unpolished and down-to-earth. And if that kind of money *was* in the family, Doris and her mother probably would have taken a private yacht to the historical island, not that sad little ferry boat that put them through that harrowing sea trip. The uncle was likely an expat who'd retired to the much cheaper islands and was doing fine with monthly withdrawals from his retirement fund.

"So, you're on your way there?" Maddie prodded, unable to shake the reporter's habit of asking lots of questions. "That's why you don't have a hotel?"

The girl nodded. "He's supposed to get us in his boat later tonight."

Boat.

Hm. Maybe the uncle *did* have a yacht. That's what rich people called them. *Boats.* Maddie thought about asking the uncle's name—maybe she knew of him—but decided she'd grilled the girl enough. "Hopefully the sea has calmed down by then," she said.

"Mom and I got here last night, and we thought it would be fun to go on a day trip while we waited for him. But now she can't move, so who knows what will happen."

"Your uncle might have to wait until she's better. You guys can get a hotel tonight."

"Yeah," she sighed. "I guess."

Maddie didn't hang around young people. She had no nieces or nephews. At 32, she had no children. A pregnancy at 30 had led to an engagement with her long-term boyfriend, but at ten weeks, the pregnancy had ended in a miscarriage. The miscarriage had resulted in thousands of dollars in medical bills thanks to crappy insurance and what seemed like dozens of appointments with her gynecologist to continually check her hormone levels, and then a dilation and curettage when the fetus didn't pass on its own.

Her boyfriend, Jesse, whom she'd known since she moved to the city in her mid-20s, had agreed to split the bills, then haggled over every dime. The miscarriage had been painful not only emotionally but physically, and she was in no mood for quibbling over medical bills, especially when Jesse made ten times the money she did.

She'd always known he was cheap—it was his worst quality—but this was an abhorrently insensitive side to him she'd never imagined. So, she'd broken up with him, and he immediately moved on to one of his coworkers—possibly the source of his insensitivity. Perhaps he'd already had something going on with her.

Only one of Maddie's friends had a child—but the child was a toddler. The typical behavior of a 12-year-old was simply out of her range of familiarity. Doris' lack of enthusiasm for her uncle's island was likely a preteen thing. Maddie vaguely remembered, at that age, being unimpressed with everything, too.

"Doris is an interesting name," she continued, driven to keep trying to connect with the girl. "Kind of old-fashioned. Those old-timey names are really making a comeback."

The girl stuck her tongue out. "Stupid name. You can call me Ruby. But don't call me that in front of Mom."

"Is that, uh, the name you'd rather have?" Maddie asked, at the same time wondering, *Why not call you that in front of your mother?*

"Doris is a—never mind." The girl brushed some crumbs off her cut-offs, then wrapped the longest clump of strings on the frayed hem around two fingers. "Just call me Doris. It's my real name. My nickname is Ruby but Mom wants people to call me by my real name."

"Oh." Pause. "Okay." Kind of an odd decision for a mother to make for a girl who was old enough to decide for herself what she wants to be called.

"You want to hear a name story?" she went on. "Maddie is short for Madison, which my mother named me because she loves the movie *Splash*." At the girl's utterly blank expression, Maddie plowed on: "You're probably too young to know that movie but it was popular in the eighties."

Another dead-blank look.

"I guess I'm lucky she didn't name me Daryl after the actress who played Madison," she continued, expecting another blank canvas. Instead, the girl said, "Daryl. I like that name."

Leaving some remnants of food for a few stray cats who sat nearby, staring regally and hungrily, the pair tossed their greasy paper wrappings into the nearest trash can and went to see if they could find an open pharmacy. They couldn't. Not knowing if Stella would be able to stomach any food, Maddie bought her a sports drink at an outdoor stall.

Then she and Doris wound their way back through the narrow maze of the *chora*. There were other strolling tourists, but not too many. Kyrie wasn't easily accessible by Athens or Thessaloniki, requiring either a plane ride and another hours-long ferry ride, or an overnight ferry trip. Plus, it was July. Most tourists, the majority of them coming from Britain, wouldn't arrive until August.

"Have you visited your uncle on the island before?" Maddie asked the girl, more to break the silence.

"Not really."

Is that a yes or no? Maddie wondered, having the sudden urge to ask the girl if she'd even *met* her uncle before.

"Well, I hope you have a good time."

The girl said nothing, staring down at her open-toed flat sandals as the pair made their way back to the studio apartment.

Maddie now had the distinct impression that the girl, for whatever reason, did not wish to move on to her uncle's island. Perhaps there was some family dynamic happening that was distressing for her. But maybe she had a naturally sullen or insular personality.

Still, there was an urge to check in, to look out for her, though Maddie had no idea how to do it without overstepping boundaries. But given that she'd likely never see the girl or her mother again, she figured there was no harm in being more nosy.

"Is that a place you want to go?" she asked, uncertain how to articulate the vaguely dark intuition creeping up on her. "I mean... you seem kind of..." The words evaporated in the air. She was stuck in that discomfiting space between wanting to get involved and wanting to be respectful. To, essentially, mind her own business. "I guess I want to make sure you're okay."

The girl stopped and stared at her, genuinely puzzled. "Okay? What do you mean?"

Now Maddie felt overreaching and pushy. She'd lived in a city too long. Worked in journalism too long. Not everything was a plot or conspiracy. Sometimes preteens were moody. She certainly had been at that age.

"About going to see your uncle." Each word felt like she was digging herself deeper into an awkward hole. "Like maybe you..." She trailed off, pretending the turquoise and silver jewelry laid out in the window of a little shop they passed had drawn her eye.

"I'm just nervous," Doris said, pulling out her hairband and rapidly redoing her ponytail. Her hair was so long and thick, it must be like a carpet on her back in this heat. But other than during the tortuous ferry ride, the girl always seemed poised and graceful. "See, he's going to pay for a private school. I kind of have to impress him. So he knows he's not wasting his money."

"Gotcha."

So much for the theory that the uncle was an eking-it-out retiree. He obviously had a plump bank account if he was going to pick up the tab for private school.

Maddie couldn't shake the feeling that something was off but decided to drop it. She'd been a journalist for many years and poking around in other people's business was her job, but she was on vacation. *And* she should be worrying about her *own* life, not that of a random preteen who was traveling with her mother and for all appearances seemed perfectly fine.

Chapter Four

*B*ack at the rental apartment, Stella was sitting up on the bed, looking much better, though still a bit peaked. Maddie handed her the drink, and Stella took a succession of careful but eager sips.

"Thanks so much," she sighed, closing her eyes. "I can't believe how sick that ride made me."

"I tried to get you some medicine but the pharmacies are closed right now. I'm sure they'll be open in a couple hours."

Stella looked at her watch. "Oh, we have to be gone by then. It's fine, I'll pick up something later. We need to get back to the ferry terminal and get our belongings." She looked up at Doris/Ruby. "You okay, hon?"

"I'm fine."

"You eat?"

"Yeah, Maddie bought me some Greek food."

"Oh God," Stella groaned, putting her hand to her head. "I'm so sorry. I can't pay you back. I've got nothing on me."

Maddie wondered why Stella didn't suggest walking to the ferry terminal together so Stella could retrieve her wallet but Maddie's ex-boyfriend's stinginess was still lodged in her mind as an abhorrent quality, so she said, "Really, it's no problem. My pleasure. The food here is so inexpensive anyway."

"Thank you," Stella said, attempting to smile.

Maddie wondered how the pair were going to make it to the uncle's boat—the mother still appeared as if she could barely move. Then the bottle of water Maddie had consumed during lunch started to weigh on her bladder. She'd always had a weak bladder, but after her short pregnancy, it seemed to have gotten a lot weaker, though she didn't know why that would be the case. But a bottle of water would take ten minutes, tops, to work its way out of her system.

"Do you think you're okay now?" Maddie asked. "You could probably get a room here for the night. It's a nice place, only seventy euros a night. Not too many people here yet."

"Oh no," Stella said, setting the sports drink on the bedside table, and shakily rising. "We should get going. We've got to get our things, then meet my cousin down at the dock. Though it makes me sick again thinking about getting back on that water."

"I get it," Maddie said, though her mind was reeling off in several directions. Hadn't Doris said they were meeting her *uncle*? She glanced at the girl, and unless it was her imagination, the girl's normally placidly blank expression betrayed an undercurrent of panic. She was staring intensely at her mother, hazel eyes wide.

The thought zipped through Maddie's mind: *They're lying.*

The intuition that had been honed over years of reporting—the one that told Maddie when something was off-kilter—was jangling insistently. The pair were on their way somewhere alright, but it had nothing to do with an uncle or cousin.

Stella approached, hand outstretched. Maddie shook it, the pangs in her bladder sharpening.

"Thank you so much for everything," Stella said. "I don't know what I would have done without you. Probably still be lying on that dock."

"Hey, listen," Maddie said. "Why don't I walk you guys to the terminal? Make sure you're alright."

"Oh no. We've inconvenienced you enough. We really should get going."

"To your cousin?" Maddie blurted. "I'd thought Doris said her uncle."

Stella's face seemed to freeze for a second, and Maddie caught that same look of momentary panic in the mother's eyes that had appeared in the daughter's. But then her expression smoothly transitioned back to equanimity. "He's my cousin. But Doris has always called him uncle."

"Ah."

Maddie glanced again at Doris. The girl was staring at her mother, and then her gold-flecked eyes roamed over to lock with Maddie's. The look in them made Maddie's breath catch in her chest. She could swear she saw fear in those young eyes.

"Listen, stay here," Maddie said, her voice tinged

with alarm. "I've got to head back into the *chora* anyway, to find my friend. I can walk you out."

"Oh no, it's—"

"*Please.* But hold on one minute, I really need the bathroom. Be right back!"

She dashed off, shut the bathroom door, and sat on the toilet. Her heart was beating rapidly. Did she really detect fear in Doris' hazel-jeweled eyes? Or was Maddie making things up in her head? If the girl was frightened of something, she could have said so when they were alone, couldn't she? As Maddie unspooled the toilet paper, an ominous thought began to creep into the back of her mind.

Could that woman not really be the girl's mother?

Doris. Then Ruby.

Uncle. Then cousin.

The girl's sullenness and apparent reluctance to travel to the other island.

The fact that the girl "couldn't remember" the island's name. Surely, she and her mother must have discussed the island extensively if they were on their way there.

Not really.

Who says "not really" about whether or not she'd ever been to that island before? It's a simple yes or no question.

Maddie quickly stood and flushed, threw her hands under the tap for two seconds and swung open the door without drying them.

The pair were gone.

Chapter Five

*M*addie sped out the door, leaving it open, as she remembered that it locked automatically upon closing, and she didn't feel she had time to grab her backpack, which had her apartment key tucked in a pocket.

There was a small hill that led to the main road, and on that road, she looked each way, but didn't see the pair. They couldn't be far, but she didn't know which way they would have turned. If she chose wrong, she'd never catch up. The main road also had many smaller roads and alleyways that bled into it, and the pair could have veered into any one of them.

Still, they must be headed for the ferry terminal to retrieve their belongings, and then the port, to meet the mysterious uncle and/or cousin who was going to bring them to his island. Maddie quickly walked back to her apartment, found her backpack, and was halfway across the room, when she stopped, staring at the open door.

Bright sunshine still poured in, despite it being almost six o'clock.

What was she supposed to say or do if she found them? Was she supposed to ask Stella to prove she was Doris' mother? Was she supposed to interrogate them as to exactly where they were going and what they were doing?

There must be police on the island—but what was she supposed to say to them either? That she'd met a mother and daughter and they were on their way to another island but the girl had said they were meeting her uncle, and the mother had said it was her cousin? That the girl wanted to be called Ruby, but for some reason, the mother was calling her Doris?

None of it made a lick of sense and she'd be lucky if police didn't turn around and arrest her for harassing tourists. The last thing she needed was drawing negative attention from law enforcement in a foreign country.

"What are you doing, Maddie?" she said aloud to herself, holding her head with one hand as if she couldn't believe her own behavior. Then she walked to the door and shut it.

A COUPLE HOURS LATER, she met her friend, Athena, at a taverna that was nearly empty. They sat outside at a table covered with blue and white checkered cloth. For Greece, it was early to eat dinner, but Maddie hadn't adjusted to the usual island dinner time for locals as well as tourists—10 p.m. or even later.

She didn't need to look at the menu, as she wanted exactly what she'd had the night before—the tomato stuffed with rice and cabbage. Athena, a former work colleague, had relocated to the island over the winter after learning that she was entitled to reclaim her great-grandparents' abandoned house and could fix it up with a grant bestowed on those who could prove island ancestry.

Athena had told her the house had a breathtaking view of the Aegean but was a complete disaster. For months, she'd been having it stripped down to the studs and everything built back up again—plumbing, electricity, flooring, roof, walls, everything. Meanwhile, Athena was staying with a distant relative who didn't speak English and she was working on improving her extremely rusty Greek.

While at *Wealthy*, Athena had always worn dark purple lipstick and heavy eyeliner, her hair pulled tightly back. On Kyrie, she was almost unrecognizable— makeup free, hair untamed and free-blowing. She'd lost that pinched *I'm a New Yorker so get out of my way* look, the muscles in her face soft and relaxed. As if she'd turned the clock back to her twenties.

The difference in her friend's appearance was so pronounced that Maddie realized she must look as tightly-strung as Athena used to. Maddie had also started to notice the signs of aging, and had even been considering getting a shot of Botox on her forehead. But who needed that when one could apparently move to a Greek island and have the signs of age and stress erased?

The two had met at *Wealthy* and became instant friends. But Athena, like Maddie, had found herself shunted to the side at the magazine. Promotions tended to go to the men. Athena had been hankering for a change. Her heritage was calling, and she looked into traveling and studying in Greece. Burrowing into her family's history, she'd discovered the house her grandmother (whom she was named after) had been raised in before she emigrated to the States was still on Kyrie. More research led to The Repatriation Project, one way that the island, which had fallen on hard times, was using to lure new residents.

While inheriting a Greek island home sounded like a dream come true, it was actually a risk, Athena had explained. The island sat on an active fault line and suffered frequent earthquakes. Most weren't that bad— but a few were, including one that had hit eight years ago, destroying huge swaths of the island. The hills had also seen so many wildfires that they were brown and singed bare of vegetation.

Add in the Greek economic crisis, which had sent streams of human capital fleeing to Europe for better paying jobs, and the island was in serious trouble. Not even its pristine beaches, medieval villages, glorious white-washed churches, and awe-inspiring monasteries were enough to overcome its lack of an airport or a port that could accommodate the gargantuan cruise ships.

Once known as the jewel of the Aegean—even supposedly the richest place on the planet for a brief spell, thanks to a tree resin unique to the island that was used to make everything from liqueur to face cream—it was now faded and struggling.

The waitress appeared with two small carafes of house white wine—in Greece, if you ordered a "glass" of white wine, you got a carafe. The locally-made wine was very good—light and crisp and, Maddie noticed, didn't cause hangovers. After a bit of small talk and drinking, Maddie told her friend the story of Stella and Doris, and her suspicion that the pair were lying about where they were going and what they were doing, and how she'd almost scurried to the ferry terminal to find them.

"Why would they do that?" Athena asked, firing up one of the "light" cigarettes sold on the island—they were white and basically tasted like inhaling air. Athena said she allowed herself one per day as a "reward" for dealing with the endless battle of getting workers to show up on time and do the work they were being paid to do rather than to lounge around smoking and gossiping. This being a smallish island, it's not like she could just fire them and hire another crew. Besides, she figured the other crew would do the same thing.

"I don't know," Maddie replied. "But the whole thing was really odd. I swear that right before they disappeared, the girl looked scared. I mean, what if…"

"What if what?" Athena asked, blowing a stream of smoke off to the side. With her heavy brows, shoulder-length, slightly coarse black hair, and dark-brown eyes, Athena appeared quintessentially Greek, though she only got that from her father's side. The rest of her was a mishmash of German, Irish, and French.

Both she and Maddie had done ancestry testing last year. Maddie's DNA contained all the countries she had been expecting—primarily England, Scotland, and Wales, and, from her father's side, Portugal, but entwined were surprisingly large strands of North Africa, Italy, and Sicily. Hence, she supposed, why she'd always managed a perfect tan.

"Well, what if… the girl is being taken somewhere… against her will?"

Athena's eyes widened as the waitress reappeared with their food. Maddie's greasy stuffed tomato was gigantic and looked as sumptuous as it had last night. Between that, the wine, the side order of French fries, and the dessert she would beg the waitress not to bring but that would appear anyway (dessert was usually on the house in Greece, and the servers didn't acknowledge the words "please don't bring dessert"), she vowed to get some serious swimming and hiking done tomorrow.

"Come on, are you serious?" Athena gaped. "Like being trafficked or something?"

"I don't know. I'm only saying, the whole thing is odd. First, her name is Doris. Then Ruby. They're going to see the girl's uncle. Then no, wait, it's the mother's cousin."

"You're jumping to the worst possible conclusion." Athena shook her head and stabbed her fork into her eggplant moussaka. "Maybe they're just drug runners."

"A 12-year-old girl? And now that I think about it, isn't Doris the girl's name in *Lolita*?"

"Dolores. I studied American lit in college, remember. Are they American?"

"So far as I can tell from the accent."

Athena stubbed out her cigarette, her gaze roving over Maddie's shoulder. "Elias!" She held up her arm. "There's one of my contractors," she said, waving. "The only one who shows up on time."

Maddie casually turned, still chewing, and saw a dark-haired man weave through a small thicket of people and head towards their table. Maddie's food caught in her throat and for a moment she thought she was about to choke.

The man was beautiful. Like a God (a Greek God if you want to be specific) coming out of the mist. Tall, lanky, jet-black hair and chiseled features. When he got right up to their table, she noticed his eyes were an exquisite blue; they radiated against his tanned face as electric as the Aegean itself.

Trying to swallow, Maddie thought how typical it was that Athena would neglect to mention she had a knee-weakeningly hot contractor. If Maddie had thought there was the slightest chance of running into a man who looked like this tonight, she would have put on a flirty sundress and at least dabbed on some mascara. Instead, she was caught with a mouth stuffed with cabbage and tomato, a t-shirt and cut-offs, and a makeup free-face that was probably glistening with sweat.

A couple of years ago, during one of their after-work drinking sessions, Athena had told Maddie she was "tired of it all." She wouldn't be dating anymore. She wouldn't be pretending to look for "the one," because there was no "one." She didn't care if she went without sex. In fact, she preferred it. Yes, she wouldn't mind a partner—someone to go to the movies with, someone to run errands for her if she got sick, someone to share her life with. But it wasn't worth the horror show that was dating in New York. After doing some research, she'd decided she was asexual. She simply didn't relate to men —or women—in that way, and she was tired of acting like she did.

"Damn, you are so lucky," Maddie had blurted. She was still stinging from her miscarriage and breakup with Jesse. Not having any desire to fuse with the opposite sex sounded like nirvana to her.

Back to the scrumptious piece of man-meat standing at their table. "*Kalispera*, Ath-eee-naa," he said, kissing her on both cheeks. His voice was slow and velvety. He looked down at Maddie and she began nervously chewing the inside of her cheek.

"This is Maddie," Athena said.

"*Kalispera*, Maaah-deeee," he said, bending to kiss her cheeks as well. Then he pulled up a nearby chair to their small table. He was wearing black shorts and a white shirt rolled up to his elbows, unbuttoned to his chest. Maddie made a concentrated effort not to stare at the tanned flesh she was sure was smooth as silk.

Athena explained that she and Maddie had worked together and Maddie was visiting from New York.

"Nyew Yooorrrk," he drawled, twinkling his light blue eyes at her. "Some my family go live to Nyew Yooorrrk. Long time ago. I need visit."

He smiled at her in that direct, flirtatious way she'd noticed from the men since her arrival. It contrasted sharply with the cloak of invisibility she had on in New York—invisible to the point where men routinely shut doors in her face. Since turning thirty, she could have probably walked into a jewelry store and scooped up all the diamonds without being noticed.

"You should definitely visit," she said, her voice coming out a couple octaves above normal, making her sound embarrassingly girlish.

"So Elias," Athena said, shoveling another forkful of food into her mouth. Maddie again thought how freeing it must be to not be crippled with the desire to impress the second an attractive man came around. "You know everything that happens on the island. Maddie met a young girl and her mother today and..." She waved absently in Maddie's direction, switching to her wine. "Go on, tell him."

Elias turned his aquamarine orbs on her. Her whole body lit up with tingles. Embarrassing.

"Well, um... I met this mother and daughter... supposedly mother and daughter... on the ferry coming back from Nalos... worst ferry ride *ever*, by the way, and..."

She realized that she had nothing interesting to say about them. Nothing they'd said or done was *that* unusual or disturbing; at least, not enough for a compelling story. "I don't know. I'm a bit worried about the girl." She shrugged. "I think living in a city too long has made me paranoid."

She laughed, uneasily. The man lived on an island paradise where he'd probably known everyone since his childhood. He couldn't possibly understand the bombardment of gory news stories one is subjected to while living in the city, and how, even if nothing violent had ever happened to you personally—and fortunately it never had to Maddie—this could make you walk around in a low-grade state of anxiety.

"What about the girl?" he asked, probing her with his electrifying eyes. Maddie tried to stop herself from staring at his mouth, which was lush and slightly sloping.

"It's just that… she's only 12. But she looked older, maybe 14 or 15. Tall, beautiful features, could easily be a model. She said she was headed to another island to visit her uncle. But she didn't seem excited about it at all."

"Hmmm…" he said, putting one hand up to his sensuous mouth and looking pensive. He ordered a glass of wine from the waitress as she passed. Then, to Maddie, "Continue."

"Her mother told me her name was Doris, but the girl told me she hated that name and to call her Ruby. And she said they were going to another island to visit her uncle, but the mother said it was her cousin. Like they couldn't keep their stories straight."

She took a sip of wine, wondering if he understood all of her tale and the slang like "stories straight." Most people she'd met on the island spoke fluent English, given the language's status as international *lingua franca*. Athena said Greeks were required to learn English in school, and most of the island's tourism came from Britain.

"I asked them to wait for me so I could walk them to

the ferry," Maddie continued, "but they disappeared while I was... um, doing something."

The man sat silent, the back of his hand still brushing along his extremely kissable mouth. Maddie noticed that the tip of his nose had a very slight roundness to it and she imagined leaning over and gently taking the bulb between her teeth. Yikes. She hoped that cringey thought hadn't migrated to her face.

When the waitress brought his wine, he took a couple of sips, then said, "Did they tell you the name of this island? Which one?"

"No. The girl said she couldn't remember the name of it. Which I also thought was kind of odd if her uncle supposedly lives there."

"There are rumors..." he said in a low voice while looking behind him and, seeing no one nearby, continued in the same low tone, "rumors about the island direct south of here. Small island, Volinos. Maybe eighty acres. Bought shortly after earthquake. Now, you can't get near. Patrolled by secure boats."

"Security," Athena corrected.

"Yes, security. You get too close, they come around —" He made his hand into a simulated bullhorn. "Yell at you to leave."

"Do you know who bought it?" Maddie asked.

He slowly shook his head, and drank more wine. "No. Some say Russian. Some say American. Others even say Greek. But rich." He paused. "Very rich."

"What are the rumors?" Athena asked, her fork poised near her mouth.

"All kinds of wild parties there. With many of young

girls. They call it… how you say…" He looked at Athena and said something in Greek.

"Orgies?" she stage-whispered. "Ew!"

Elias shrugged and slouched back into his chair. "That's what they say. Man always bring the girls there for—what you say—*owr-gees*."

"How would anyone know this?" Maddie asked. "If no one can get near the island."

He tossed his palms up in a *Who knows?* gesture. "People have ways, yes?"

"Is anyone there besides this man?"

Elias gave a languid stretch, then leaned forward, bringing his voice down so low that the boppy bouzouki Greek music playing over the outdoor speakers nearly drowned out his words. "They say all kinds of rich men go to island. Movie stars. Political. All kinds of big men. He bring them over on his boat from here, from there, from everywhere. Island is protected."

Maddie felt sick to her stomach, remembering the look Doris—or Ruby—had given her right before she'd urgently dashed off to the bathroom. The look Maddie had interpreted as fear. Maybe the girl was a runaway who'd met up with Stella, who'd offered to "help" her. The next thing the girl knew, she was on her way to Greece. To a private island. Where no one could reach her.

"Elias," Maddie said. "If people suspect he's bringing underage girls to the island, why hasn't anyone done anything?"

"Who to say underage?" He looked a bit surprised. "Only rumor. What you want anyone would do?"

"I don't know. Can't someone go check it out?"

He shook his head, bemusedly, then purred, "You Americans."

* * *

Back at the rental studio, Maddie logged into *Wealthy* magazine's *Wealthiest in the World* database.

If anything knew about rich men, it was *Wealthy* magazine. Most of them were clamoring to get into it. Some of them, like old monied Rockefellers and Astors, were not. But if one of them had recently bought Volinos island, it could very well be noted in the database. A general Internet search had come up empty.

Typing "Volinos Greek island" into the database's search function, she got a hit. A man named Dexter Hunt. Looking through his rather short biography, there were notes at the bottom, and one read, "Bought Greek island, Volinos?? Source: J.C. Schwarzman."

Dexter Hunt, she could see, had not made it onto the list of the world's richest people, simply because the magazine's researchers couldn't verify his assets enough to confidently include him. He was one of the many men and a few women who were contenders for the list, but remained off of it.

Hunt was a hedge fund manager, and hedge fund managers were notoriously difficult to value, given that a hedge funds assets weren't public. It was fairly easy to value someone like, say, Elon Musk, as the majority of his wealth was due to a public company, Tesla. For the most part, one need only do some math—the amount of shares Musk owned (also public information) multiplied by the price of the shares. Naturally, it was a tad more complex than that, but not by much.

Dexter Hunt had been the chairman of Hunt Management for 24 years. He was 45 years old. He was divorced. He had no children.

He was in the database not only because one of the magazine's regular sources, J.C. Schwarzman (himself a money manager) suggested that he might be a good candidate for the list, but also Dexter Hunt had several times made the news as he was one of the lead investors in a private space exploration company, Dex-X. He'd already launched himself into high Earth orbit via capsule and was planning to break Apollo 13's miles-from-Earth record. A man who had enough money to spend it on adventures outside of this planet was a good candidate for being one of the richest people on it.

It was a small lead on the "rich man" who might own Volinos, where Ruby could be headed, but it was hardly definitive proof. *Wealthy* got tips all of the time and plenty of them turned out to be false. Maddie had no idea who had put the tip about Volinos into Hunt's file.

Whomever logged into the database could be identified by their name and a date stamp but individual notations couldn't be traced unless the writer added their name and this one hadn't.

Maddie shook her head. Between Elon Musk, Jeff Bezos, and Richard Branson, she had no idea why billionaires had such a preoccupation with space. Perhaps Earth had proven too easy for them to conquer.

Chapter Six

The next day, Maddie took a ferry to the island's most glorified beach—Kalaria. The remote beach was accessible only by a small boat that went twice a day. The beach was utterly pristine, thanks to being unreachable by car or scooter. It had none of the staples of some of the other "organized" beaches— costly umbrellas and beach chairs, a nearby taverna or food hut.

The ferry took about an hour to get to the beach from Kyrie's main port, right outside of the *Kastro*, then anchored. Three hours later, it would depart. If you missed it, you had to wait several hours for its next appearance. If you missed it again, you were stuck there all night.

After a swim, Maddie sat on her folded beach towel. The beach, with its white candy pebbles, was too uncomfortable for her to lay the towel flat. The glossy, iridescent water showed straight through to the white pebbles, causing glittery, silvery prongs of light to sparkle along the surface. The prettiest, most unusual water she'd ever seen.

The beach cove was protected by a perpendicular, soft-white, limestone bluff, on which she could hear baby goats bleating mournfully. Gulls and falcons swooped and cawed.

She'd walked away from the other tourists, who had made a beeline for the northern shore's most famous photo-op: a rock bridge that curved naturally over the water. The scene was stunningly picturesque, but Maddie couldn't stop ruminating on the girl and what Elias had told her about the "orgy island."

Could Maddie really have happened to run into a young girl being trafficked to a private island owned by an obscenely wealthy man? But she also knew she was piecing together vague observations into the most sinister scenario.

And she had a good idea why she'd do something like that.

It was now late afternoon as Maddie had taken the second boat, but the sun was still strong, especially as the beach contained no shade. Getting hot again, she took another swim, treading water as she stared up at the bluff, watching white and brown goats, no bigger than thimbles from her perspective, weave their way along its craggy valleys, bleating in a sad tone that made her wonder if they were lost. But they couldn't be lost. They lived there. She couldn't imagine how they managed to keep their balance and not tumble off the sheer drop.

Then she noticed a house atop the bluff, the only one she could see. It was a traditional cuboid white-washed home with blue shutters and Mediterranean style archways on a large terrace that jutted out over the limestone cliff.

As the area seemed so remote, she had no idea how the house had even been built. There must be a road somewhere on the other side.

A young woman walked along the home's bright white terrace; its wall hung with the island's ubiquitous magenta bougainvillea. Maddie's pulse jarred awake from its lazy swim. The young woman turned towards the sea. Her hair was long and rusty-blonde—wheat colored. She was pale, thin, and young.

Maddie couldn't believe her eyes. She was almost certain she was looking at Doris/Ruby. Quickly, she paddled through the water, bringing herself to the shore. White pebbles poked painfully into her bare feet and she wobbled her way to her towel making *ouch* gasps. From this angle, she could no longer see the girl or the home's terrace, only its peaked orange-tiled roof.

She spun her towel around her wet, bikini-clad body, looking for a way to get up to the house, and finally spotted what appeared to be a thin foot trail snaking up the bluff. She pulled on her cut-offs, a sleeveless t-shirt with the name of her local yoga studio on it, and her flip-flops—hardly ideal footwear for a trek up what was essentially an almost perpendicular mountain.

The sun continued to relentlessly beat down, and she dug into her backpack for her floppy hat, then jammed it over her head, her thick auburn hair in a low ponytail.

About 15 minutes later, she was almost at the top of the bluff, and she could see the white-washed house towards her right. At least thirty feet below it, Maddie stood panting and surveilling the area, but there seemed no way for her to get to the front of the house. The foot trail had disappeared into thick rock.

She cupped her hand around her mouth and called out, "Doris!" After about ten seconds, she cupped her hand again, this time calling out, "Ruby!"

Just when she thought that no one was going to appear, to her utter amazement, the girl's beautiful face peeked out over the top of the terrace. Not surprisingly, Ruby looked bewildered at hearing her name called.

"It *is* you!" Maddie yelled up, squinting her eyes against the sun. The air was blindingly bright, and the sun's rays bounced off the white of the house. She'd taken off her dark sunglasses so she could get a good look if the girl appeared, but now she retrieved them from where they were hooked on her cut-offs and replaced them on her face. "I thought I saw you from way down there on the beach!"

"You have to go away!" the girl called in a reedy voice. She looked behind her, then back to Maddie. "My mom is out getting food."

"Why do I have to go away?" Maddie planted her flip-flops harder into the thin trail and climbed atop one of the white, pock-marked limestone rocks. "What's going on?" she asked, her face scrunched up against the bright sunlight. "You didn't go to the other island?"

"No," the girl called down. "The waves were too rough last night. So, we leave tonight."

Maddie kept doing her best to scramble atop the rocks so she could get closer to the house but it wasn't easy. If she had sneakers on, it would have been easier. Millions of years of wind and water had beaten the rocks to a buffed sheen.

"Whose house is this?" Maddie asked.

The girl didn't answer, looking back over her shoulder for several seconds, then down at Maddie again. "A friend of my mom."

"Listen, I only want to make sure you're okay."

The girl crinkled up her nose. "Why do you keep asking me that?"

"I don't know. Maybe I'm being paranoid. But if you need any kind of help…"

"I'm fine," the girl sighed out in an exasperated manner.

"Are you going to an island called Volinos?"

"Mm." The girl looked antsy and shrugged. "Where did you hear that?"

"A friend told me about the island being near here and owned by a rich man."

"I don't know." The girl shrugged again.

Maddie realized it was possible that the girl really had no idea where she was going. That her "mother"— Stella—had fed her some kind of story.

"Is Stella really your mom?" Maddie blurted.

The girl widened her eyes, then shrieked, "Of course!"

Maddie was caught between starting to feel like a complete imbecile, and being determined to claw past the girl's unwillingness to open up.

"Why did you say I should leave?" she asked.

Ruby looked back over her shoulder, then leaned

over the flat terrace wall, which came up to her shoulders. "I'm fine, Maddie, but everything is a secret, okay?"

"What do you mean *secret?*"

"If I told you, it wouldn't be a secret!"

"So you're going to an island and it's a secret? Is the man you're meeting really your uncle? Or your mother's cousin?"

"That's part of the secret!"

"No, no," Maddie stammered, kneeling on a knobby edge of a rock, trying to inch her way higher. "I know you don't know me, but sometimes adults have bad secrets, and…" Her leg slipped out from underneath her, a grainy section of the rock's surface scraping along her bare knee. "Ah!" she yelled. "Shit!"

She carefully lowered herself to the flat rock below, and looked up again. Ruby's face was lost in a glaze of white sunshine.

"I'm worried you're going somewhere bad," Maddie called up.

"It's not bad! I don't know why you think that!"

"Because you seemed kind of scared back at my studio."

"Umm…" The rays dissipated enough that Maddie could see the girl had one finger dangling from her mouth. "I'm a little scared because this is a big deal. I was chosen out of tons of girls. It's an honor."

Chosen out of tons of girls?

Maddie's mouth dropped open—it was exactly as Elias had described. Her heart pounded thickly in her chest as she frantically wondered how she could get the girl out of this situation.

"*What's* an honor, Ruby? Do you even know?"

"I know, but I can't tell. You have to understand."

"Why did you tell me your name was Doris?"

"I *told* you. I have two names."

This was getting her nowhere. Maddie surveilled the house again, trying to figure out a way to get to the front, but the rocks made it impenetrable from her location.

"Maybe your mom can tell me the secret? I'm really curious. I won't share it. When is she getting back?"

"No, she'll be angry if she knew I told you this much. I'm only telling you because you seem worried. But everything is fine. *I'm* fine."

Maddie's knee began to sting sharply and she looked down to see a thin rivulet of blood trailing down her leg. She *had* to get to the front of the house somehow. She *had* to confront Stella. But the house was behind a fortress of rocks.

Suddenly, the girl whipped her head back. "Oh! I think that's Mom. I hear a scooter."

"I'm going to stand here until she talks to me," Maddie yelled up.

"No, you have to go or I'll get in trouble."

"Please, Ruby! Tell her to come talk to me."

"Bye, Maddie!" She shook her hair, which was glowing golden in the sun, then disappeared behind the terrace wall.

"Shit," Maddie sputtered under her breath, her knee throbbing painfully. Then she heard a long, piercing horn blast emanating from below on the beach. It was the boat she'd come in on—alerting people to reboard. She vaguely remembered that one of the ferry workers had explained as they came down the ramp that there would be three warning blasts before the boat departed.

If she didn't get to the boat before it left, she'd be here all night. With no shelter. No food or water. She had finished up her bottle of water and bag of chips about an hour ago and her stomach already had a hunger-pang emptiness to it and her throat was growing more parched by the second. She desperately wanted to get on the boat and to its small snack bar.

Besides, even if she managed to get Stella to come to the terrace, the woman would only give Maddie some story. She certainly wasn't about to confess anything nefarious. And she likely wouldn't allow Maddie inside the house. Sleeping outside all night on a craggy bluff with God only knows what animals—besides the baby goats—lurking around, didn't sound enticing in the slightest.

"Ruby!" she called again as if the girl would reappear and say something that would definitively confirm or dispel her worst suspicions. But Ruby was gone.

Maddie looked back at the anchored boat and could see people on the beach heading towards it. If she didn't start down now, she'd definitely be here all night. Finding a napkin inside her backpack, she wiped her bloodied leg, then reluctantly started to traipse down the bluff.

Chapter Seven

$\mathcal{T}$he boat docked, and Maddie walked distractedly down the gang-plank, guilty and disappointed with herself. She should have stayed on the bluff, calling up to that terrace all night long if needed, until Stella appeared and gave her a satisfactory answer about where Ruby was being taken and for what purpose. If it turned out Maddie's darkest suspicions were wrong, and if she got into some kind of trouble for harassing the pair, then fine. At least she would know that the girl was safe.

"Maaahh-deee!" she heard. Startled to hear her name being called in a masculine voice, she looked towards the row of outdoor cafés that lined the pier. A dark-haired man was standing near a small table, hand held high. It was Elias.

He looked as scrumptious as she remembered—even more so, as he was slightly dressed up in a nice pair of dark blue jeans and a form-fitting white t-shirt that showed off his excellent physique. Despite her preoccupation with Ruby, Maddie's heartbeat kicked up at the sight of him.

"Hi!" she said, walking over, hoping she didn't look unbearably frowzy. The wind on the ride back had, despite her ponytail, whipped her hair into a tangle, and she was again make-up free. Only some clear SPF lip balm on her lips. Before she knew what was happening, Elias had grabbed her arms and done the European greeting—a kiss on both cheeks.

"Sit, sit," he said, indicating the empty chair across from him. "How do you do? Let me get you a drink."

He waved at a waitress who appeared and Maddie ordered a glass (carafe) of the local white wine, even though before her lay a large menu illustrated with a wide array of colorful tropical drinks.

"Done working?" she asked him.

"Yes, left an hour ago."

"Athena says you're the only one who shows up on time." She smiled, but inwardly cringed, as she might have inadvertently insulted his friends.

Thankfully, he laughed, showing off good teeth— somewhat uncommon, she'd noticed, on the island. "Yes, the rest are lazy *tempélis*, but what can I do?" He shrugged good-naturedly. "Where you come from? You go see a beach?"

"Yes, Kalaria. It's beautiful. One of the most stunning beaches I've ever seen. You're so lucky to live here."

"Ah, I only come for work in summer. I live in Athens. But I grow up here in Kyrie."

The waitress reappeared with Maddie's wine—she

was young, tanned, pretty, and noticeably voluptuous. As the waitress and Elias made eye contact, Maddie had the suspicion the pair knew each other quite well.

"*Yamas!*" he said as the waitress left, clinking Maddie's wine glass with his squat glass of something milky-looking, probably Ouzo. "You try the Yastika?" he asked, referring to the island's famous tree gum that was converted into liqueur and everything else imaginable.

"First purchase. Bottle of it back at my hotel."

"Excellent. My family come from the Yastika *chorio* —village. You know the story of the village?"

She shook her head.

"When the conquerors come, they slaughter almost everyone on the island, except those who live in the Yastika village. The conquerors always want the Yastika and only those in the village know how to—how you say —culvate it."

"Cultivate?"

"Yes, cultivate. So, my family survive many massacres. But there was another one—the Turks. This time they slaughter all the nobles in the Yastika village. A young woman run with her baby up into the mountains, to a village called Kremos, at the very top. As the Turks come up the hills, the women all jump so they not be raped and enslaved. The woman with the baby—she jump with baby in her arms. Woman die but the baby— my great-great-great-great-grandfather, Constantine— live." He smiled and lifted his glass to her. "If that baby not survive, our family line die out."

Maddie was speechless. She didn't know whether to offer condolences or congratulate him.

"How—how was he found?" she stammered.

"His mother's body cover him long enough until the Turks leave, and when some come out of hiding, he cry and they find him. This what I always am told my whole life."

The wine started to create a pleasant buzz in Maddie's head as she tried to absorb this dramatic and tragic story.

"Remember the young girl I told you about? The one who may be going to that island owned by the rich man—Volinos?" she asked.

"Yesssss?" he said, full of interest, eyeing her intently.

"I saw her at a house in Kalaria."

He shook his head. "Impossible. No homes in Kalaria."

"But there was. It was way up on top of that cliff. A white-washed home with a large terrace. I spoke to her."

"Ah, not on beach. On hill?" He put his finger to his lips. "I think I know the house you mean. Only house in area."

"Do you know who owns it?"

"Only more rumor. Rich Russian, rich American, rich British. But not Greek."

"Well, the girl was in there. She's leaving tonight for the island. I couldn't get her to tell me if the island was Volinos, or who she was going to meet. She may not even know."

Her scraped knee began to sting, so she took her cocktail napkin and patted its pink, raw flesh.

"What happen there?" he asked.

"Slipped when I climbed up the bluff to talk to the girl."

Elias grabbed his chair and dragged it closer to her, so close she could smell his slightly minty cologne. "Why you worried about this girl?" he asked. "Why you so sure she not with her mother?" He seemed genuinely concerned and curious—not judgmental.

The darkness rushed up on her. She could suppress it for long periods of time, sometimes years. But then, usually if she was stressed, but sometimes out of the blue, it would light up her mind, start it whirring, make it impossible to sleep, impossible to think clearly. Sometimes it only lasted a few minutes, sometimes days.

She had only told two other people about what had happened: Jesse and Athena. But she was about to tell this virtual stranger. She didn't know why, but the sun, the sea, the wine, his blue eyes and sensuous face, his silken voice, and, most of all, the dramatic story of his ancestors, made her want to tell him.

"Probably because when I was her age, something bad happened to me. A friend of my father's. He was always at our house. We trusted him. I trusted him." She looked down into her wine glass, and took a long, ragged breath. "I shouldn't have."

Elias surprised her by putting his hand over hers. In America, she would have interpreted this as a poorly-timed come-on. But she could tell that the Greek people were more demonstrative. She didn't feel invaded or irritated. The touch of his hand soothed her.

"That's terrible," he said.

"So, you see, it's that..." The back of her throat

started to burn as she tried to swallow back tears. "I guess she's… reminding me of me at that age."

She plastered her free hand over her lips, determined not to start crying in front of him.

He gave her hand a squeeze, then polished off his drink, and plunked it on the table. "Then drink. Finish. We go to house. See what we can see."

"Really? You know how to get there?"

"Yes, of course. Kyrie not so big. But first we get you —what you call—Bad-Aid?" he asked, trying to peer around the curve of the table to see her leg.

"Band-Aid." She smiled.

He placed money on the table as she finished the dregs of her wine. As they left, Maddie caught sight of the pretty brunette waitress watching them. She didn't look happy.

* * *

About 20 minutes later, they pulled up a long, dirt road in Elias' sporty little red Fiat 500. The interior was cramped, but she didn't mind being in such a tight space with him; in fact, she liked it.

The rear seats looked suitable only for children or very short people, but the car was perfect for tooling around the island, and Elias told her it was fully electric —a benefit in an area with exorbitant fuel prices.

Despite being eight o'clock at night, it was still extremely light out. Summer days lingered long in this part of the world. Maddie had read that Kyrie had the longest sunny days of anywhere in Greece.

Eventually, the paved road dwindled into dirt and then into tall grass that had clearly been driven over many times, and then that finally came to an end at a high, white-washed wall that extended around a property beyond which nothing could be seen.

They stopped the car, got out, and walked up to the wall, which had a rusty metal entrance gate that would fit a vehicle as small as Elias' car. There was a silver keypad on the side of the gate, but no call button.

"Wait here, I have idea," Elias said. He walked several feet to his Fiat, opened the tiny trunk, and out came a ladder that he proceeded to unfold. "That wall not so high." He promptly walked over and placed the ladder against the wall. Then he looked at her, gesturing casually at its steps.

"You go over, jump down. I throw ladder over, you come back out."

"Are you crazy?" Then, realizing that sounded harsh, added, "How will we get the ladder back out?"

"Grab the ladder, pull it up." He shrugged. "Not so hard."

"I—I really don't think it's going to work. I'll get stuck over there. Or the ladder will."

He shrugged again. "I buy new ladder."

This sounded like a sure-to-fail plan, but she couldn't think of an alternative. Just then, they heard the sound of a motor growing louder and they both stepped back from the gate, which opened. Out drove a little black car, but it had to stop as the Fiat was blocking its path. In the driver's seat Maddie could see a lone woman—and it wasn't Stella.

She was an older woman, maybe in her sixties, with dark hair. Maddie momentarily worried the woman would start yelling at them, or call the police, but Elias made his way confidently to her driver's window, his strides long and self-assured.

With Elias here, it didn't seem like any trouble could come to them—that this was a slightly dangerous but fun caper, the type that can happen in a foreign country on vacation. Like the time she and Jesse had been invited by complete strangers to have dinner at their house in Marrakech. Or how she'd gotten lost in the byzantine streets of Venice and spent hours wandering aimlessly until she happened upon her hotel.

"*Kalispera,*" the woman said. Elias leaned down and the pair spoke for a few minutes in Greek with Elias gesticulating towards the house beyond the wall. Then Elias hopped in his car and moved it as the gate closed and the woman's baby car bounced off down the bumpy, overgrown "road."

"Well?" Maddie said, walking to his side of the car.

"She clean house." He pointed back towards the gate. "She say no one inside. But earlier she say people there, and they all went down to the beach. House empty now."

"Did you mention the girl?"

"Yeeessss," he said in that drawling way she'd noticed a lot of the Greek men said "yes." "She say she talk only to man and woman who speak Greek. She pretty sure woman is British, her Greek bad. They pay her, then they all leave down to Kalaria. She not pay attention to the others. My guess? They left on a boat from that side. Very private. You could come from Volinos, or any of the islands, pick up people, and leave." He made a *poof* gesture with his hands, indicating the boaters would disappear into thin air. "No customs. No port. No nothing. Passports should be logged but—" He shrugged. "—who would know if they not?"

* * *

"HE WAS my father's college buddy," Maddie said, sipping on her sweet and tangy glass of Yastika. After leaving the Kalaria area, Elias had driven her back to her studio apartment, and he'd said with a friendly, open smile, "Yastika while we watch the sun go down?"

Something about the way he said it was so amiable —consistent with his demeanor this entire time—that she didn't think twice about inviting him inside. Besides, if he made a move on her, it wouldn't be the worst thing in the world. Not by a long shot.

They sat on her rather large terrace, him on the lawn chair, her on the short couch, watching the sun slowly sink into the crystal Aegean. She stared trance-like at the water, not wanting to stare directly into the sunset and scorch her retinas.

Then she'd had the urge to tell him everything. Her concern about Ruby had opened up a pathway and the need to share it with someone again, and it seemed easy to do with a stranger. Probably because if she regretted telling him, it wouldn't matter. She'd never see him again after she went back to New York.

"They were best friends. I'd known him my entire

life. When I was 13, I got it into my head that I was in love with him—it was a crush. I was just beginning to figure out the dynamics between men and women, and to feel attractive."

"How old was he?"

"Somewhere in his late thirties, like my dad." She paused. "My mom and dad went on a long weekend away for their anniversary. They completely trusted him to watch me. It took me years—*years*—to realize what happened that weekend was wrong on his part. Wrong, illegal, immoral. He must have known it too, because he basically stopped coming over after that. I don't know what he told my parents to explain his disappearance. Then I learned he was engaged. She was his age. I was completely crushed."

"You didn't tell your parents?"

"No. By the time I thought maybe I should, my father was dying. Daniel—that's the man's name—and his wife, the same woman he'd started dating right after what happened—started to come over to help my father. Driving him to chemo. Bringing groceries for me and my mother. I felt there was no way I could tell them something like that right then. Plus, I liked his wife. She was so nice to me. It felt like it would be some kind of betrayal to everyone—to her, to my dad—if I told. I wanted my dad to die in peace."

The sun shimmered along the horizon in its last dance before disappearing behind the curve of the Earth. The sky darkened to a deep navy-violet, the bright, plentiful stars made their appearance, and the moon tossed ribbons of silver along the water. The temperature was perfect.

Except for the conversation—the one she never could have anticipated having here in Greece with a man she'd only met twice—it would have been the most exquisite tableau imaginable.

"After my dad died," she continued, "Daniel and his wife moved. I haven't seen him since. Now it seems pointless to tell my mom. For what? She'd feel awful it happened. Probably blame herself." She paused, sipping more of the sweet Yastika. "But one time, while my dad was really sick, almost near the end, I was alone with Daniel in the kitchen and his wife wasn't there, or was elsewhere in the house. I made some kind of remark, alluding to it. Because, honestly, sometimes I'd convince myself I imagined it. I wanted to see his reaction. So that I could know if it had really happened."

(What had she said to him? Could she remember?

I can't believe this is happening to him, Maddie. He's too young for this.

Sometimes people are too young for things, Daniel.)

"What did he say?"

"First, he looked at me blankly. Just blankly. Then his face went totally red. Just *red*." She held her splayed hand near her face. "Almost purple. I thought he was about to have a stroke. Do you know then I felt *bad*? Felt *bad for him*. So, that was the last time I tried anything like that."

"It was wrong," Elias said. "He was wrong."

Maddie numbly nodded. It was good to hear someone say it so unequivocally.

"It might seem like I'm out-of-control about this young girl but I keep thinking of myself at her age. I was curious about boys, about dressing up and playing at being sexy—but I wasn't ready for the real thing. Not at all. And certainly not with a grown man, a friend of the family. But I also keep thinking it's possible everything is fine with the girl and my past is badly affecting my perception."

"The girl told you she was chosen out of many girls?"

"Yes, something like that. And whatever she was chosen for was a secret."

Elias sighed, scanning the horizon, then turned his gaze on her. It was now completely dark, with only the moon for illumination, and she couldn't see his eyes' astonishing shade of blue. "It does sound strange. But it could be nothing. Maybe she win contest—trip to island. Maybe she model. Beauty—how you say?—pagan."

"Pageant," she smiled. "I thought of all that, but none of it adds up. Do you think I should go to the police here?"

"I know police. I know everyone. They would need proof, yes? Like in America." He sipped more Yastika, then stared down disappointedly at his glass. "Good but not so good as my family's Yastika. I bring you a bottle."

A couple hours later, they said their goodbyes. Elias kissed her on both cheeks, but didn't try to move his lips to hers, then strode back up the hill to his Fiat. The waitress at the port café might be his girlfriend, though he hadn't mentioned her. Or he could simply not be interested.

His mild flirtation was the way she'd noticed most of the island men, of all ages, acted towards her. "*Kalimera*, pretty lady," various men would greet her as she made her way through the *chora* in the morning for coffee, smiling and making little bows. She could definitely get used to this. A far cry from the doors closed in her face that she got back in New York. (She didn't ask them how they'd instantly surmised she was an English-speaking tourist, but they did.)

Though she was disappointed she didn't get to feel how Elias kissed, there was no point in getting involved. She'd be leaving in two weeks—back to the buzzing city and her stressful job. Sure, a vacation fling would be tempting, provided Elias wasn't attached elsewhere, but as he worked on Athena's house renovation, Maddie feared she'd then spend her time back in the States squeezing her friend for information about him.

Perhaps she and Elias would email each other for a bit. Even make well-intentioned plans to meet up again. But it would dissolve as both were tugged back into their daily lives an ocean apart. While some of Maddie's friends tittered about holiday hook-ups, or hook-ups in general, they had never suited her. She was too sensitive, fretted too long and too hard on things not destined to be hers.

Maybe it was a side effect of her "Daniel situation" —as she termed it in her mind. She'd been so disgustingly naïve, thinking what had happened between them had meant something. At 13, she'd fully expected that the weekend he initiated her into sex was the start of a great love affair. Oh sure, they might have to hide it for a few years, but she'd been certain that, maybe after a period of resistance, her parents would approve! How could they not? They adored Daniel!

She'd lived in a hopelessly ignorant fairytale. It had been predation, but her still-developing, barely-out-of-childhood neurons had seen romance. Where had she gotten this idea? Movies? Books? She couldn't even blame them as she could think of no movie or book she'd ever consumed where it was permissible for a 13-year-old to have a relationship with a guy in his late thirties.

She supposed it was what it appeared on the surface —a young girl entering puberty and beginning to develop feelings for the opposite sex, whose fancy had latched onto a handsome, kind man she felt safe with. It had been up to *him* to not allow that childish infatuation, that ignorance, to go where it did.

It made her stomach clench with disgust remembering how she'd put on her prettiest dress for him that weekend, parading herself in front of him, and the way his amber eyes had lit up when he saw her. Made her nauseous to remember how, after he disappeared into his marriage, Maddie had spent a few years fantasizing he might change his mind and return to her. He hadn't been a predator in her mind but a prince.

A therapist, if she'd bothered to see one, would probably diagnose her with "Daddy issues" but she couldn't think why that might be. Her father had been a good one, spending plenty of quality time with her. He'd been a dependable, decent man, who had loved Maddie and her mother.

It was only when she reached her twenties that much darker thoughts began to burrow in. It was like she'd finally come out of Plato's cave, blinking in the blinding daylight.

Was Daniel a relentless, repeat predator? What she'd interpreted as a genuine friendship, had that really been a patient, intricate, and premeditated grooming process? Had he done the same to other young girls?

Daniel and his wife, Chelsea, would go on to have twins—a boy and a girl. Amos and Amity. (Maddie was 15 when the birth announcement arrived at her house. "What adorable names!" her mom had squealed as Maddie tried not to throw up in her mouth, queasy not only with their arrival but their hipster monikers.)

As Amity grew up, a terrible thought began to take hold… would Amity's friends be safe around Daniel?

But at that thought, Maddie's brain would always go to war with itself.

He wouldn't do that to his daughter. He loves her.

He loved Dad. He did it to me.

Daniel had been the best man at her parents' wedding, in almost all the wedding photos. After Maddie was born, he'd been the first person to come to the house, holding her as a wrinkled, pink-fleshed newborn. She'd think of this when she'd become angry with her parents—asking herself why they'd left her alone with a grown man. Even one they'd known forever. An hour is one thing—but for three days?!

But her parents wouldn't have been able to conceive of a man who could hold their daughter as a newborn, and then do the thing he did. Sometimes, the mental tug-of-war would spiral into rage, to the point where it was difficult for her to breathe. The only thing that eased the unbearable tightness in her lungs and furious tumult in her soul was the idea of avenging herself on Daniel.

She imagined tracking him down and, in front of him, telling his wife and daughter what had happened.

(Would they believe her?)

Then her anger would do a U-turn—why hurt *them*? They hadn't done anything wrong.

But shouldn't they know what he was—or even still is? Shouldn't they at least protect his daughter's friends?

He's in his fifties now. He wouldn't still be like that.

What are you talking about? The world is filled with fifty-something scumbags.

Even if I tell Chelsea, she isn't going to end her marriage because of something that I say happened years ago that he'll likely deny. She's been married to him for years. Has children with him. She barely knows you. And if I tell, that means Mom will know. Why burden her with that? Why tell her something that will torment her? I only have one parent now.

Round and round it went. Grappling with the pain and shame, and still, at other times, coming to some kind of higher-level understanding, a Zen Buddhist enlightenment. Human beings are stupid, fragile, weak, and at the mercy of their most animalistic impulses. It's all well and good to hope that people behave honorably their entire lives *but they do not*. It's madness to expect it.

In her queen-sized temporary bed with its plump, oversized pillows and silky-soft, fresh-smelling white sheets, Maddie tossed and turned, exasperated that her

short vacation on this picturesque island had degener-
ated into the old turbulence.

A vision of Ruby loomed behind her eyelids. Such a
beautiful girl. Smooth, clear skin the shade of a dark
peach. Waist-length, sinewy honey-colored hair. Forest
green eyes flecked with hazel-gold. Long, coltish legs. A
girl who has no idea of the sinister danger those attributes could attract—and may have already attracted.

Chapter Eight

RUBY

This island is even prettier than Kyrie. It's unreal to me that one man owns it. One man! How lucky he is!

Mom and I are staying in this awesome apartment overlooking the water. From here, I can barely see another island, and beyond that is Kyrie.

I have to stop thinking about Maddie, and how upset she looked when I saw her the last time. I shouldn't have told her what I told her, but I didn't know what else to say to get her to go away. She seems convinced that bad things are going to happen to me. She's way too nosy. But I like her because I'm sure she is only looking out for me.

Anyway, it's all Mom's fault. She told me to say uncle, and told Maddie we were going to meet our cousin! What a stupid mistake. And she's always telling *me* not to mess up?! She's the one who pukes her guts out on the boat and ends up on Maddie's bed, and she's the one who says cousin instead of uncle. No wonder Maddie thinks I'm being kidnapped. Thanks, Mom.

A man came to pick us up this morning, and brought us around the island in what looked like a military golf cart. He told us to call him Max. I got the feeling that wasn't his real name. The man who owns the island, we're told to call him Mr. John.

Max told us that sometimes people come by a helicopter, but sometimes by boat. The island is windy, so sometimes the helicopter can't fly. And the water can be very choppy, so the boat can't ride. He said after we see the island, we'll have a nice dinner at our apartment, get a good night's sleep, and tomorrow I'll meet Mr. John.

Today, we had breakfast on the balcony. We could order anything we wanted, and I ordered chocolate chip waffles with whipped cream and watermelon!

In the hallway of our apartment are pictures of Mr. John. He's tall, handsome with a square jaw, like he belongs in the movies. He looks maybe in his forties. For some reason, it makes me feel better knowing he's not super old, though he's kinda old. He's always standing with important people. Mom pointed them out and was all, "Oh my God, there's Mr. John with the princess!" or "Wow, Mr. John knows so-and-so" and she'd name a big star.

It's really crazy to think he wants to meet me, that he picked me!

Oh, and the closet was full of dresses MY SIZE. Gorgeous dresses. Max said I can keep them all but to pick one to wear to meet Mr. John tomorrow. He said Mr. John was as excited to meet me as I am to meet him, that he can't wait to "see the beautiful girl who won over so many other girls." So, after dinner (I'm pretty sure I'm going to have the LOBSTER!), I'll try on all the dresses for Mom and she'll help me decide which one to wear.

I really want to share pics of myself in the dresses. Everyone would be so jealous. It's so much better than when Olivia went to Las Vegas and we all had to look at her photos on Pikchur for like a year. But Mom has already told me a thousand times (maybe a million) that I can't tell anyone. That this is all TOP SECRET. Plus, we weren't allowed to bring our phones or laptops so there's no way to take pictures anyway!

Mom says it will be worth keeping everything quiet because we're going to get all we wanted, like a house on the beach, and then I can put up photos of that.

Well, I guess I should get ready for dinner now. Maybe I'll have the steak instead of the lobster but I think I can probably have both.

I really, really hope Maddie isn't still worried about me. She doesn't understand. I'm in such a big thing, it's so secret, NO ONE can know about it. But me and my mom know. And we have to prove we can be trusted.

Chapter Nine

a couple of days later, Maddie still felt unsettled, grappling with a gnawing sense of guilt over letting Ruby slip away from her, and bogged down with unsavory memories of Daniel.

Over the years, she'd mostly managed to seal off those memories in a far corner of her mind so she could go on about her life with equanimity. Now it felt as if the bolts had been pried off, the door pulled wide open, to the point where she could picture Daniel's face, hear his voice, more clearly than she'd been able to do in many years.

She decided she'd walk to the *chora*, get her usual coffee, and drink it while gazing at the sea. That would cheer her up. She couldn't allow enjoyment of her one vacation this year to be blighted because of wild theories over Ruby or memories of what had happened to her so long ago.

Besides, she'd learned over the years that anything she spent this much time worrying about was destined not to be an issue. She remembered a few years ago when a woman she only ever conversed with online had vanished. Maddie had spent weeks trying to track her down. When the woman popped up almost a year later, her only explanation was that she'd been "taking a break." Maddie felt ridiculous for putting so much mental energy into the woman's disappearance.

It was the things on which she didn't spend a moment's rumination that came out of nowhere to upend things.

She was on Kyrie, a stunning island. The sun was shining in glorious white-yellow, sparking off the calm, turquoise Aegean, its vast expanse visible beyond the glass doors of her terrace. The sky was a marvelously clear robin's egg blue without a thread of cloud. Later, she'd meet Athena for lunch and was looking forward to her usual: a traditional Greek salad and a glass of the local white wine.

Flickering at the edges of her melancholia was a more upbeat feeling—the hope that she'd see Elias again. Maybe he'd stop by after work, given that he'd promised her a bottle of his family's brand of Yastika.

The thought made her smile to herself. She looked forward to seeing his electric blue eyes, his easy smile, and to bask in that laidback, charming way he had about him. She cringed a little when she thought about what she'd told him about her past. Although she knew she'd done nothing wrong, she was still unaccountably embarrassed by it, as if she carried some responsibility for it as well.

The walk to the *chora* refreshed her spirit, as she

suspected it would. A few of the men said *Kalimera* and did their little bows, and she greeted them back. In New York, these types of casual exchanges simmered with danger, with Maddie never knowing if the hello's and good morning's would turn to hurled abuse if she didn't respond exactly the way the passing men expected she should. But it wasn't like that here. Sometimes she responded, sometimes not, and always the men smiled graciously and moved on, not seeming to expect anything more from the encounter.

After coffee at a café overlooking what she was coming to think of as the world's best view—the Aegean —she headed back to her apartment with not much more to do than read, swim, and laze the morning away until it was time for lunch. Even thoughts of Ruby were lessening their grip on her mind, and she was beginning to accept that she'd interpreted the girl's words and behavior in the worst possible way because she'd seen them through the prism of her own experience.

Everything is fine. I'm fine.

Ruby had been adamant about this. Who was Maddie, who'd only spent an hour or so with the girl, tops, to act like she knew more?

She could see her apartment peeking out from behind the green hedge and coco palm trees in front of the building. Her heart swelled, feeling free. She was determined to savor the rest of her vacation. There would be enough stress and anxiety back at her job and her noisy Hell's Kitchen studio apartment.

(It wasn't until she'd moved in that she realized there was a stoplight in front of the building, where cars would line up, their occupants endlessly leaning on their horns. But it was so difficult and expensive finding a place in the city, that she had yet to be able to bring herself to move.)

It was then that a man came skipping by her. He was wearing black shorts and a white biking shirt with red stripes on the arms. And, yes, he was *skipping*. It was an athletic, masculine form of skipping, arms stretched wide, knees bent almost to the chest, but it was still skipping.

It was such an out-of-the-norm maneuver that she felt in her bones the man must be American. The skipping screamed *entitlement*. Not only that, despite perfect vistas for jogging, biking, and yoga, she'd seen none of it on the island. Greeks got their exercise from swimming and climbing the ubiquitous steep steps around the hilly terrain. And she certainly hadn't seen any skipping.

The man then turned into the driveway of her apartment building, skipping down the curve of the small hill, below her line of vision.

Her stomach gnarled with a strange foreboding. Something about the man seemed familiar, the skipping absurd and arrogant—like someone who wanted to get under her skin. As she came up over the hill, she could see the man was sitting in the apartment's front patio area, where the owners would set out bowls of tomatoes, pears, plums, and figs that they grew on their property. The man was gnawing on a fig, and she wished she didn't have to walk right by him to get to her suite, because she had the bad feeling the skipping douchebag was going to try to talk to her.

At the bottom of the hill, she tried to walk quickly and surreptitiously past the man when he turned in her direction, wiping his dripping lips with one of the white cloths left on the patio table. Maddie's heart nearly stopped and her mouth fell open.

The man only stared at her. After calmly wiping his chin, he said, "Fancy seeing you here, Splash."

Mouth still hanging open, Maddie was unable to move. Her heart rate accelerated, her mind tearing off in a dozen opposing directions.

The man was her coworker. A coworker she happened to dislike. And for some unfathomable reason, he was here in Kyrie. Not only in Kyrie but at her rental apartment.

It occurred to her that perhaps he'd been sent to find her because something was happening back at work that needed her attention. She had an article that had been pushed back, and before she'd left, she'd added Sider-atos and its main phone number into the magazine's internal database in case the story went to press and anyone had questions on it. While editors had her cell phone number, she hadn't been able to make her SIM card work, and was currently relying on plentiful Wifi around the island to communicate with Athena via WhatsApp.

But none of that made any sense. Her story was a fluff piece—nothing so important that Logan Bernman (the skipping coworker) would have been sent all the way from New York to find her. Plus, he wasn't an editor. Additionally, he could have emailed her or called Sideratos and left a message, she would have gotten back to him through the work email system.

"Beautiful island," he said, breathing in deeply, and taking in the area with a look of satisfaction. He always looked like that—as if the world belonged to him.

"What are you doing here, Airport?" she finally snapped.

Airport was her nickname for him, as Splash was his for her. A year ago, at an afterwork drinking session attended by a small group of coworkers, the topic had turned to how each person had been named.

Amid the usual stories of being named after grand-mothers or sobriquets randomly found in a name book, Logan and Maddie's stories stood out—Maddie named after the mermaid character in the movie *Splash*, Logan because his parents had met at Logan Airport. All night, they'd drunkenly called each other Splash and Airport. Somehow, they never came out of it.

"Calm down," he said, picking at the bowl in front of him, then holding out a golf-ball sized green piece of fruit. "Fig?"

"*Why* are you here?"

She was utterly baffled and had lost the ability to speak calmly. Could his presence be a fantastical coinci-dence? No. He must have gone into the work database and found out where she was. Then he'd actually taken a ten-hour flight to Athens and one of the not-easy routes to Kyrie.

"Just relax and—"

"Don't tell me to *relax*." Ugh, didn't men know

telling a woman to *relax* was the equivalent of waving a red flag in front of a bull?

If it had been any other work colleague, Maddie would have been surprised and confused, but not upset. But she and Airport—Logan—had had too many clashes.

He was the type who instinctively knew every editor to brown-nose. He'd been rapidly promoted up the hierarchy so that, despite the fact that they'd both started in the reporter pool at the same time, he was now a Senior Reporter, while Maddie was still two rungs below him (it went Junior Reporter, Associate Reporter, Senior Reporter). During that time, she'd had to fact-check his stories, and he hers, and it had never gone smoothly.

Not only that. The night they'd drunkenly shared their "how I got my name" stories, the pair had—she still cringed to think about it—hooked up back at her place. At the time, it had only been six months since her break-up with Jesse, and she hadn't yet been on a single date. She'd been vulnerable and lonely, and had found Logan show-offy but funny and better looking as her alcohol consumption increased.

The sex, what she remembered of it, had been good, but the next day at work, the awkwardness between them was palpable. Whatever chemistry that had alchemized between them the night before had evaporated by morning. They were then like two magnets repelling each other.

They never again spoke of what had happened, a silent agreement to forget it.

"I'm not stalking you," he said, stretching back on

the patio love-seat as if he had all the time in the world. "I want to help you."

"Help me?" she screeched, then lowered her voice, fearful that the apartment's owners would think she was making a scene. "Get to it, Logan. Why did you follow me on my vacation? Half way around the world?"

"I'll tell you, if you'll cool your jets and sit."

Maddie walked over to the sitting area, legs shaky with livid adrenaline, and lowered into a wicker chair. She grabbed a hard green fig and began squeezing it like a stress ball.

"I saw you went into the richest database," he said. "I saw you logged into Dexter Hunt's file. I'm the one who added the note about Volinos, maybe a couple of years ago. And I saw that you're staying here," —he pointed out past the apartment building, towards the Aegean—"and Volinos is right out there."

"Keep going."

"I also needed to take my vacation time or I was going to lose it, so I thought I'd come out, see what you've got going on with Hunt."

"You were able to get vacation approval in three days?"

"I might have not exactly told them where I was going. And maybe that I had a family emergency."

Despite her dislike of him, Maddie had a certain grudging admiration for Logan. Whether it meant kissing ass or lying, he knew how to expertly handle the powers-that-be at *Wealthy*.

A part of her wished she could be more like him. For a while, it had looked like she wouldn't get to leave in

July, as too many other reporters had requested time off that month. Luckily, another reporter had changed her request. It had never occurred to Maddie to simply lie and say she had a family emergency. Yet Logan was the one speeding up the masthead, and she was the one languishing.

If she was smart, she'd stop resenting him and start imitating him.

"I've been trying to dig up information on Hunt for years," he continued, "but he's a slippery sucker. Can't get any contact information." He again gazed around the patio area, at the meticulously trimmed green hedges, impressed with the scene, as if he'd been the one to pick out the rental. "I've always wanted to see Greece, so it's not all about Hunt. But if I can research *and* get some sun, why not? If it comes to anything, I can probably get *Wealthy* to pay for the trip or at least write it off."

Leaning forward, a flap of his hair fell over one squinty brown eye. He always managed a bit of a slob vibe, with dark brown hair perpetually askew, work shirts continually slung over his waistline, and pants bagged up along the hem. When he walked, he kind of lurched. How she'd found him attractive enough to have sex with him one night was beyond her—not even all the booze excused it.

"Why were you skipping?" she asked. It wasn't what she wanted to ask, but it came out of her mouth.

"It's great exercise."

"You looked ridiculous."

"Wouldn't be the first time. So, Splash," —he picked

up another fig and began peeling it— "What's up with Dexter Hunt? You confirm he owns Volinos?"

"No." She crossed her arms. "And even if I did, why would I tell you?"

Despite the fact that the reporters were supposed to be a team, working towards the common goal of making *Wealthy*'s richest people list the best it can be, the reality was that promotions were doled out based on accomplishments like getting exclusives, so every reporter was in competition with every other reporter.

"Because I know things and you know things," he said, "and we could combine things we know and then we know more than we each know. You know?"

She laughed. Typical Airport.

"You've already been promoted over me," she said, trying not to sound too bitter about it but not succeeding. "If you cracked anything with Hunt, you'd get another promotion and I'll still be stuck in the reporter pool."

He smiled, more like a smirk, sagely shaking his messy head. "It's that kind of thinking that's holding you back."

The nerve of him thinking he understood what was holding her back. What was holding her back was that he could spend two hours shooting the shit in a male editor's office (and all the important editors were male), and only succeed in bonding with the editor—which gave him a huge advantage on assignments and promotions. Maddie didn't have that freedom. Walking into an editor's office, closing the door, and flopping on his couch for an hour of private, shoot-the-shit time would only invite trouble or gossip or both.

All the women reporters saw what had happened to Annabeth Sciandro.

She'd been a rising star at the magazine. Three covers in one year—almost unheard of for a lowly reporter. But she'd made the huge mistake of starting a relationship with one of the top editors. When they broke up, she only lasted a few months before getting pushed out.

Maddie had seen how Annabeth had gone from respected to held in contempt, with everyone saying how she was only getting plum assignments because of her boyfriend, never mind that she'd come into the magazine blazing, and had done a ton of great reporting before she'd ever begun dating an editor. But it didn't matter. The women were gossiped about, picked apart, and had to watch their every move. The guys, not so much.

(No one had anything untoward to say about the married male editor who made out with the 22-year-old female intern, in flagrant view of everyone at the Christmas party. In fact, he was promoted shortly thereafter.)

The double standard had finally caught up to Maddie about four months ago. She'd been given a top notch assignment: to interview an elusive British retail billionaire. She'd even get to go to London for it.

But while making arrangements with the billionaire's assistant, she'd learned he wanted to meet in a hotel suite. Maddie had seen in the tabloids that this particular billionaire had a penchant for womanizing, and she didn't want to risk finding herself in an uncomfortable position, so she declined, suggesting that they meet somewhere neutral, like a restaurant or his headquarters.

The next thing she knew, she was called into her editor's office and told she was off the story. The editor had decided someone else would be more suited for this particular assignment. That someone happened to be the man who'd followed her to Greece and skipped by her on the road about ten minutes ago.

Maddie had clearly been taken off the story because the retail billionaire must have complained she was being "difficult." Since then, she hadn't been offered any assignments by the editors and was having a much harder time getting her own pitches approved.

She had the ominous sensation that, like Annabeth Sciandro, she would soon be pushed out, told that she and the magazine weren't a good match. While that might be true, it's not like it was easy to get decent-paying staff reporter jobs. If *Wealthy* let her go, who knows when she might find another one.

The pressure she was absently applying to the green fig made it break apart, oozing sticky pink juice over her palms. "Dammit." She snatched up a cloth napkin and tried to wipe the stickiness off.

"If you don't mind, I'd like to enjoy what's left of my vacation," she told Logan, standing.

"Think about it," he said. "Dexter Hunt is wily. He's like Jay Gatsby. No one can figure out how he got so rich. Sure, he's a hedgie. But hedgies don't usually become billionaires. And this guy is a billionaire, more than one trusted source told me. I can't trace who owns Volinos but I think it's him. How does he afford it? How does he have mansions all over the world? How can he buy a private space rocket?"

Logan was good. He knew steering the conversation to the mysteries of the uber-rich would get Maddie's mind turning away from his boundary-busting trailing of her to Greece towards the bigger questions.

Where *did* Dexter Hunt's money come from? And was he not only rich and space-obsessed... but a pedophile?

"Look, Splash—*Maddie*. I know you haven't been treated fairly at the magazine. The Sergey Brin cover alone should have gotten you promoted to Senior Reporter. I guarantee you that if anything comes out of Dexter Hunt, I'll go to every editor and plead your case. I've made some friends there. I can make it happen for you."

"Am I supposed to thank you for something that should happen without your assistance?"

"Yes."

He grinned. At this point, she got the feeling he was pressing her buttons. He liked to do that.

"*Adio*, Airport." She tossed down the fig-juice smeared cloth, hiked up her tote bag, and headed for her room, calling back, "Make sure to try the stuffed tomato."

* * *

"*Logan*?" Athena looked gobsmacked. "You're kidding me."

"He skipped by me. *Skipped*! Who does that?"

The waitress deposited their small carafes of white wine and poured half of them into their glasses. "It's good exercise," Athena said, nodding. "Not just for kids."

Maddie guzzled a long sip of wine, something she'd wanted to do since she saw Logan. Then she looked over the menu even though she already knew what she wanted. The Greek salad.

The tomatoes here were so red, they looked like overripe watermelon, and no tomato in the States could remotely compare to a Greek tomato's bursting flavor. The Kyrians were proud of their tomatoes. Maddie had seen wreaths of cherry tomatoes hanging on doors and rafters all over the island. Athena had told her it was the local way of ripening them.

The pair ordered and the waitress disappeared.

They were sitting at an outdoor café along one of the myriad alleyways that veined the oldest part of the island, the *plaka*. Many of the homes were crumbling and padlocked, abandoned for years or even centuries. Because it was so arduous and expensive to haul debris off the island, most abandoned houses stayed that way.

But the area was still teeming with cafés, clubs, and restaurants.

"Do you think he came for you?" Athena asked. "You guys did hook up that time."

"Ugh, don't remind me. I'm about to eat."

Athena laughed.

"No, he's here because he thinks I sniffed out a story about a billionaire and he wants in."

"Which billionaire?"

"His name is Dexter Hunt."

"Never heard of him."

Before she quit the magazine, Athena, like all the reporters, had done her time helping to compile the richest list. The world's richest people weren't so different from everyone else—they also loved to be in the press, and many of them called *Wealthy* personally, revealing assets and even emailing bank statements. Of course, whatever a billionaire told you they were worth, you usually knocked it down by half, because they loved to exaggerate.

But Dexter Hunt was an enigma, and clearly not someone jonesing to have his name in *Wealthy*. In fact, he seemed perfectly fine with not having his name anywhere, as Maddie had been unable to find any profiles of him or even articles quoting him. Nothing in the *Wall Street Journal*. Nothing in *Barron's*. Hedge fund managers were usually all over the financial press, as having their name out there drummed up investors. Only the most elite of them didn't need to bother, because their funds were closed, their clients very few, very rich, and very private.

Maddie had only been able to dig up bare bones information, with him being mentioned in passing or identified at a few important events.

"I hadn't heard of him either," Maddie said. "But Logan's been following him. He saw I went into the guy's file and that the island he might own is right near here, so he hopped on a plane to come and try to steal the story."

"Story? What story?"

"There *is* no story. I don't even know if the guy owns Volinos. All I have is what Elias told me, the tip Logan got, and my own imagination."

"Well, stories are built on less."

"True. But I'm not concerned with getting a story. I'm only concerned if a 12-year-old has been taken to something called 'orgy island.'"

Athena peered doubtfully at her over the lip of her wine glass. "It's okay to be concerned with both."

"I know, I'm only saying, my first priority is that girl's safety. Not a *Wealthy* exclusive. Anyway, I've convinced myself I'm jumping to the worst possible conclusion."

Their meals were delivered and both dug in. Maddie savored the creamy feta cheese and the spectacularly tasteful tomatoes. Athena had ordered the same.

"All *I'm* saying," Athena stressed, "is that if you're going to stay at *Wealthy*, it wouldn't hurt to break open a big story about a mysterious billionaire and his crazy island. *And* help the girl. If either thing is real."

"What are you suggesting?"

Athena grinned, her dark eyes flashing mischievously. "Two heads are better than one."

"You're saying I should work with Logan."

"Would it kill you?"

"It might."

Athena chortled and drizzled more olive oil on her salad, then dusted it with fresh sea salt, which came in a tiny china teacup. "He's not so bad. I think he likes you."

"He doesn't like me, and I don't like him."

"Sounds like the beginning of every romantic comedy ever."

"And every murder."

"Funny. What about Elias?" she prattled on. "You'll have to decide between two men. Oh, poor Maddie. Will it be the brash American reporter or the charming, blue-eyed Greek guy?"

"For your information," Maddie said, spearing a tomato with her fork, "Elias isn't interested either. He spent hours at my apartment the other night and didn't make a move."

"Did *you*?"

"Of course not."

"And *you're* interested, so what does that prove?"

Maddie pondered, sipping her wine. Athena might have a point. At least about Elias.

As for Logan, Maddie was still too irritated about him swooping in to take over the retail billionaire story for her to want to work with him. From what she could tell, he was a good (not great) reporter, but she suspected whatever they might be able to unearth about Dexter Hunt would only serve to raise Logan up to an editorial office, and do nothing for her.

Still, it seemed that Logan had more information on Hunt than anyone else had, thanks to whatever sources he'd been cultivating. And if a young girl—perhaps many young girls—was in trouble, then it would be worth it to put up with him.

Chapter Ten

*a*fter lunch, Maddie took a swim in the fabulous Aegean. The beach at the bottom of a rocky incline behind Sideratos was small, tucked into a cove, and never had many people on it, in fact, usually she was alone. The water was shallow for a long stretch—seemingly, she could walk for a full minute before the water became deep enough that her toes couldn't touch the bottom.

Of course, the water was so crystal clear that she could see her own body, as if the sea was rippled, permeable glass. Then she lay out for maybe an hour but couldn't relax, knowing that Logan was in the same building and possibly even keeping watch out his terrace onto the beach—and her—below. While she could perhaps forgive him for coming to the same island, that he'd gone so far as to book an apartment in the same rental was extremely agitating.

You got gills under there, Splash? He'd murmured in her

ear as they'd waded back through the crowded streets from the bar that fateful evening.

Mermaids don't have gills, dummy, they have a fin.

Sorry. Fin. I bet you have a hot fin.

She lived in Hell's Kitchen, and him in Union Square, but he'd offered to walk her home before he caught the subway. The next thing she knew, they'd been making out on the sidewalk, and soon enough he was following her up the four laborious flights to her minuscule studio. At the time, she could only think of Jesse, and how he'd already moved on, and she was still stuck in relationship (and sex) purgatory.

Logan wasn't her type—too full of himself, too smug, too "brash" as Athena had put it—but he was the first man she'd had any desire to crawl into bed with since her breakup. Why, she wasn't certain. Perhaps *because* he wasn't her type. There was no chance she'd fall for him.

Still, at the borders of her mind, she knew it was a bad idea to sleep with a coworker. If things didn't go well, it would be awkward. If things *did* go well, it would be awkward. There was no winning. But her level of intoxication was such that these objections were easily quashed by the desire to forget Jesse and have some physical pleasure (hopefully) for an hour or two. What the hell.

As the Greece sun baked her back, Maddie buried her face deeper into the crook of her elbow, trying to ward off the memory before it went any further. Ugh, what a mistake. Thankfully, he'd gotten up early, said a quick goodbye, and left.

As soon as she'd sobered up after he left, all she'd thought about was how their hook-up was going to get around the office. Even if he didn't tell anyone, her coworkers out at the bar saw them leave together, and had witnessed them bantering flirtatiously all evening. They'd know what was up. And, sure enough, that's what had happened. Only a day later, Athena, who hadn't even accompanied them to the bar, had IM'd her through the work system: LOGAN???!!!!! You holding out on me, girl??!!!!!

Deciding she'd had enough sun, Maddie slipped on her jeans cut-offs and headed back to her studio. It wasn't until she stepped out of the shower, pulled on a loose sundress, and sat down at her computer that the back of her neck prickled.

Her laptop was open and the password bar had one dot in it. When her screen awakened, the password bar should be blank. The only reason she could think that there would be a dot inside of the password bar was if someone had tried putting in a password, then deleted it when it didn't work, but mistakenly left one letter.

Her gut tingled uneasily, the blood in her veins starting to pump thickly and forebodingly.

Getting up, she snatched her keys from the desk, went outside, and shut the door behind her. She tried the door handle, and it opened.

Didn't the door lock automatically? She was almost certain it did, which is why she was so careful to bring her keys with her even if she only stepped outside to grab a fig or orange from the bowls on the patio. She didn't want to risk that one of the island's *Meltemi* winds would push the door shut behind her and she'd be locked out.

Sometimes the owners, a married couple named Karen (from Norway) and Kostas, were gone all day long and she didn't want to risk having to wait for their return before she could get back into her apartment.

Inside, she traced her steps through the small kitchen, the short hallway with a closet, and then the bed and desk area, casting around for any other sign that *someone* had managed to get in. The garbage pail underneath the desk still contained her paper coffee cup from the morning, so it wasn't that the cleaning lady had arrived. Besides, why would the cleaning woman try to get into her laptop?

Inside the closet was a small, built-in safe. She pressed the lock's combination—her birth year—and eyed her passport and a small pile of American dollars and euros, all undisturbed.

Although she still felt strange and uneasy, one dot on her password bar wasn't enough proof of forceable entry to make her seek out another place to stay. But she couldn't shake the sense that *someone* had been inside snooping around.

And she could only think of one person who'd want to do that.

* * *

It didn't take long to see him. Maybe an hour. Maddie had settled herself under the patio's white awning, book in hand, and waited. Eventually, he came trundling up around the side of the building, from the steep stone steps that led to the beach area. They must have just missed each other, or he'd prudently waited until she'd left before going for his own swim.

He had a towel wrapped around his hips, his chest was bare, and suddenly the night they'd spent together came surging back at her full-force. She remembered that as soon as he'd shed his clothes, she'd been pleasantly surprised that underneath the slovenly habiliment was a well-formed body. Sans clothes, some men were a disappointment. Logan had been an unexpected improvement.

Laying her book down on the couch, she tried to keep her line of vision above his neck. "Were you in my room, Airport?"

"Excuse me?" he said, acting as if he'd only seen her as soon as she spoke. He stood adjusting his towel in a slightly-threatening way, as if he might deliberately drop it, revealing whatever was underneath—then *that* memory rushed back at her. She started to lose her bravado, felt her cheeks flushing and the words she wanted to rap out at him instead came out flustered and uncertain. "I—I just wanted to know if you went into my room."

"Your *room*? Splash, I don't even know where your damn room is."

"It was in the database. You saw it like you saw the island and the rental address."

"Well, I don't remember it. And no, I wasn't in your room. What kind of bizarre question is that anyway?"

She shook her head, fumbling to pick up her book,

still trying to avoid eye contact with his bare chest and hanging towel. "Never mind."

He ambled over, and sat down, legs spread in that insolent way some men had, then reached for a fig and began peeling. Damn it, why had she confronted him? Of course, he was going to deny it and now she'd have to sit here and answer his questions.

"You gonna tell me what's up?" he asked.

She studiously kept her eyes on the pages of her book, though she couldn't read any of it. "I don't know, the door normally locks automatically, but it was open. And it seemed like someone tried to get into my laptop."

"And you think it was me."

"Who else would it be?"

"Maid?"

She snapped her eyes up to him. "*Maid*? I've met her. She's perfectly nice, and no, it wasn't her."

"Well, it wasn't me."

"Fine."

She closed her book, stood, and was about to get out of there, when he said, "I want to tell you something about Dexter Hunt. It's completely confidential, not in the database."

"Alright," she sighed, wishing he was wearing clothes. It was difficult to concentrate on what he was saying. "I'm listening."

"Not like this," he said, indicating his towel. "Tonight. Let's do dinner."

"I'm meeting Athena."

"Ahh. I'd heard she'd run off to Greece. I just didn't

know where. I'm not insulted that you're not inviting me to meet up with you guys. Alright, I'm a little insulted. How about a drink beforehand? I really think you should hear this, and I'd rather not get into it while I'm half-naked."

* * *

THE PAIR WALKED to the *chora*, and then to the tavernas that lined the port. Most of them looked similar—restaurants and bar areas in the back, and long rows of small tables that sprawled to the boardwalk right along the water, which was lined with boats.

Many of the boats gave tours of the surrounding islands or acted as water taxis, ferrying tourists to the harder-to-reach beaches. The island had a bus system, but from what Maddie could tell, buses came infrequently and most people used the boats to get around. There were also little fishing boats, identifiable by their multicolored stripes and tangle of nets draped over their sides.

Maddie and Logan didn't speak much on the five-minute walk to the port. When they did speak, it was strained, casual talk about work. They settled on the second taverna they saw for no real reason other than that it had an empty table right at the boardwalk.

Greek service could be excruciatingly slow, and Maddie was desperate for a drink that would slough off the edges of her annoyance with Logan. Fortunately, a server quickly appeared and took their orders. They forced more awkward small talk until their drinks arrived. Both had opted for a local specialty—a Yastika Mojito.

"Delicious," Logan said. "You picked a great island. Was it because Athena's here?"

"Mostly. But I'd also read about it, and I liked that it had a lot of history, with medieval and Byzantine architecture, and isn't too touristy."

"I can't wait to see more of it." He eagerly rubbed his freckled hands together, then sipped more Yastika. She had an odd feeling of pride that the island passed muster in his eyes. Why she should care about that, she didn't know. But she didn't like that he seemed to think his trailing her to Greece was going to be accepted as a non-creepy thing to do. It wasn't.

"Look, Logan," she said. "What you did is really unacceptable. You could have gotten in touch with me and asked if it would be okay to come here, work on a story with me."

"I was afraid you'd say no."

She rolled her eyes. "Whatever. So what is it you want to tell me about Hunt?"

He took another couple of sips of his drink, as if he'd tell her in his own sweet time, then said, "Couple of my hedge fund guys claim they know him pretty well. They're irked with him, think he gets away with a lot of tax evasion stuff. So, that's what they think about this island, which they swear is Volinos, of the North Aegean islands. He bought it through a series of shell companies, has greased up every influential palm in the country, and manages to get all kinds of tax breaks and grants on ghost projects. They think his fund is a way for the elite rich to hide their money. But here's the thing," —he put down his drink, and wriggled forward—"they swear he's pals with everyone, and I mean *everyone*. Up to and including the president."

"The president?"

"Yes, of the U.S. of A. And that Hunt's figured out a way to hide clients' assets while making them a hefty return. Because of that, he's basically untouchable."

Maddie tapped her fingers on the table, absently people watching, but her mind thrumming with questions.

"Why not go to a Swiss banker?"

"Because he's giving them a triple digit return on investment *while* concealing the investment."

"That sounds impossible."

Logan shrugged. "It's close to impossible which is why my guys are pissed and out for him."

Maddie took in Logan—his wrinkled white t-shirt printed with "Hedgehogs—Hedgies like to hog" (whatever that meant) and khaki shorts with too many pockets that hung down to his knees. His overgrown hair almost grazed his collar, and he had a rabid intensity in his chocolate brown eyes. There was something repellant about him, and yet she couldn't bury the distasteful suspicion that if she had a few more drinks, she'd end up in bed with him again. Angry sex felt like the only satisfactory way to fully express her irritation with him.

"Well, I have another theory," she said.

"Great." He excitedly rubbed his hands again, then picked up his Mojito. "Let's hear it."

"I suspect he's running a large pedophile ring."

Logan literally choked on his drink. Eyes bugged, he repeatedly slapped his palm on his chest, coughing, for at least thirty seconds. The choking fit was dire enough that Maddie started to get nervous. "Are you okay? Take some water." She tried handing him one of the glasses of water on the table.

"No-nuh—" He shook his head a few times, and eventually was able to take a long, ragged breath. He looked at her with watery eyes. "Damn, that was a bad time to be in the middle of swallowing. You're not being serious?"

"Very."

"Come *on*. The president hanging out with a pedophile?"

"Maybe the president is a pedophile, too."

He threw his head back in a loud guffaw, examined his glass and, seeing there was nothing but ice left, craned his neck around for the waiter.

"You don't believe me," she said.

"You don't want to work together on this. That's fine, I get it."

He was shifting around in a restless way and she wasn't sure if he was hailing the waiter so he could pay and leave, or if he was going to order another round.

"I met a girl," Maddie went on. "She says she's 12 and I have no reason to doubt that. She was with a woman who was supposedly her mother, and I caught them in a few small lies. The girl told me she's on her way to meet her uncle on some nearby island, and that he was going to pay for her schooling, and then later she tells me she 'won' over many other girls, and that winning was an 'honor.' And she couldn't tell me what she won because it's a secret. Who 'wins' something from their own uncle? Who, by the way, the mother called her 'cousin'? I go back and forth on whether this is anything. But I can't completely shake the feeling that it is."

"We're going to be waiting a while for the waiter, aren't we?" he asked distractedly.

"Are you listening?"

He turned back around, fiddling with his straw, mouth turned downward in disbelief. "Sorry, that doesn't sound like evidence of a pedophile ring."

"What evidence do you have he's hiding client assets and evading taxes?"

"Two reliable sources who haven't misled me yet."

"Why can't he be doing both things? Evading taxes *and* running a pedo ring?"

Logan made eye contact with her, his reportorial side finally kicking in. "Did this girl say she was on her way to Volinos?"

The waiter approached and they quieted their conversation until they ordered another round, and he left.

"No, but there aren't that many islands close by."

"Splash," he groaned, staring out at the sumptuous blue sea for a few moments before eyeing her. "We can't bring anything this outrageous, not to mention libelous, to *Wealthy* unless we have something big to go on."

"No kidding." She leaned forward, until she could smell him—a vague whiff of sea salt, Irish Spring, and that special city bouquet of dirty subway tiles and roasted chestnut carts. "I want to get on that island. But no ferries go there, obviously."

"How well do you swim?" he asked, grinning.

"Not *that* well! And it's got security that runs off anyone who tries to get close."

"How do you know that?"

The waiter returned with their drinks and she lifted hers, holding it out to him in a jaunty *salut*. "You're not the only one with sources."

And, because she was a little buzzed, she winked.

Chapter Eleven

RUBY

$\mathcal{M}$om and I agreed on which dress was the nicest to wear to meet Mr. John: It hung down to my knees and was green and blue with a flower and pineapple pattern. Mom said the green in the dress really brought out the green in my eyes.

Then Mom braided my hair into a plait. She thought that would look more "classy." But when Max came to pick us up, he said how pretty I looked, but then brought Mom off to the side and spoke quietly to her. When she came back, she said, "Let's let Mr. John see all your hair, sweetie," and undid my plait. My hair spilled down over my shoulders and to my back. I was bummed because I'd thought the plait was really nice and it took Mom a while to get it right.

Then we got into the buggy thing that looks like a souped-up golf cart and we drove down a very long hill, and then up another long hill. We must have been driving for about 15 minutes, clear to the other side of the island, and the view was amazing.

Blue water as far as I could see, so incredibly dark blue, with light blue and emerald along the shore. The prettiest view I've ever, ever, ever seen and I wished so badly I could take a photo. I know I'm not supposed to tell anyone where I am, but I feel like in a year when I have nothing to look at to prove I was here, I might start to doubt it, to think this was all a long dream.

Finally, Max drove us up another long hill, and then a house came into view. It stood atop the hill and looked nothing like all the other homes I'd seen in Greece. Instead of white, it was made of glass, but you couldn't see into it. It was like a huge square with many other squares coming out from all sides of it. It was interesting looking, like no house I'd ever seen, but not as pretty as the little white houses or the white churches with dark blue domes. I wondered why a man with as much money as Mr. John would want kind of an ugly house.

A tall gate opened, and the cart went through and we parked in a really large garage. Inside was a red sports car that looked like the kind of car only a very, very rich man would own, though I don't know how he could drive a car like that on these little roads. Maybe he keeps it here for show.

In the house, Max brought us to an incredibly large room that had ceilings that went far, far up, and now I understood why Mr. John had a house like this. Because it felt like you lived outside. The glass was perfectly see-through from inside and all around were the island and the water. My heart was pumping quickly because it was so crazy beautiful and I thought I could not ever see a more insanely awesome house, and any house I ever went into after this would be a silly house.

Max told us to sit on this very, very long white couch. It was so white I felt like maybe it was brand new and no one had ever sat on it before. I stared at the walls, where all kinds of photos and art was hung. Some extremely large pieces that took up much of the wall, and then some so small I couldn't see what the pictures were.

But one thing I did see was a photo of a beautiful woman with her back turned to the camera. She was blonde and naked, her face peeking over her bare shoulder. She looked really familiar to me and when I looked closer, I realized it was Marilyn Monroe. I'm pretty sure.

Seeing a naked woman, even a famous one, made me nervous. I thought again about why I was here, and I looked over at Mom, who was staring with glassy eyes at everything, and I got the feeling she'd sort of checked out. She tends to do that when she's overwhelmed. I really needed her to not check out, because I was about to check out myself.

It was maybe thirty seconds later that it happened. A man came into the room.

At first, I didn't think there was any way this was Mr. John. I'd built him up in my head as being a superhero, but he was this small, kind of frail-looking man. But when he came closer, I realized he only looked small because the room was so enormous. In reality, he was really tall. He looked older than the photos I'd seen on the wall back in our room, but not that much older. He had a wide jaw and his hair was brown except for a lot of silver around the sides.

When he got very close and took my hand, I noticed his eyes were dark blue, and his lips were kind of pink for a man. He shook my hand, smiled, and then shook Mom's hand. He had nice, straight, white teeth. I thought maybe they were fake. He had on white pants and a white shirt that was long-sleeved and casual but somehow you knew the outfit was really expensive.

"It's so nice to meet you both," he said.

"It's nice to meet you too, Mr. John. Thank you for having us," Mom said, sounding like a little girl meeting her idol.

Then he looked at me again, and this time, he really *looked*. His eyes went all up and down my body more than once, in the way I'd begun to notice that men did on the street, but even more intensely. I felt really uncomfortable and wanted to run out of the room.

"Are you nervous?" he asked.

I tried to answer and say no, but I couldn't talk. There was a big lump in my throat.

"Yes, she's nervous. We both are," Mom said. "We've never done anything like this."

He didn't even look at Mom, but kept staring at me, and he was smiling a little, so I knew he liked what he saw.

"You look exactly like your photos and video. Which is good. Sometimes people don't. It's a risk bringing people here because they get here and have to go back home. But everyone had reported how you looked the same as your photos, so I was optimistic."

I nodded at him. I'm pretty tall—five-foot-nine—and a lot of guys are shorter than me, but he was a few inches taller. I don't know how he looked so small when I first saw him.

He put his hand over the top of my hand as he still held it, and said, "Are you ready for this adventure?"

I nodded and this time managed to get some words out of my mouth. "I think so."

His smile drooped a little. I got the feeling I'd said the wrong thing. After all, he chose me out of so many girls, and he could have easily found someone much more excited, so I said, "Yes, definitely. I can't wait." My voice sounded younger than what I normally sound like —kind of chirpy and weird.

"I understand you're nervous," he said, patting my hand. I wished he'd stop holding it. "But this is going to open your eyes in a way that will be incredibly beneficial for you. All of the other girls your age—they won't get to experience anything like this. They'll go through life never knowing everything you know. Isn't that marvelous?"

"Yeah," I said, and wanted to tell him to let go of my hand. I started to kind of tug it back, and then he dropped it, thank God.

"Are—are there other kids here?" I blurted out.

Mr. John got very silent, and his blue eyes went flat and got a little darker.

"I'm sorry, but we won't be able to talk about anyone else on the island. I know you're curious but everyone has their right to privacy."

"Sure," I said. "That's fine." I felt so stupid and

ashamed for asking such a dumb question. I wondered if he would change his mind and tell us we needed to leave. To be honest, I was torn. I wanted so badly all the things that had been promised to us, but at the same time, I wanted to run away and forget we came here. I wanted to go back to Kyrie and have a sandwich. Maybe meet up with Maddie and tell her not to worry about me, that nothing had happened. That I'd gone to the island and met the man, but then Mom and I had left.

"My girl," Mr. John said, in a deadly serious way. "You do understand that this will change your life, and it will be fun, I promise that, but it's also top secret, right?"

I nodded. Again, I couldn't speak.

"Your Mom signed important documents. If you break the secret, there will be severe repercussions. You know what that means?"

I kept nodding. I felt my lower lip starting to tremble. "Y-yes."

"Good."

The warm, welcome look came back into his eyes, and his lips curled up into another smile. He seemed much more friendly again.

"Then ladies," he said. "I invite you to enjoy yourselves. In order to protect everyone's privacy, you can't wander around the island unattended, unfortunately. But you've met Max, and he is here for you. He'll check in regularly and will always be available outside of your house if you need anything. He can take you to some beaches at certain times. We have a beach here that has pink sand. You won't find it anywhere else. And Lucy, the lady who brought your dinner and breakfast, is available by the house phone. Just call her. If there's something you want that isn't on the menus, no worries. It will be made for you. There's fresh catch every day."

"Thank you so much, Mr. John," Mom said, almost breathless.

I knew she was nervous too, but the way she was acting was sort of sickening. Because she sounded so humble and grateful, like we were nothing, and Mr. John was God.

And it seemed about *her*, and how *she* wanted to quit the bar and go back to school, and not about me and what I might want. Like she didn't even think for a second that I might find this all too much, too big and overwhelming, and I wasn't ready for it. Maybe I didn't want to know everything I was going to learn. Why was no one here giving me the chance to change my mind?

But I couldn't back out now. I didn't even know how to leave.

"You are so welcome," Mr. John said. His voice was very smooth, like one of those voices you hear on the radio. "Thank you for giving birth to a girl with this face."

He put his hand under my chin, and the touch made me want to rip my face away, but I didn't. So glad his hand only stayed there for a few seconds.

"Now," he said, "in five days will be the most important day." He smiled again, and it was the smile of a man who truly thought he was doing me the biggest favor you can ever imagine. "You'll get to meet my special friend."

Chapter Twelve

The next day, Maddie and Logan walked to the port and approached one of the first small boats they saw. A weathered man who looked like he'd spent decades' worth of summers being pruned in the sun was untangling a net. The boat was larger than the tiny fishing boats also lined along the port.

"*Kalimera*," Maddie said. "Are you for hire?"

"Possibly," the man said very slowly in an accent thick enough that she immediately sensed communication would be difficult.

"We'd like to go to Volinos island. Can you bring us?"

"Vol-eee-nos?" He scratched the side of his head, his black hair wavy and plentiful. He had the hair of a man in his thirties and the face of a man in his seventies. "No, no one go Volinos."

"What about just by it," Maddie said, pantomiming with her arm, trying to convey a boat sailing on by the island without stopping. This isn't what she wanted to do, but she had a vague plan of jumping off the boat and swimming to the island if they could get close enough. What she'd do if and when she got on it, she had no clue. The time to think about that was later. "We only want to see it."

The man regarded her with black, weary eyes, and an expression that conveyed he had no patience for this spoiled American who thought she could get whatever she wanted by asking more than once.

"No Volinos," he said, succinctly, then turned his back and began untangling the netting again.

"That went well," Logan said under his breath as they left and walked down the boardwalk looking for more boats.

The next boat had a sign on the boardwalk saying it could be hired for island excursions. The captain spoke much better English, and was clearly more tourist-oriented, but he gave them the same spiel.

"Ah, no," he said, shaking his head, looking bemused. "No Volinos. But we can go to other islands. You see Skelios? They film movies there."

"Why can't anyone go to Volinos?" Logan asked, sounding a little confrontational. Maddie felt like telling him to keep his New Yorker attitude in check.

"Because it private," the man said, adamantly. "No one allowed."

"What would happen if we went anyway?" Logan challenged.

The man shrugged, looking like he wished the pair of them would go away so he could hit up the other tourists on the boardwalk for business. "You can try," he said. "Maybe nothing happen. Maybe you arrested. Who knows?" His eyes roved past them, towards a couple strolling along who seemed a better bet for hiring him for something he could actually do.

"Well, thank you. *Efharisto*," Maddie said.

"There must be a place where we can hire a motorboat. Or sailboat," Logan said as they continued down the boardwalk, which was becoming more crowded as the morning wore on.

"You know how to sail?" she asked, skeptically. Logan had once told her he was Brooklyn born and bred. Brooklyn might be surrounded by water but it wasn't exactly known for its sailing.

"Well… no."

"And I don't feel like getting lost in the Aegean with you."

"Could be fun," he said, bumping her arm with his in an insinuating manner. The way he said it made her realize that he remembered their night together. She'd somehow convinced herself that perhaps he'd forgotten it. She stopped and turned to him, squinting her eyes, as she'd forgotten her sunglasses.

"Don't get any ideas, Airport."

"*Ideas?*" He looked affronted. "That was called a joke. And don't flatter yourself."

"Let's keep asking. All we need is one person to say yes."

"All you need is your head examined. We're not getting on that island. And it's too hot and you're too annoying." He wiped his sweaty brow with the back of his city-pale hand. "I'm going for a swim."

At that, he strutted away, disappearing behind a group of people with that odd forward-lurching gait he had, as if he had every right to take up as much space as possible. Watching, she felt a surge of resentment at how he could move through life expecting, and generally getting, everything else to move out of his way, everything to work out for him.

He was the type who parked in handicapped spaces with no repercussions. He could tell the petty tyrants of corporate life what to do, and instead of arguing, being dismissive, or ignoring him, they simply did what he ordered, and did it quickly and with a smile. If he raised his voice, he was "decisive." If he messed up a project, the mess would be given to a woman to fix, and he'd get the promotion.

And if, on the rare occasion, someone—Maddie, say —told him he wasn't going to get what he wanted, then he'd toss an insult and strut away, without an ounce of concern that this could backfire or bring consequences.

Then Maddie realized the hot surge of sensation in her gut wasn't resentment.

It was envy.

* * *

BACK AT HER STUDIO, Maddie changed into her bikini, determined to swim off the sour taste of a morning of "no" from every boat captain she'd approached. They'd all said the same thing—Volinos island was off-limits.

There was a knock at her door and, figuring it was the cleaning lady who was checking to see if the studio was occupied, Maddie opened it. But it was Logan. He stood big and bulky before her in black and red swimming trunks and that same "Hedgies" t-shirt, his wet hair plastered across his wide forehead. The sun was already deepening the color of the freckles scattered on his temples and neck.

Not for the first time, Maddie stared at him and couldn't register whether he was good-looking or not. At some angles, his heftiness appeared bold and masculine. At others, he seemed doughy and bleached out.

"Sorry," he said. "I didn't mean to snap at you before." His gaze trailed down her body, then hurried back up to meet her face, his pale cheeks flushing pink.

"Forget it," she said, returning to the bedroom area of the studio. She knew Logan well enough to know he didn't need an invite to follow her inside. She wanted to put clothes on if she was going to have any kind of conversation with him, and grabbed her cut-offs from the bed. They were stiff, smelling of sea and sand. She really needed to wash them.

"I just got frustrated," he said. "So I came back and emailed a bunch of the billies I've talked to over the years. One of them has to be in Greece or have a friend in Greece with a yacht."

"It's worth a try, I suppose," she said, slipping on a t-shirt over her shorts, and grabbing her new beach towel, which had a map of Kyrie on it. "You didn't alert them to what I'm suspecting, did you?"

"Of course not. I only said I'd like a ride to Volinos island. I assume you didn't have any luck?"

"Nope. All said the same thing, 'No Volinos.'" She

pulled her tote bag over her shoulder and stood before him, feeling small in front of his heft. "I know how much I annoy you, so maybe we should work on this thing separately."

"Hey," he said, putting up his palms in a gesture of *detente*. "It's clear I annoy you, too."

She laughed. "You might have a point there. But I don't want this to degenerate into squabbles. If there's a girl—or more than one girl—in trouble, I want to help her. That's it."

"Me too."

For once, he looked completely sincere, and Maddie began to feel a little guilty about how prickly she'd been with him. But she squared her shoulders and shook off the feeling, remembering how she'd felt *bad* about her remark to Daniel. How she'd taken on guilt that was not hers to take on. It had been *Logan* who'd busted boundaries by showing up on her vacation.

"Are you sure?" she asked, casting around for her sunglasses. They'd proven elusive on this trip; she was always misplacing them. "Because I feel like it's all about a promotion for you."

"I'm not going to lie. A promotion would be nice. But obviously if this dude is really running a pedo ring, I want to help stop it. I know you think I'm an ogre but I'm not."

She had to laugh at the word "ogre." He'd described himself better than she could have done. Finding her glasses in the bathroom, she slipped them onto her face and waved her arm to indicate he should head toward the door.

"Then let's try to get along. This is about something bigger than us."

"Agree, Maddie. Agree. And I'm sorry I brought up… what happened. Between us. I won't mention it again."

"You just did."

She grinned as she showed him out. Logan brought out the devil in her.

Chapter Thirteen

"*S*ounds like he's keeping you on your toes," Athena said.

The pair were having dinner at Marmita, one of the many little restaurants you could stumble upon while threading through the byzantine alleyways of the hilly *plaka*.

Athena had lived here long enough that she had her favorite tavernas, and this was one of them. The owner had come out to give her a boisterous greeting and lead them to a front table. He then personally delivered a large plate of grilled *horta* with lemon, anchovies fried in olive oil, and small glasses of Yastika, without them asking. Athena explained it was something Greek taverna owners did—they were proud of their food and loved to pile visitors with it.

Maddie rolled her eyes at Athena's remark about Logan and sipped her tangy-sweet Yastika, which reminded her of Elias and his Yastika-producing family.

She was unsure if he'd bring her the bottle he'd promised or if he'd only said that to make conversation.

"There's something about Airport—Logan as you know him—that really gets on my nerves," Maddie said. "I try to control it but I can't seem to."

"It's called sexual tension," Athena said, jiggling her brows.

"You're confusing me with this stuff," Maddie teased. "You're asexual but constantly talking about sex."

"Not for me. For *you*."

"It's definitely not sexual," Maddie said. "It's partly that he took over that story from me, the London billionaire. He's a mansplainer extraordinaire. Do you know one time we got into an argument about what it's like to own a dog? He's never *owned* a dog. I had a dog for nine years. Somehow, he knew more about dog ownership than I did." She rolled her eyes again, this time so hard they hurt. "He once told me the worst thing that ever happened to him was that he didn't get into Harvard. He was being serious. And he was promoted over me and I've done as much work as he has. You ever watch him walk? He *struts*. He's so cocksure that nothing bad will ever happen to him. It's not like that for girls."

"Well, he can't help that he was born with a penis. He does have a penis, doesn't he? I mean, you saw it, right? And did other things with it, am I correct?"

Athena chortled, enjoying her ribbing, as Maddie pantomimed gagging.

"I'm just tired of the penis pass," Maddie said.

"He's not going to turn down a promotion because you weren't offered one too," Athena responded, getting into lecture mode. "No woman would either. In fact, I would have taken a promotion if they'd offered one, which they didn't. And thank goodness for that, because it opened my eyes. You can have the sleet and snow, the noise and rats. I'll take the Aegean, the sun, and the fantastic Greek food."

"Speaking of which…" Maddie said as the owner and a waiter were beside the table, dispersing plates of bread with olive paste, zucchini fritters, cherry tomato balls, honey cheese balls, pots of moussaka and sea bass, and a bottle of the local house white. Then the owner and Athena made small talk in her rudimentary Greek until he backed away, smiling all the while, keeping his eyes on the table as if worried his diners might disappear.

Maddie and Athena divvied up the food, gape-mouthed and gleeful, with much fawning commentary. After about 20 minutes of this, they were satiated enough to return to regular conversation.

"Maybe we should invite Logan out for drinks," Athena said. "I feel kind of bad he's roaming around the island by himself."

"Please, no. I've had enough of him today. Besides, he came here on his own. I'm sure he's finding ways to amuse himself."

Just then, Athena raised her arm. "Elias!" she called.

At his name, Maddie's heart skipped a beat before she even saw him. She turned in her chair, and he was strolling up the steep hill with long and languorous strides, wearing white pants and a navy-blue dress shirt that Maddie knew was going to make his mesmerizingly blue eyes even more mesmerizing. As he got close enough that she could see them, she wasn't surprised to realize she was right. Every time she clapped eyes on this man, he got more attractive. She felt irrationally happy to see him, happier than was warranted given how little she knew him.

"*Kalispera*," he said, leaning down to double cheek-kiss each of them. Maddie caught a whiff of his minty-woodsy cologne, leaving her pleasantly lightheaded.

"Sit down," Athena said. "Help us eat. Panos keeps bringing out food we haven't ordered."

"That's *xenia*," he said, sitting next to Maddie, who was almost giddy that he'd chosen her side of the table. "We Greeks believe in feeding our guests."

He looked at Maddie and she grinned foolishly, thankful that he saw her looking presentable. She had on a short, playful dress she'd found in a local shop, her waist wrapped in a leather belt, and had let her hair naturally dry into beachy waves and had on mascara and mauve lipstick. She knew she wasn't a grand beauty —nor had she ever had the desire to be one, it seemed like a lot of hassle—but she thought she cleaned up rather well.

A couple of hours later, they paid the bill (Panos having refused to charge them for at least half of the food) and went for a walk along the boardwalk. Athena began to stretch and plead exhaustion. Maddie had little doubt Athena was trying to be a pal by leaving her and

Elias alone. Though she hadn't seen Athena's house yet, she knew it was several miles from the *plaka*, up into the remote hills, so they said their goodbyes, and Athena headed to where she'd parked her car.

Elias and Maddie kept on the boardwalk, then turned into the street that would eventually meander around to her studio. "I have something for you," he said. "If you come to my car."

She followed him to where he'd parked his Fiat and he opened the door and took out a bottle of alcohol. "Yastika." He grinned. "Best kind."

* * *

BACK AT THE STUDIO, Maddie put her key into the lock but the door wouldn't open. She jiggled the handle several times, thinking perhaps she was drunk enough that she'd done something wrong, though given all the food she'd consumed and the long walk she'd taken with Elias after dinner, she didn't feel drunk. Then it dawned on her: She'd locked the door instead of unlocking it— because it was already unlocked.

Maddie turned the key in the other direction and the door opened, with Elias close behind her. She glanced quickly around her room but didn't notice anything out of place. Perhaps the cleaning lady had forgotten to lock it when she'd left.

"Can you get some glasses in the kitchen?" Maddie asked Elias, who said, "Of course," and headed to the small kitchen with the bottle of Yastika.

Maddie took this opportunity to beeline to her

laptop on the desk. The password protection bar didn't appear, the laptop's contents were available for anyone who may have opened her computer.

She clicked into her security settings and realized that her computer was set so that she only needed to enter the password every three hours after sleep mode was activated. But she'd been out of the studio for more than three hours.

This meant during the initial three hours she'd been away, someone could have opened the laptop, awakening it, and gone inside without typing in a passcode. Afterwards, the three-hour limit would start back up again, which is why she was not seeing a password bar now.

Getting up, she hurried to the safe inside of the closet, pushed the passcode, and checked its contents. Her passport and cash were still sitting there undisturbed.

Elias reappeared and smiled at her. His winning smile was enough, for the moment, to ease the suspicion that again someone had been inside of her studio.

* * *

ON THE TERRACE, Elias poured them each a squat glass of the Yastika. The bottle was clear, its logo sporting the Greek "evil eye." The light and dark blue shaded eye symbol was ubiquitous on the island, staring out of shop windows, plastered on souvenirs and jewelry. The eye was meant to ward off bad juju.

The Yastika brand was called Doukas, which Elias

told her was his family's name. It meant "Duke." His family was descended from nobility and had been on the island since the 1300s, when Kyrie was ruled by Venetians.

"*Yamas*," he said, tipping his glass to hers. Maddie echoed him, trying to replicate his inflection exactly, with the stress on *Ya*, not *mas*. She sat on the short couch on the terrace and, this time, instead of taking the chair across from her, Elias glided down next to her. His nearness made her ovaries pulse. (Cheesy, yes, but that's exactly what it felt like.)

Since breaking up with Jesse two years ago, she'd dated here and there, but nothing had ever gone past a third outing. Something about a fourth date indicated things were moving forward in a more real way, and so the third date was always the end of the journey. Sometimes, it was the guy who never got in touch again, and Maddie would be a little disappointed. Other times, it was she who stopped responding to communications or would send a canned email such as, "Although I enjoyed our time together, I don't feel we're the best match…"

She felt she had a lot to give a relationship but deep down worried she was damaged in some fundamental way; that her father's death when she was only 16, her experience with Daniel, and her relationship with Jesse, all had snapped an essential cog, leaving her unable to trust and be vulnerable the way that relationships required. So many people had disappointed her, failed her, that she couldn't tell if this was the way things were, or her expectations for her fellow humans were too unrealistic.

Elias—with his warmth, charm, relaxed manner, and yes, maybe even the fact that he lived so far away— drew her to him in a way she hadn't experienced since she'd met Jesse almost a decade ago.

"Why are you working on Athena's home and not in the Yastika business?" she asked him.

He waved one hand. "Yaskita business very hard. Mostly old ladies collect the sap. They're much stronger than me." He flexed one bicep, then laughed with his airy, masculine laugh. "And I want to live in Athens. I love Kyrie, it my home, but I like city life. One day, maybe, I take over company. Right now, my father and older brother run it. It used to be much bigger. Sell all over Europe. But after earthquake and economic crisis, things get tougher. They're better businessmen than me, so they're trying to get back to what it used to be."

"You're right," Maddie said, savoring the taste of the Yastika. "This is better than the other brand."

"I told you."

He leaned towards her and for a moment her heart spasmed in anticipation that he was about to kiss her. But he didn't. He was only leaning towards the table in front of them, to place his glass on it.

"You have husband, Mahdee?" he asked.

"Husband? Not at all." It hadn't occurred to her that he might assume she was married. In America, everyone checked out the ring finger. Perhaps that wasn't a thing they did here.

"Why not?" he asked.

"I don't know," she said, flustered. She wasn't going to tell him about Jesse, their short engagement that ended with her miscarriage. She'd already revealed more than she was comfortable with for the amount of time she'd known him. "It's not something I really think about. You have a wife?"

"Oh no," he said, slowly shaking his head. "No, nooo."

Maddie realized something. He hadn't known her relationship status before. In Greece, people tended to get married earlier than in New York. He must have assumed she was married or, at the very least, in a committed relationship, given her age. Of course, he didn't know her age unless he'd pumped Athena for information, but she was probably clearly older than the marriageable age in Kyrie.

Since she was a bit buzzed, she said, "That's good," and gave him what she hoped was a flirtatious smile.

He laughed that airy laugh again. It signaled pure, almost childlike, joy. In the past, she'd noticed that if she didn't like a man's laugh, she couldn't be attracted to him. In fact, she'd once gone on three dates with a perfectly nice older man, a neurosurgeon, whom she was desperately hoping to develop an attraction to but his snickering, high-pitched giggle had unwillingly repulsed her. Why a laugh had to appeal to her senses for there to be any chance of procreation, she didn't know. No wonder she was still single!

"How old are you?" she asked.

"Three-zero," he said, pantomiming the numbers with his fingers. "My mother, she very much like me to get married, have babies. I'm old now, eh?"

"You're decrepit," she said. "Your time has come and gone, my friend."

She didn't know whether he understood her sarcasm but when he clutched his heart and pretended to pass out for a moment, she knew he did. It was nice to be around a guy with a sense of humor, they were rare finds in New York.

"Elias, today I tried to hire a boat to bring me to Volinos," she said. "But no one would do it."

He nodded somberly. It was now completely dark out, that other-side-of-the-world dark, with a waxing moon that appeared so much brighter and closer than it did in New York, throwing silver ripples on the darkened sea.

"No, they all know. Volinos private."

"But you said there were rumors of the island being the scene of parties and orgies. How would anyone know that if no one can get near it?"

He thoughtfully sipped his Yastika, staring out at the sea. "Who knows how rumors start?"

"Would you do me a favor and take me to anyone who has talked about the island to you?"

He contemplated this for a few moments, then turned to her. "You still worried about the girl?"

"Yes and no. A part of me thinks I'm imagining the worst things because of what happened to me. The thing I told you."

"Yes, I remember. I wish this thing not hurt you anymore, Mahdee."

"Thank you," she said, laying her head back on the couch so she could stare straight up at the bulging moon. "But another part of me thinks I've stumbled into something big. And I don't know what to make of this, again, it could be my imagination. But twice I feel like someone has come into my studio and was looking around. Trying to get into my computer."

"Who?" He sounded rather shocked. "I know Karen and Kostas," he said, naming the studio's owners. "They never come in without permission."

"Oh, I don't think it's them. There's a coworker who's on the island and he's the only person who'd have a reason to want to spy on me, but now I don't think it's him either. Maybe I'm losing my mind." She tilted her face towards him and smiled.

"Here is your mind," he said, placing his hand on the top of her head. "I find it for you."

Then he leaned in and kissed her.

Chapter Fourteen

*T*he next day, Maddie couldn't help continually smiling to herself as she headed down the stone steps to the rental's back beach, towel slung over her arm. Elias hadn't left her room until the sun peeked over the horizon, a ring of fiery red blending into a spectrum of orange hues, the air tinted amethyst.

He had not put pressure on her to have sex, but after an hour or so of kissing and fondling, she'd felt like she would die if they didn't. So, they had, and it had been absolutely wonderful.

She was leaving in a little less than two weeks, and he would return to Athens at the end of the summer, but she felt it would all work out as it should.

Intellectually, she knew she shouldn't let a fantasy of them being together roll out ahead of her, but felt it starting to unfurl against her will. Romance had seemed such a difficult thing back in New York, jagged with obstacles and disappointments, but suddenly, it seemed so easy. How had she not seen how easy it could be? All you had to do was meet the right person.

Plenty of people did long-distance relationships. And Athens and New York weren't so far apart—a ten-hour plane trip. Less with a strong tailwind.

Plenty of people started out long distance before figuring out a way to be together. Not that she should be even considering this kind of thing given that she hardly knew Elias, but plenty of people also got together after extremely short periods. Plenty of people! She may not know any of them, but she'd at least read about them.

I was solo backpacking around Spain when I met Manuel in Barcelona. We hit it off right away and haven't been apart a day since. We have two kids and will celebrate our tenth wedding anniversary this year.

Hadn't she read that somewhere?

She was in such a state of dreamy bliss and vague future-planning that she didn't notice Logan until she was almost right on top of him. He practically blended into the beach's white pebbles. There was no one else but him in sight.

"Morning," she said, feeling trapped. There was no way for her to leave without seeming excessively rude. Much as she didn't want to spend too much time with Logan, much as he was still her number one suspect for breaking into her studio, she needed him to be her ally on digging up information on Dexter Hunt.

"Morning," he said, propping himself up on an elbow. "I could do without these pebbled beaches."

"Yeah, me too." Her mind was whirring with how she could find a place not near him. The beach wasn't that big. Spotting some shade under a small tree, she decided to head for it.

"Careful in this sun, Airport," she said, starting to walk away. "You're a lot paler than I am."

"Hey, Splash," he called out. "I might have a lead on Volinos."

Turning, she pulled her wide-brimmed hat lower to shade her eyes from the sun. He took a container of sunscreen with "100 SPF" on it out of his shorts pocket and slowly, as if she had the entire day to stand watching him, began applying it to his neck, face, and shoulders. She could tell his leisurely pace was meant to push her buttons, so she decided to pretend she wasn't annoyed, which she knew would annoy him. *Two can play this game, Airport.*

Finally, he tossed the sunscreen to his towel and went on, "I heard from one of my billies. He's adamant no one will get near Volinos. Word has gone around that there is something big going on on that damn island this week. That Hunt's got heavy hitters over there."

"Like who?"

"Like who?" He smirked. "You think anyone would know names? But major people. Like maybe Bill Gates. Jeff Bezos. Maybe..." He paused. "...the president."

"That's a lot of maybe."

"My billie says security will be extra tight. No way a yacht can sidle up. Hunt gets guests there on his boat or chopper, no one can bring their own transport."

"Does this mysterious source know what's happening this week?"

"All kinds of speculation. Major investment opportunity? Secret wedding? But the biggest rumor is that he's going to invite the richies to reserve their place in space. Not rocket them up and spin them around. Invite them to live on a special space station. A luxury one, with caviar and champagne, not the freeze-dried kind, surrounded by the stars, sun, moons, and planets. Talk about location, location. Talk about an unparalleled view." He made a frame with his hands. "Of course, it'll cost 'em. Most expensive condos of all time. Who knows how he'll manage it, but my source tells me he might."

Maddie pondered this. Sounded like the kind of crazy thing an eccentric billionaire would attempt and even more eccentric billionaires would buy into. But it also sounded like a nice cover for something more nefarious.

"So your sources have gone from thinking he's evading taxes to that he's starting the world's first luxury space condo?"

Logan stood and began adjusting his swimming trunks. Maddie wanted to avert her eyes but was strangely riveted by the motion of long, black, wet shorts rubbing against his pasty but flat stomach.

"Things change," he offered. "So I was thinking. What if the girl you met was invited to the island because she won some kind of school science fair contest? That would explain the big secret and why she might have given you a fake name."

"Could be. But if he's such a genius, such a science fanatic, why is everyone saying he throws wild parties and has orgies?"

"Are you saying nerds don't like sex, Splash?" He

stopped shifting his trunks and wiggled his slightly unruly brows at her. "Because I assure you they do. And, no, I'm not hitting on you."

"Well, thanks for the information, Logan. I suppose that could be what this is all about. I sincerely hope so. But I'm not going to stop poking around just yet."

She pulled her long Kyrie-map towel tighter around her arms. The sun was beginning to beat down relentlessly on her bare shoulders, and she wanted to get into the shade—and away from Logan.

"I'll see you later," she said, waving at him.

Halfway to the shaded area, she heard him calling her again. She turned and he was ambling towards her, pebbles clacking under his leather sandals.

"Look, I don't know if I should tell you this. I've been debating it all morning."

Now what? she thought, irritably, but only stared at him. A luminous glob of white sunscreen balanced precariously on his clavicle. He was squinting down at her with a solemn expression that said he had some kind of news and not of the welcome variety.

"That guy who spent the night at your place," he said. "His name's Elias?"

Maddie's mouth popped open. She was so taken aback that she couldn't think of a thing to say, and even if she could, she'd lost the ability to answer him.

"I saw him come out in the morning," he continued. "I'm only two doors away from you. I was up early, getting coffee and figs."

"I—I don't..." She shook her head, still too flustered to know what to say. "I don't... *Why?*"

"Because he was sitting next to me yesterday at a taverna on the port. He was with a hot chick and they were pretty cozy. They were speaking Greek, so I don't know what they were saying, but she kept calling him Elias. Definitely seemed like the same guy who came out of your room. He looked right at me and said '*Kalimera.*'"

"What do you mean 'cozy'?"

"Cozy as in she was sitting on his lap and they were exchanging spit cozy."

"I—I don't—" she sputtered defensively, inexplicably feeling as if she was being accused of something. "I don't know why you're telling me this."

"If it's an island fling, hey, kudos. But in case it was a bit more, I thought you should know. Don't want you to get hurt, that's all."

"It's really—really none of your business."

But she knew her rattled reaction had made it his business. Had made it patently clear to him that his tidbit of information was not only unexpected but very much undesired.

"Just thought I'd mention it. Probably shouldn't have." He wiped his wide freckled forehead, raked his hair back, and said, "Sorry. Should have kept my mouth shut."

He walked off, wobbly from the pebbles underfoot, and Maddie made her way to the shaded area, which, in the ten minutes since she'd first seen it, had become speckled with sun. Throwing her towel on the white pebbles, she eased down cross-legged, staring into the sparkling water, dismayed, disappointed, and feeling like an utter fool.

* * *

TAKING her scooter up into the hills to Athena's new house, the wind on her face, the sun blazing on her arms, she couldn't stop thinking about what Logan had told her.

Sitting on his lap and exchanging spit cozy.

Unbelievable! Elias went from making out with one woman to—a few hours later—making out with Maddie. Exactly how people caught strep throat!

She couldn't shake off the feeling of being duped, even though she knew it was her own fault for letting her fantasies run away with her.

But she *had* asked him if he had a wife. He'd said no. If this "hot chick" (Airport really needed to throw that part in, didn't he?) was Elias' girlfriend, he technically hadn't lied, but he hadn't been honest either.

At the top of the hill was a crisscrossed wooden gate with the street number Athena had given her, and outside were parked several work trucks. The gate was open, and Maddie drove into the dirt driveway, astonished at the size of the white-washed house. It was two stories and sprawling, with what looked like a smaller guest house to the side.

As Athena had never given the impression she came from money, in fact, quite the opposite, Maddie was speechless. There was also a large yard out front shaded by several silvery-leafed olive trees.

"*Kalispera*," she said to one of the workers after managing to kick down the stubborn stand on her scooter. "Is Athena home?"

The man nodded and smiled pleasantly but she got the distinct feeling he hadn't understood a word she'd said, not even the name Athena. He pointed and she followed the direction of his finger to the side of the house, towards a man who was kneeling on the ground, layering cement onto a brick wall.

The man was shirtless, clad in paint-splattered jeans, and had his back to her. She instantly recognized the body shape—Elias. The first man was sending her to the best English speaker. The very man she had no desire to speak to right now. She tried surreptitiously heading towards the blue portico over a door but Elias turned and saw her.

"Mahdee," he said, putting down his trowel and striding towards her.

Before she could stop him, he'd walked right up and kissed her on the mouth. His lips were the same soft lips that had turned her into quivering jelly last night and, despite herself, his bare-chested nearness made her mouth go bone-dry with lust.

Mere hours before, she'd had him naked in her arms, had her face pressed up against his smooth, deliciously manly-smelling skin, and this wasn't something she could block from her mind easily.

"So happy to see you," he said. "Athena is back of house. Wait till you see the view."

"Sure," she said, tone flat.

Elias' face drooped as if he sensed that she was unhappy. "Something wrong?" he asked.

"Can you come here?" she asked, indicating that they should move away from where two other men were layering the brick wall.

With a bewildered expression, he followed her to the side of the house, where a tall hedge gave them shade and privacy. She took a deep breath, then forced herself to look into his eyes. They were the same breathtaking blue as last night but now she felt they held secrets.

"Do—do you have a girlfriend?"

He slowly put his fingers to his chin, as if she'd asked him an advanced trigonometry question.

"Girlfriend? Why you ask this?"

"Because a friend of mine saw you with a girl last night, right before you met Athena and me for dinner. It's fine if you do. But if you do, I can't see you again. That's not me."

"Mmm," he said, in deep thought. She could tell by his drawn-out, pensive reaction that it was true. "You must mean Caterina." He looked at her with something like sadness pooling in his eyes. "Yes, Mahdee, I admit that Caterina and me…" He trailed off, shuffled his feet a few times, then sighed dolefully. "We know each other since children. Her family and my family always think we get married someday. But… we more like good friends."

"Good friends who have sex?"

"Ehhhh…." he said, voice croaking. "You Americans very, eh, what is the word…"

"Direct?"

"Yes, direct."

"Is she the waitress who served us that time?"

Maddie remembered the dark-haired, curvy waitress at the port taverna who'd given her side-eye as she'd left with Elias to go to the Kalaria house. Just the kind of woman Logan would think was a "hot chick."

"Ahhh," said Elias, once more seeming as if Maddie had thrown him a challenging mathematical conundrum. "I think you mean Anjeliki. She waitress at Bon Pressa." He studiously contemplated the area somewhere over Maddie's left shoulder. "Or maybe you mean Nefeli. She waitress at Cosmo."

"More childhood friends?"

This time she couldn't help smirking as Elias at least had the decency to look deeply embarrassed. He'd once said he knew everyone. She didn't know he'd meant carnally. Now it made sense why he'd "just happened" to have a condom in his back pocket last night.

"You were a very popular little boy," she said.

"Oh, Mahdee," he moaned, dramatically pressing his forehead. "What can I say? What can I do? How I correct this?"

His pleading tone and expression were almost comical. Must be a Greek thing. Where Maddie came from, men barely had emotions, let alone the operatic ones currently on display.

"I did not know I would spend the night with you," he went on. "Make love to you. I couldn't help it. I'm only a man. Not table. Not chair. Man!"

She struggled to control a smile tugging at her lips. His performance was so histrionic that she was on the verge of slow clapping. "It's fine, Elias. I just hope you're keeping everyone apprised. Girls don't like liars."

"Liar?" he huffed, his palm flying to his nut-brown chest. "Not me." He took her hand, staring into her eyes with his soul-baring blues. "I like you. I want to be with you again. All other girls, I will tell them to go away."

"Oh, don't change your life for me," she said, trying to twist her hand away. "Where's Athena?"

He increased his grip and led her back around to the front of the house, to a door of distressed purple hues, with a metal knocker in the shape of a gracefully drooping hand. She'd noticed the island was brimming with beautifully decorated and painted doors. Since most of the homes were white-washed, she supposed this was the one way for the houses to have a burst of color and unique expression.

"Come inside," he said. "Wait till you see house." Right before they were to enter, he pulled her under the portico, his arms tight around her waist. "You not mad at me anymore, no?" he asked, hopefully.

The crazy thing was, she wasn't. She realized that Elias was a stereotypical charmer, who likely had a string of women from here to Athens. But he managed it with such affability that she couldn't be angry with him. Besides, it was her own fault for reading more into things than she should have. She *did* feel like squirming away from his embrace, but resisted, instead saying, "Not mad. But when can I talk to anyone who told you about orgy island?"

"Tomorrow?" he said. "I take you to my friend Yiannis at the port."

"Sounds good."

"And you kiss me more, no?" he asked, grinning.

"One thing at a time, Elias," she said, and couldn't help laughing.

* * *

On the other side of the house, Athena walked Maddie around the property, which was about quarter of an acre and looked down upon the vast blue expanse of the sea on three sides.

"You never told me your ancestors were loaded, Athena," Maddie teased. "I would have been nicer to you all these years."

Athena snorted and brought Maddie to a lemon tree that had dropped half its lemons. She began plucking them off the ground, examining ones that were in good shape, and plopping them in the little basket she was carrying.

"My great-grandfather was a successful merchant. Olive oil, silk, and things. I'd always heard that but didn't know much about it. Then my grandmother emigrated to the States and that was the end of the money side. Thanks, Yia Yia!" she shouted to the cloudless sky with mock bitterness.

"Then you got funding to restore the house from a group here?" Maddie asked. She'd only heard the very basics from Athena.

Athena sniffed a plump lemon, placed it in the basket. "Yeah. The Repatriation Project. A ton of locals fled after the last earthquake and I guess the municipality was getting kind of desperate. I stumbled upon the opportunity while doing research to visit. Next thing I knew, I had a house. It had been sitting empty all these years. I had to promise to live on the island for at least ten years." She tossed a puckered, browning lemon back to the ground. "I suspect they were looking for breeders to repopulate the island. Well, my uterus is retired. Not that it ever had a career. But they didn't need to know that."

"Did you have an interview?"

"No, but an extensive application. Though because I could prove my ancestry, it didn't take that long to approve it. Maybe a few months."

"That's fantastic. Damn, I need to find out if my long-dead relatives have any homes lying around I can claim."

"Get on it, girl."

At the edge of the property, they could see the sea looping around the island and spot many ships in the distance.

"Sooooo," Athena drawled. "Going to spill? What happened with Elias?"

"He's a nice guy, very cute," she said, too embarrassed to admit they'd had sex. "But a little too active in his personal life for my tastes if you know what I mean."

"Hm, not surprising. That's par for the course around here. The locals love to pick up tourists."

"Oh, these are local gals. I hadn't even gotten to the tourists yet."

"Shocker," Athena said, deadpan.

"What's alarming is how quickly I started

daydreaming I was going to run off to Athens to be with him."

"Oh, Mad. He's so tasty, I don't blame you. And maybe you're ready to find someone and settle down. It's been a while since the whole Jesse fiasco."

Maddie sighed, dragging her eyes away from the spectacular view. How lucky Athena was that she'd get to wake up every day to this. At home, Maddie had a view of the grimy tenement buildings across the street, laundry hung out on fire escapes to dry. Occasionally, she was treated to the view of the barrel-bellied man in one of those tenements who liked to stand at his window in his underwear.

But she wondered if she could ever live in a place like this. Wasn't it so special because Maddie wasn't seeing it every day? If she lived here, this view would soon become monotonous, expected, even boring. And much as she loved Greek food, she was already craving her local Chinese, Thai and sushi takeout joints. And a good slice of pizza. She'd noticed one Italian restaurant in the *chora*, but that was it for variety. Nothing is delicious when you have to eat it every single day and night.

"You might be right," Maddie said. "But I also think it has to do with what happened to me as a kid. Remember? With my father's friend?"

"I remember."

"Lately, ever since I met that girl Ruby, I can't stop thinking about it. It's making me feel kind of weird and clingy." For a moment, despite the sizzle of peak afternoon, she shuddered. "It might even have made me imagine a nonexistent pedophile ring."

What she didn't tell her friend was that ever since she'd arrived on the island, its dry, warm clime had plunged her into deep REM sleep, and she was having some of the most intense, detailed dreams of her life, like movies playing on the backs of her eyelids.

Many of the dreams had to do with Daniel. He looked as he had 20 years ago, and in the dreams, Maddie was her current age of 32 but every bit as attracted to him as she'd been as a lovestruck teen. His wife, Chelsea, was often in the dreams too, looking plain and maternal, and sometimes the twins, always toddlers, made appearances.

There were many variations on the dreams (in one, all of them were putting on a musical at some hole-in-the-wall theater) but there was one constant—the dreams were suffused with the sensation that although Daniel had a wife and kids, it was Maddie he truly wanted, and the pair were on the verge of being reunited.

Upon awakening, the dreams would fill her with a deep sense of melancholy and shame. Once her attraction to Elias solidified, he blessedly began pushing Daniel out of her dreams, replacing him with his own much more acceptable presence. This, she realized now, had made her bond to him in a way that wasn't rooted in the reality of their relationship or who he was.

"Why don't you hunt that dirtbag down and confront him?" Athena demanded.

"What's the point? It's been 20 years. There's no case against him anymore even if I wanted to go that route. And he'll only deny it. Do you know if he denies it convincingly enough, I might believe him?"

"Come on, Maddie. That's absurd. *You know* what happened. I wrote to one of my own jerks a few years ago. Found him on social media. He actually apologized. Said he was really screwed up in high school. In some weird way, it made me feel better. If you give this guy a piece of your mind, it might make you feel better too."

Maddie only gave a little shrug and stared into Athena's basket. "Never thought I'd see you with a basket on your arm, picking lemons like a country girl," she said.

Athena proudly examined her pickings, approximately a dozen perfectly-formed, bright yellow lemons. "You know what they say," she grinned. "When life gives you lemons…" She hooked her arm through Maddie's. "Make Yastika lemonade."

* * *

THAT NIGHT, Athena dropped Maddie off at her studio after the pair had dinner. Sometime tomorrow, Athena would pick Maddie up and bring her back to the house so she could retrieve her scooter, which she didn't want to drive after their afternoon of guzzling spiked lemonade.

As Maddie approached Sideratos around midnight, she spotted a light on in the window of the studio two doors down from hers. She knocked, assuming that Logan, like her, was still on New York time and wide awake. Within thirty seconds, he answered in shorts and a black t-shirt, filling up the entire doorway with his bulk, his expression only mildly surprised at Maddie's presence.

"I wanted to thank you for telling me what you saw," she said. "I didn't take it well but I'm glad you told me."

"Oh, um, that's good," he said, slouching against the doorframe. He had a square glass in his hand, and the sharp, licorice-y odor identified the contents as Ouzo. "I've been feeling bad that I said anything. Like not only did I break some kind of international bro-code but I also got yelled at."

"Don't feel bad. Goodnight."

"Sure you don't want to join me for a nightcap? I'm not hitting on you. Well, I probably am a little."

She stared wearily at him for a few moments with a *nice try* expression before waving goodbye. This time, her own door was properly locked, and inside, she checked her suitcase and its tiny padlock, where she'd stored her laptop. From now on, she wouldn't leave it out in the open.

Chapter Fifteen

RUBY

*M*om and I had the most amazing dinner tonight. Definitely the best one I've ever had. There was steak and lobster, lasagna, all kinds of vegetables, salad, ice cream, this delicious creamy pudding cake with chocolate frosting, and Mom had champagne and I had soda.

After the plates were cleared away, tea was brought in and we were told Mr. John was going to join us. I could barely move from so much food but when I heard Mr. John was coming, I got nervous. I thought I might throw up. Maybe he'd take one look at me and, this time, realize he'd made a big mistake.

Which in some ways would be terrible, but in another way, not so bad, because I'm definitely trying not to think hard about everything and panic. If I start thinking too hard about it, my breathing gets quick and my heart starts to flutter like butterfly wings.

Mr. John came in and smiled at us. He was wearing

all black. A black long-sleeved shirt and black pants. He had on the brightest watch I'd ever seen. It was so bright you could tell it was real gold and that every other gold I'd seen was fake. I tried to stop myself from staring at it.

He asked us if we enjoyed our meals. "Oh, yes," Mom practically gasped. "It was the best meal we've ever had." While that was true, it was irritating how she answered for me.

A woman with short dark hair who was standing in the corner came over and put a folder down near Mr. John. I recognized her as the woman with the British accent who'd talked with Mom at the hotel in New York. I'm pretty sure she'd said her name is Glenda.

But this time, she didn't speak to us. She handed Mr. John a folder, then backed away. For a few minutes, he did nothing but read and ignored us, which was awkward. I tried to sip my tea but I was too nervous, and kept the teacup up to my lips but didn't swallow, which was even more awkward.

"Karolina Ruby," Mr. John finally said. "What a beautiful name for a beautiful girl."

I tried to say thank you but my throat was thick, and I could feel that Mom was disappointed that I didn't say anything but Mr. John didn't seem to notice.

"You are a very rare girl," he went on. "Your ancestry chart says you have 24 different trace regional ethnicities in your DNA."

I knew Mom's family was originally from Canada and Dad's was originally from Morocco but that's all I knew. So right now, Mr. John knew more about me than I did.

"Most Americans, myself included, have eight or nine." He kept turning pages. "You have North African trace DNA, Dutch, French, Spanish, Italian, Irish, Syrian, Russian. Your ancestors migrated and inter-procreated an excessive amount."

"I knew about some of that but some of it is a surprise," Mom said. "Russian? Syrian? I have no idea which side of the family that is. How fascinating."

"This variety is what gives Karolina Ruby such a distinctive look, and at the same time one that many ethnicities would feel comfortable with and attracted to," Mr. John said. "This makes her very valuable to us."

I remember when I'd had to spit, over and over, into a little tube for Mom and she'd told me the modeling agency was going to test my DNA but I hadn't known why. I had to do it again as soon as we got to the island.

"You also passed our emotional intelligence tests with flying colors," Mr. John said. "You're curious, studious, open to new experiences, mature for your age, and resilient."

I liked that he was saying so many nice things about me though I don't think I'm anything that special. And I really didn't think I was mature for my age. But maybe I am. Some of the girls my age act so ridiculous. I started to relax and managed to sip some tea. Who doesn't like hearing nice things about themselves?

"We also appreciate that you and your mother aren't on social media," he said. "It shows us you don't feel the need to share everything that happens to you with strangers."

Oops. Mr. John didn't seem to know about those

few years when Mom had a social media account for me and tried to get a modeling career started through that. It was only because of Dad that she took it down. And I guess Mr. John didn't find my Pikchur account, which I only use to share pictures with about 20 friends. Mom doesn't know about it and I use a different name.

I didn't fill him in.

"Your age is on the young side for what's ideal but you look a little older. Thousands of studies, not to mention millions of years, have shown that attractiveness is closely tied to perceived fertility. That may not be politically correct but neither is nature. There are millions of variables on attractiveness but that's the core of it. If I put you in front of a thousand different people, from a thousand different cultures, the majority of them would affirm that you visually please them. Of course, there are always the outliers. There's no pleasing some people."

He sighed and laughed a little as if he'd made a funny joke. Mom started to laugh with him. Then I automatically laughed, even though I wasn't sure what was funny.

"Symmetry is universally valued," he continued. "Body modification is common and popular all over the world. Long necks in parts of Africa, Asia, and India. Large breasts in many Western countries. Rubenesque when food is scarce, rail-thin when it isn't. What's considered attractive in one era may go out of fashion or even be considered barbaric the next. We can't account for all tastes, all the time. We can only work with statistical odds, and statistically, Karolina, you're an above average bet."

This was all pretty flattering. I guess. He kind of lost me in there. But I did always feel I was pretty, and that I'm kind of unusual, for one, I'm taller than most of the girls and even a lot of the boys. I mean, that's why I wanted to be a model. Unfortunately, this isn't what I'm here for.

"Equally as important, your mother is supportive of our endeavors." He smiled, showing those weirdly straight white teeth. Unlike his gold watch, I'm pretty convinced they're fake.

"Of course, Mr. John," she said, practically bowing at the table. Gag.

"That's *very* important," he said. "Parental approval for minors."

He closed the folder and stared at me. He had an uncomfortably direct stare. Sometimes he looked at me like Mom does when I bring an A home from school. Like I'd done something great. Only I knew I hadn't done anything great—not *yet*.

"How are you feeling about everything, Karolina?"

"You can call me Ruby," I practically whispered. "Everyone does."

"That's fine. Code name Doris. That was my favorite aunt's name."

I nodded, thinking how I'd told Maddie my real name. If Mom knew that, she'd be upset. So would Mr. John.

"I—I feel fine," I said. But he must have guessed I was lying because he leaned forward and said, "Tell me the truth. Are you nervous? I don't blame you if you are."

I nodded, feeling a little bit on the verge of tears. I'm not sure why. It seems like everything will change after this. Like I won't be a kid anymore. Mom finally sensed how nervous I was because she turned and held my hand.

"But you're so lucky to get to meet Mr. John's special friend," said Mom.

"I know. I just feel like…" Ugh, I really didn't want to blow this opportunity for Mom and me. I kept thinking of the beach house. College. Mom quitting the bar.

Mom's hand squeezed around mine. I couldn't tell if she wanted me to talk more or was warning me to shut up.

"What?" Mr. John said. His dark blue eyes had grown darker, to where maybe I thought they'd never been blue and I'd only imagined that. They were a little flat, though his voice was warm. Did he feel bad for me or did he think I was wasting his time?

For a second, he reminded me of that creepy older guy who hangs out near my school trying to talk to me and my friends as we walk home. Sometimes the dude follows us in his car, staring at us like Mr. John is staring at me now, like he wants me but doesn't like me at the same time. I knew I was disappointing him by questioning anything.

"Will I be the same after?" I asked him, barely able to get the words out.

Mr. John looked blank and he slowly started to shake

his head. My stomach dropped. I felt I'd said the wrong thing.

"Of course you won't be the same," he said. "Ruby, you will *never* be the same." He paused for what seemed a long time, then said, "You will be so much better."

Chapter Sixteen

"*Maddie*," said Elias, who'd begun saying her name with more of an American accent, which was a shame. She missed his slow "Mahh-deee" drawl. "This is Yiannis."

The pair stood on a dock on the southernmost tip of the island—an area she hadn't seen before, one filled with boats but easily a half hour's drive from the main port. Yiannis had a traditional Greek wooden fishing boat, a *kaiki*, 16 feet long, white trimmed in red. His age was a bit of a mystery—his hair was wavy and thick but mostly silver and his face, coated with a bushy silver beard, was plump and sun-reddened. Maddie guessed he could be in his fifties. But she wouldn't make any bets on it.

"*Kalispera*," he greeted her. It was early evening and still quite light out, that brand of mellow buttery light that she'd not noticed anywhere else in the world. Like most of the men she'd met on this trip, Yiannis looked friendly and content. Who wouldn't be, Maddie supposed, living life on the teal blue water, basking in the sun and salty fresh air, knowing most everyone on the island, having a true sense of community? And no horns blaring. Can't forget that.

Elias spoke to the man in Greek but Maddie could pick out the word "Volinos" mentioned multiple times. The man was nodding and following along, then began speaking in halting English, gesticulating around the dock area with one weather-beaten hand.

"Girls come here. Get on boats." He waved his hand off into the Aegean. "Go to Volinos. Young, pretty." He drew his hand along his craggy face, as if describing himself, then laughed. Maddie noticed his teeth were yellowed and rickety. The island apparently didn't have the best dental care system judging by the mouths full of ailing teeth she'd witnessed—Elias a notable exception.

Elias spoke more to the man in Greek. They went back and forth, then Elias said to her, "Yiannis has driven by the island many times. He says there is a big house on the highest hill, all dark glass. Sometimes he sees a man outside on a terrace, sometimes the man has a young girl with him."

"How young?" Maddie asked.

Elias turned to translate but Yiannis understood. "Erm," he said, eyes rolling up, seeming to mentally count in English. "Fifteen, 16?" He shrugged. "Hard to say. Some look very young, some older. Maybe in twenties."

Maddie knew that just as she couldn't pinpoint Yiannis's age, the girls going to the island could be much older or much younger than they appeared. In fact, there was every possibility that the billionaire was under the impression the girls were of legal age even if they weren't. How many people asked for identification before getting intimate with someone?

Still, if there were underage girls being trafficked to his island, Hunt's ignorance of their true ages wouldn't be a defense. They looked young enough, at least judging by Ruby, that he should have made certain of their ages.

"How many girls have you seen?" she asked.

"Maybe five or six this year. Maybe same amount each year. Maybe he like girls, yes?" His eyes twinkled at her as if this was a completely natural penchant and why Maddie would be interested in such a thing, he had no idea.

"Do you ever see older people with the girls? What might be their parents, or a mother or father?"

Yiannis looked as if Maddie's English had finally run away from him so he turned to Elias, who translated.

"Ah, yes," Yiannis said. "Sometimes. Older ladies. Mothers maybe. Sometimes older men. Fathers? Maybe."

"Is there any way to get on this island, do you know?"

Yiannis turned to Elias and the pair spoke for a few minutes, Yiannis gesticulating with straightened arms and lots of pointing. Maddie got the feeling he was giving instructions as to how this might be possible, and sure enough, Elias confirmed it.

"He says the island has many little coves. A small boat could pull up and anchor but the island is very rocky. Would be extremely difficult to climb up from the beaches."

Yiannis interrupted him. Elias kept nodding, asked a couple of questions, then turned to Maddie again. "He says on south part of island, there is a small cove where it looks like rocks are low and people could climb over them and then keep going into the main part of island. Would be hard to see at night. At day, secure boats patrol island and would see anyone coming." It took Maddie a moment to absorb that by "secure" boats, Elias meant security boats.

"But he get goods delivered all the time," he continued. "Food, drink, toilet paper. Everything. All is delivered on dock at north of island. All deliveries checked by secure. Maybe way to sneak on delivery boat. Or..." He tapped his finger on his mouth. "Delivery boats come once a day. Yiannis says he see them at ten in morning. Wait until boats dock with delivery. Could be good opportunity to sneak on the island."

* * *

"We did good, no?" Elias asked as he parked his Fiat across from Sideratos.

"Thank you, Elias, that was really helpful. I'd still like to get on the island but I have no idea how to drive a boat. I could pretty easily end up in the middle of nowhere."

"I take you," he said, his tone indicating that the discussion was closed. "South end of island, small cove. We will find."

"Oh, Elias," she said, all of the recent coolness she'd felt towards him quickly melting. "I couldn't ask you to do that. I mean, we could get into a lot of trouble."

"Better I come with you," he said. "I'm Greek national. Something happen, better I can help."

"I—I can't ask you to risk yourself on what could be a wild goose chase." Elias looked perplexed and she laughed. "It means something that could go nowhere."

She stopped; he was staring at her with tenderness and true concern in his eyes. It wasn't surprising he was catnip to the women on the island—more than being handsome, he seemed like a genuinely good person.

"My point is this could all be nothing and I don't want you getting in trouble for it. Do you think if I offered Yiannis enough money he'd take me? He could drop me off and come back a few hours later?"

"Mahdee," he said, reverting to his drawling pronunciation. "I borrow Yiannis' boat. I take you. No more argument."

Much as she didn't want to drag Elias into something that could potentially be a big mess, it did make a lot more sense to not only bring a Greek citizen, but one who spoke good English. He might have to be called upon to explain their presence not only to Greeks but to Dexter Hunt himself.

She had a feeling Hunt was going to listen to a citizen of the country where he was residing more than he was going to listen to an American. The problem was she still didn't know what either one of them would say to him if they were found.

"You know how to sail?" she asked.

"I'm Greek," he said as if that was sufficient explanation. When she kept staring expectedly at him, he continued, rotating his forearms in demonstration, "Yiannis's *kaiki* is motorboat. Just steer it."

While one part of her wanted to get on Volinos as soon as possible, even tonight, another part of her was frozen with apprehension. It all seemed so crazy. How had she gone from what was supposed to be a fun, stress-free vacation full of sun, swims, good food, and quality time with Athena to… *this*?

Sneaking on to a well-connected billionaire's private island. This could end very badly. Any jail time at all didn't appeal to her—but jail time in a foreign country? Every guide book you read exhorted you to avoid such peril at all costs. How would she get a lawyer? How would she get back to the States? Trespassing was one thing—but what if she felt compelled to break into a residence?

And if Dexter Hunt had a secret as dark as an island that was a law unto itself when it came to abusing children, what might he be willing to do to protect this secret?

"We should go in the morning when delivery boats come," Elias said. "Too dangerous to climb rocks at night."

While she knew this was true—scrambling up the path on the bluff at Kalaria beach in the broad daylight was difficult enough—the idea of traipsing around the island at a time when anyone could easily see them didn't make much sense either.

"Elias, I think the only way to do this is to go directly

to the island and not try to hide. Anchor and say we got lost and need directions. That should give us enough time to at least scope things out a little."

"No one will believe that," he scoffed. "Islands very close together. Kyrian like me, lost? Impossible."

His excessive pride in that statement made her smile.

"Then let me think. But I feel we need to have a better plan or we'll be there for five minutes before someone hauls us away. I can't risk getting thrown in a Greek jail—or even worse, some crazy billionaire's basement. I don't want that to happen to you either."

"Then we think. We plan."

She was so grateful for having someone along with her on this bizarre journey—someone taking her fears seriously and willing to do more than nod in sympathy at her, but willing to risk himself as well, that she had the almost unstoppable urge to kiss him, but didn't dare.

Once she kissed him, there would be no sending him home. He'd shortly be inside the studio and her bed. Then her mind would be held hostage wondering about other girls he was with when he wasn't with her because she didn't believe they would magically disappear. Not exactly how she wanted to spend the remainder of her short vacation. Trying to crack open a potential pedophile ring was enough drama.

She leaned in and quickly hugged him, then turned before she could see his expression and was out the door. "Thanks. We'll talk soon, okay?"

He leaned over the seat and peered up at her. "Maddie, I'm sorry about the girls. It's an island. We get bored."

"I get it. I'm not a prude," she said, sensing disappointment coming off him as he realized she was about to scurry off. "I just know what works for me and what doesn't."

"Prune?"

She laughed, said, "*Kalinihta*, Elias," and hurried across the street even though it was empty.

* * *

At her door, she was about to head in when she heard, "Hey there, Splash," and turned around. Logan was sitting at the apartments' patio. She smelled the sickly-sweet odor of tobacco and saw an orange glow.

"Didn't know you smoked, Airport," she said, heading back in his direction.

"Just a light cigar." He leaned his head back, staring up into the starry night sky. "I have to say, you picked a great place to vacation."

"And Hunt picked a great island to buy, considering it must have all the same attributes this one does."

"True." He tipped his head back up, took a drag off his cigar.

She was torn about whether to let him in on her plans to ambush Volinos with Elias. A part of her was worried he'd mess it up for her somehow—if they got approached by security, she didn't want him copping an attitude and potentially getting them into more trouble than they'd already be in.

Elias had an easy charm about him—not to mention he was a neighbor—so she hoped, along with whatever story they'd concoct, he'd be able to placate security guards. But she also felt a bit underhanded hiding her plan from Logan, especially when he appeared to be working his sources and keeping her in the loop.

She decided to go with her gut and her gut was telling her to keep him in the dark for now. For all she knew, he was doing the same thing to her. Wouldn't put it past him.

"Was that Athena?" he asked, gesturing towards the street.

"No. But she does say hello. She's been busy with her new house."

He nodded, not looking like he believed that, and dragged on his cigar. He blew smoke out in front of him, staring off into the night. "So that was Prince Charming?"

"It was Elias, yes."

"Okay, Splash," he sighed, tapping his cigar on a glass ashtray on the table. "Glad to know it worked out."

Just then the apartments' owners, Karen and Kostas, came around the side of the building, having apparently been enjoying a night swim on their beach. They made greetings and headed into their apartment, which was on the side of the rentals.

"We're just friends," Maddie clarified, not sure why she felt the need to do so. It was none of Logan's business. But it also happened to be the truth. For now.

"I only hope he doesn't..." Logan murmured.

"Sorry, what?"

He looked straight at her. "I hope he doesn't hurt you."

Maddie's chest grew tight with irritation. Especially since Logan hadn't exactly been kind to her after their night together last year. Why was he now so concerned about her feelings?

"Any news on Volinos?" she asked.

"Nope. You?"

"Nothing." She shrugged. "Probably nothing going on anyway. I've got a florid imagination."

"Apparently so." He put out his cigar, stood, and stretched. She was again struck by his towering physique —over six feet tall and fully fleshed out with broad, muscular shoulders. Against her will, her mind traveled back to their night together.

Her breathing quickened and she realized with some horror that she was somewhat painfully attracted to him. Attracted in a very different way than she was to Elias, who, if he could keep it in his pants with other women, was the kind of man she could imagine being in a long-term relationship with. She could never imagine that with Logan. Something about him repelled her on a molecular level.

But she still had the animal urge to close the space between them, reach up around his neck, and draw his mouth down hard on hers.

"Night, Airport," she said.

"Night, Splash."

Chapter Seventeen

*I*t was now almost midnight, but Maddie's mind was sharply awake. She decided she'd have a glass of Yastika to try to soothe her into sleep. But there was only one thing she could think of, the thing that kept coming into her dreams.

Daniel Pewter.

He'd be in his late fifties now. She didn't know where he lived. He'd disappeared shortly after his marriage to Chelsea and birth of the twins. Once in a while, Maddie's mother would say something like, "I wonder whatever happened to Daniel."

But as he'd essentially been Maddie's father's friend more than hers, Maddie's mother never said more than that. Besides, adults seemed to understand that adult life —spouses, kids, mortgages, jobs, health problems—had a tendency to get in the way of friendships.

Her mother had her own busy life—she still taught English at a high school, and was extremely active in various hometown social clubs (gardening, books, civics, democracy, women's rights, on and on…). It wasn't surprising that she didn't sit around pondering what had happened to her late husband's best friend, even if, at one point, he was one of her closest friends as well. If her mother was particularly hurt by Daniel's not circling back to keep her up-to-date on his life, she never mentioned it.

Maddie never asked about him either. After that weekend, she could barely say his name aloud, as if her parents would instantly pick up strange vibes if she did, and start questioning her.

But Maddie remembered that Daniel would wistfully talk about California as a place he wanted to relocate. He'd visited there several times, and always felt at home with the laidback lifestyle, the balmy weather, and especially, the open roads and mountain vistas for motorcycle riding. He was never specific about where in California, at least that Maddie could recall.

Just me and the road, Maddie Madster, he'd say. *Me and the California road.*

At the time, any mention of him moving so far away, of not seeing him regularly anymore, would make her heart contract with fear.

"No, Daniel, you can't move," she'd said one time. "Dad would be so hurt."

"And you, Maddie Madster?"

"Me, too. Me most of all."

Ugh. She cringed at the memory.

"Daniel Pewter, California" typed into a search engine brought up a few people on LinkedIn, none of whom, she could tell by age and profession, were him. It also brought up two men on social media, but neither of them had a picture of themselves on their profiles, and there was no other identifying information. His twins' rather unusual names—Amos and Amity—would probably be a better bet.

Amos was nowhere to be found but Maddie got a hit on "Amity Pewter" right away as she was a minor social media celebrity, with slightly over 300,000 followers, and a modeling agency's email as a contact.

Maddie stared and stared. It had to be Daniel's daughter—how many other Amity Pewters in the world could there be? Not only that, many of her posts were tagged "Los Angeles, California."

Amity had shoulder-length, dirty-blonde hair; high, square cheekbones; thick, expertly-molded eyebrows. It was the eyes that convinced Maddie this had to be the right Amity; she could see Daniel in the light brown eyes rimmed with long, delicate lashes.

Maddie had always been a sucker for soulful eyes, eyes that looked contemplative and a little sad, and Daniel had those like no other man she'd ever met. She remembered thinking his eyes had been the exact color of the brandy in the crystal bottle in her parents' cupboard, suffused with amber-golden light.

Amity, who must be 18 now, appeared to be living the typical west coast lifestyle. Posed in various bikinis (she was tall, with a flat, muscular stomach), she frolicked on the beach and had posted a wide array of selfies. Sometimes her posts—Amity with a jug of wine, Amity lying on the grass in a black knitted turtleneck dress, Amity running in a field in a white trench coat and white go-go boots—were marked "Paid Sponsorship."

Maddie realized she'd mindlessly scrolled through a dozen photos and it would only be a matter of time before she spotted the teen with one or both of her parents, so she put the phone down on the glass table on the terrace. Her heart was pounding so furiously that air caught in her chest, triggering a short coughing fit.

She had gone all these years not wanting to know what Daniel was doing, where he was, what his life was like. Why was she doing this? And *now*? Didn't she have enough crazy stuff on her mind?

But something was driving her. It was more than meeting Ruby. It was more than Athena's words, *Why don't you hunt that dirtbag down and confront him?*

It probably had something to do with her age. She'd be thirty-three in a month. The age at which, if she wanted children—and she was fairly certain she did— she needed to start thinking seriously about it. Yet she hadn't been on a single measly date in, well, she'd lost track of how many months exactly. Three? Four? Could it even be five?!

Sure, the New York City dating scene would tax anyone's patience. But it wasn't only how mind-numbingly disappointing city dating could be. It was also her past. Her lack of trust. Her fear of being vulnerable.

Somewhere in the back of her mind was the continual drumbeat, *Is this what all grown men do? Is this what they're all like? Will I marry a man who, behind my back, seeks out minors for sex?!*

Sure, her father had been a good man. But he'd died on her when she was 16. So, the good ones died?

These thoughts weren't exactly rational, but they plagued her nonetheless.

And that led back to Daniel.

But she wasn't certain she wanted to confront him. It was one thing to have dreams about him. She could wake up from those—shake them off with a shower, a cup of coffee, have them submerged under the routine of her day. But to see the reality of him… she wasn't sure she wanted it in her mind.

With shaky hands, Maddie went to the search bar in Amity's profile. Now her heart was inside of her throat, throbbing erratically, and her hands had grown cold and tingly. She was having such a visceral, physiological response to the possibility of seeing him, she felt sure if she took her blood pressure it would be sky high.

Putting down her phone, she wandered to the kitchen and poured another small glass of Yastika, the Doukas brand, from the bottle that Elias had shared with her before they ended up in bed together.

Then she returned to the terrace. The night air was soothingly warm. The sky was dark velvet, the stars brighter than she'd seen them in years. The water glowed silver, the moon was fantastically white. She drank until her panicky physical responses calmed and warmth flowed into her fingers and chest.

Why not see him here, on Kyrie, where there was so much magical beauty that would balance out the darkness, could tame the turbulence of her soul? How much more depressing it would be to see him while in her tiny, rundown Hell's Kitchen studio with the car horns blaring outside. If she was ever going to do it, to look at his face again, why not do it now?

She picked her phone up again and stared at Amity's search bar. She typed, "D… a … n …"

Several Daniels popped up but none of them had his last name. Relief mingled with disappointment.

What would you say to him even if you managed to reach him?

I'd ask him why. He could have told me, 'Look, I know you have a crush on me, but you're a kid and I'm an adult.'

But he didn't do that. You already know why. Because he wanted sex. He didn't care about you as a human being. Why do you need this confirmed? What do you think he's going to say that will make you feel better?

Maybe nothing. Maybe I only need him to see me. To hear me. Maybe this gorgeous daughter who looks like she's doing so well in life, at least on social media, looks up to him. Maybe she worships him. Maybe he's a hero to his wife and kids.

But I know he's not a hero.

I know what he did.

There's one person on this planet who knows.

I want him to know I know.

Emboldened by this clarification within herself, Maddie backtracked on the search bar and typed, "C… h… e… l…"

Chelsea Pewter came up. The circle next to her name was so small that at first Maddie couldn't make out the shapes inside of it, but soon enough, the shapes crystallized: Two heads, tipped together so they were almost one.

Instantly, she knew it was a photo of Chelsea and Daniel. Every physiological alarm she'd managed to quiet exploded back triple-force. Her hands shook, her heart fluttered wildly, her breathing went shallow and rapid.

Daniel. He was wearing sunglasses. But it was him. He was still married to Chelsea. Still happy and in love.

And she started to cry.

* * *

Back inside, she set the phone down somewhere and tried to sob quietly, acutely aware that Logan was two doors away. She didn't want the humiliating sound to travel through the glass doors and onto her terrace and perhaps over to him.

She wasn't sure why she was crying, exactly. The rush of emotions at seeing him was too much to explain to herself let alone to anyone else. Anger. Curiosity. Self-pity. The unfairness of it. Him breezily living his California dream with an adoring family; Maddie paralyzed, unable to move forward into the life she wanted.

After about 15 minutes of this, her tears dried and she felt strangely tranquil. In the bathroom, she splashed water on her face, then refilled her glass of Yastika, noting that the bottle was almost empty and she'd have to either ask Elias for another or find a store that sold the Doukas brand.

She considered letting this be the end of her search but, as if controlled by remote, picked her phone back up from her bed and wandered to her desk, staring at the screen and sipping Yastika.

Chelsea's photos were benign—flowers, sunsets, her in yoga poses. She looked fantastic—sculpted and tanned—much sexier than the plain, matronly vision of Maddie's dreams.

Maddie had to scroll down, down, down before she stopped at the same photo that Chelsea had as her profile shot—one of her and Daniel, both smiling, heads tilted together, a halo of sun rays behind them. The photo was tagged "Big Sur, California." Because of Daniel's sunglasses, Maddie couldn't get much of a sense of how he'd aged, but he appeared essentially as he did in her memory, though his hair was shorter.

She kept scrolling and found only one more photo of him. He was sitting atop a motorcycle, wearing jeans, boots, and a black leather jacket. His arms were crossed and he smiled carefree and proudly at the camera. He was not wearing a helmet and his blondish-reddish hair was windblown, the longer hair of Maddie's adolescent memory. The caption said, "My dear handsome husband, I love you always!"

Maddie felt as if something heavy was on her chest, stopping her from breathing freely. She realized she'd put down her drink but had no memory of it. She also realized she was grinding her teeth but couldn't stop even though her dentist had made clear at her last dental appointment that if she didn't stop grinding her teeth, or start wearing a mouth guard, she was going to be looking at tens of thousands in dental bills one of these days.

I love you always!

Oh, really, Chelsea? Would you love him if you knew? You probably would, wouldn't you? Because you'd simply refuse to accept it was real.

At this point, Maddie was fairly drunk and only wanted to curl up in the comfy bed, thankful that Yastika was pretty strong stuff. Vision bleary, she plugged in her phone and set the alarm for 7 a.m.

She would not remember clicking "Follow" on Chelsea's profile.

Chapter Eighteen

"*What* a piece of garbage," Athena sneered. "Imagine being married to him and having no idea he once raped a 13-year-old."

Maddie put down her glass of water. A little worse for wear from her Yastika consumption last night, she couldn't bring herself to have her usual glass of wine with her Greek salad. The local wine may not cause hangovers, but too much Yastika certainly did. She and Athena sat outside at the same café in the *plaka* where they'd had lunch once before.

Maddie had told her friend about her inebriated trawling of Chelsea's and Amity's social media accounts last night.

"I don't like to use that word," Maddie said.

"Why not? Because you didn't try to fight him off? Doesn't matter. You were a kid; he was an adult. Simple. Wrong."

"I know it's wrong, but I don't like to use that word. It's my preference."

"Are you going to tell the wife?"

"No. What's the point? How would it change anything?"

"If it was me, I'd say something to *him*, at least. Let him know how much it messed you up."

"I'm afraid he's going to deny it, and then I'll be more pissed than I already am."

"I'm sorry," Athena said, reaching over to touch her hand. "I've had my own crap, you know that. But what happened to you is really wrong. Having a crush on an older man isn't an excuse to—the word you don't want to use."

"So, I want to tell you something, but you can't tell Logan."

"Tell Logan? I haven't even seen him since he came here. What is it?"

Maddie looked around, as if Logan might lurch out of one of the narrow, cobbled streets.

"Elias is going to take me to Volinos island. On a boat."

"No shit." Athena's mouth fell open. "What are you going to do once you get there?"

"I have no idea. Look around. See if I can find Ruby? I'm not sure."

Athena began to slowly shake her head, her face pinched with disapproval. "Not sure that's such a hot idea, Maddie. You could get arrested. You really want to piss off a billionaire while you're in a foreign country?"

"Well… I could explain myself. Or Elias can explain it. He's a local, maybe everyone over there will listen to him."

"Maddie," said Athena, forking some feta and cucumbers into her mouth, still looking cynical. "This isn't the States. It's a bit more freewheeling when it comes to sex, you know?"

"The age of consent is 15," Maddie said. "I looked it up. Ruby, if she told the truth, is only 12."

"But you have absolutely no proof she's being trafficked. Nothing she said—at least from what you told me—even remotely indicates she is. I'm just saying…" She heaved a sigh. "If you get into some kind of trouble, I can't help you. It's not like I have contacts here. I'm an American and trying to fit in. I can't get into a big thing."

"I'm not asking you to. Elias is going to help me."

"Elias wants to get in your pants, girl."

Maddie squirmed. "He already has."

Athena nearly choked on her wine. "Dayam. Why you always holding out on me? How was it?"

Maddie rolled her eyes. "It was great but it only happened one time. Now we're just friends."

"Ermkay," Athena said, dubiously. "Anyway, I'm sure he has no idea what you're even talking about with this pedo ring thing."

"Of course he does."

"No, he *doesn't*. He's doing the Greek thing and trying to be friendly. You're really going to risk getting him in trouble, too?"

"The whole thing was his idea, Athena."

Maddie was getting deeply irritated. Athena had seemed as if she understood and sympathized with Maddie's suspicion, but now she was acting like Maddie was a nut. A troublesome nut. Perhaps her friend had been out of a newsroom for too long, and had lost all ability to sniff out nefarious activity.

"Like I said, he's trying to please you," Athena rattled on. "He has no idea what he's doing or talking about, and has no sense of the ramifications of getting on the wrong side of a guy who's rich enough to own the island next door and who must know every single important person around here and has paid them off to boot."

"Okay," Maddie said, her food sticking uncomfortably in her throat. She knew that Athena had a good point—and suddenly she felt stupid about dragging Elias into something that was potentially nothing but an overreaction on her part. "So you think I should forget this whole thing."

Athena sighed, pushing her plate away as if she couldn't stand the sight of the leftover tomatoes and crumbs of feta sitting forlornly on her oily plate. "I don't know, Maddie. I wouldn't want to be the one to tell you nothing's happening over there if something *is* happening over there. But I also don't want you or my main contractor sitting in some sort of jail. Like, where *is* the jail on Kyrie? I have no idea. Does this billionaire dude have his *own* jail? I don't know that either. I don't know anything and I just moved here and the locals can be very welcoming on the surface but, underneath, they can be really hard to crack. I've got to live with them, you know?"

Maddie sat slumped over, unable to take another bite. Her gut was churning. She not only was potentially putting Elias in harm's way, but her actions could affect Athena as well.

The only thing to do was accept that she'd made a mistake, a misjudgment, and push it all aside. Push aside that look of fear she'd thought she'd detected on Ruby's face. Push aside those small inconsistencies in Ruby's and Stella's stories. Push aside Ruby's own words, that she was involved in something that was secret.

Push it all aside and enjoy what she had left of her vacation.

"You're probably right," she said, defeatedly.

"I—I just… I don't…"

"It's fine," Maddie said. "Sorry I dragged you into this nuttiness."

"You're my *friend*," Athena said as the waiter came over, depositing their bill on the table. Maddie took this opportunity to make things up to Athena by pulling over the coverlet and inserting her credit card. Athena put up a short, obligatory protest, then thanked her.

"I want you to do what you feel you need to do," she continued. "But go into it carefully, you know? This guy is going to have security and they could be armed. Saying, 'Hey, sorry, I thought you were a pedophile. My bad,' isn't going to win you any friends. If you seriously think this might be going on, I'd suggest researching it back in the States, where you'll be safe. What good will it do any girls in trouble over there if you're nabbed and sent back on the first boat, or to a holding cell, or they shoot you on sight for trespassing?"

"Shoot me on sight?" Maddie laughed nervously. "Come on, this is Europe not the States!"

"Well, I don't know what happens on a private island like that." She reached over and grasped Maddie's hand. "I can't have you get hurt. I can't."

* * *

BACK AT SIDERATOS, Maddie took a swim, then a shower. Taking a break from alcohol, she poured a glass of orange juice and wandered to the terrace to watch the sunset in a couple of hours.

It was then she noticed that one side of the sliding glass doors was open about an inch. Her skin prickled again with the feeling that someone had been inside her room. Of course, she could have left the door open herself, especially with how intoxicated she'd been last night. But she'd been strict about making sure the door was fully closed as she didn't want bees (which were plentiful on the island) or mosquitoes getting inside her room.

She walked out to the terrace and leaned over the side, where there were several feet of space between her terrace and whomever had the room to her left. She'd never seen anyone on that terrace. To the left of that apartment was Logan's.

This was the first time she realized how easy it would be for anyone to get on to her terrace, as the ground was only a few feet below it. Anyone who was even the tiniest bit athletic could push up on the wall and sling themselves over.

The back area of the complex was simple enough to get to as well, there was no gate or security, and all anyone had to do was walk down the short drive and around the building. Maddie had not bothered to lock the terrace door as she'd been working under the mistaken assumption that her terrace would be impossible to get on to from outside.

Back inside, she walked to the front door and turned the lock, immediately realizing what might have happened. Someone could have come into her studio through the terrace door, then gone to the front door and locked it, not wanting to risk being surprised while inside. What the intruder didn't realize was that the door locked automatically when Maddie left—so when the person locked it, they were really *unlocking* it.

Naturally, this was all speculation. Maddie could tell by the orderly arrangement of her personal products on the sink counter and the new towels hanging on the wall bar that the cleaning lady had been inside. The woman could have gone onto the terrace to look for empty bottles or glasses and not closed the door all the way. But given the other small signs Maddie had seen that someone else had been inside snooping around, the open terrace door served to deepen her suspicions.

The only people who knew she was staying here were Logan, Athena, and Elias. The prime suspect was obviously Logan, but why? At this point, so far as he knew, they were working together on anything involving Dexter Hunt. Perhaps he suspected she was holding out on him, which she was.

As for Elias or Athena, she couldn't imagine why either one would want to get inside her room. But as a reporter, Maddie knew she had to look beyond the obvious, and that meant looking beyond Logan.

Retrieving her laptop from her locked suitcase, Maddie sat on the terrace with it propped in front of her and, not really knowing what she was looking for, tried to find whatever she could about Elias.

He didn't have a social media account, at least that she could track down. But it was easy enough to locate the website for Doukas Yastika Spirits, which was in both Greek and English. In the "About Us" section, she read:

The Doukas Family—led by Petros and son Alexander—are direct descendants of Sofia Doukas, who threw herself and her baby off the cliffs at Kremos rather than be captured by Turks. Miraculously, her baby, Constantine, survived and went on to keep the Doukas lineage alive.

We are the longest continuous producers of the unique "tears" of the Yastic tree that has been cultivated exclusively on Kyrie since Homeric times. With our patented copper stills and centuries of expert distillation, Doukas Yastika offers an unrivaled and purely authentic taste and experience.

There was a picture of Petros and Alexander standing side-by-side in a grove of Yastic trees. The trees were green and bushy, with short, gnarled trunks. Many of the trees were leaning almost to the ground. While the elder Doukas had the weather-beaten face common on Kyrie, Alexander, appearing somewhere in his late thirties, was dark and striking, though not nearly as good-looking as Elias (at least to Maddie's taste). However, the family connection was undeniable as both of the men shared Elias' eye shade of electric sapphire.

She went to the tab labeled, "Yastika and Kyrie."

This section spun a tragic tale of a people who were essentially held hostage by their ability to cultivate a resin that, for mysterious reasons having to do with soil and climate, couldn't be reproduced anywhere else in the world.

(Though folklore has it that when an officer in the Roman navy was dragged near to death by horse for refusing to repent his Christian faith, he collapsed under a crop of Yastic trees. The trees cried for him, producing the precious resin.)

Whether their conquerors were pirates, the Persians, Romans, Venetians, Genoese, Ottomans, or Turks, Yastika workers continually had their lives spared, but only in exchange for harvesting the resin for their current oppressors. Yastika cultivators let the resin harden on their hands to show they were valuable to whomever currently occupied the island and shouldn't be killed for some minor infraction.

It wasn't until the mid-nineteenth century that the native Kyrians were allowed to go into the Yastika trade for themselves. (Kyrie wasn't even an official part of Greece until the early twentieth century.) It was around this time that the Doukas family opened its first distillery.

Once in high demand all over Greece and Europe, Yastika eventually waned in popularity, crowded out by wines, craft beers, and various spirits. Additionally, a large percentage of the island's precious Yastic trees were destroyed in various wildfires, and its distilleries damaged in various earthquakes, especially the one from eight years ago.

But starting a few years ago, Maddie noticed there was a burgeoning revival—the sweet liqueur getting more international press and distribution. She even found a few brands that were being sold in the States. The Doukas father and son were making a valiant attempt to keep its centuries-old family business alive despite enormous difficulties.

Maddie thought about the history of this island. Kyrie had been under perpetual siege from classical antiquity to World War II and was populated by inhabitants who had learned to cooperate and assimilate with multiple conquerors for their survival. The island may no longer be menaced by pirates or colonizers, but it was definitely still vulnerable to modern-day threats: fires, earthquakes, loss of human capital, economic crises.

An island in trouble.

A billionaire next door.

If Dexter Hunt had purchased Volinos with the idea of turning it into a personal fiefdom for his illegal fetishes, then it would be smart to have the larger island near him—Kyrie—on his side. He could use its port to dock his yacht and pick up girls. He'd keep a house on Kalaria beach for temporary boarding.

Maddie got up and paced back and forth a few times, in distress at where her mind was insisting on going next.

Athena. One of her best friends. She couldn't dismiss the fact that Athena knew where Maddie was staying and which room—Maddie had showed it off to her the night of her arrival. Yes, she'd been with Athena today at lunch, and her friend couldn't be in two places at once.

But Maddie had also told her friend her plans to swim when she returned to the studio, so Athena could have simply knocked on the door and when Maddie didn't answer, taken that as her opportunity to come around the back and enter via the terrace doors.

But what connection could Athena have to Dexter Hunt?

The same connection, she supposed, everyone on the island had. They lived here, and he lived next door.

Stopping her pacing, she returned to her computer and did a search for "The Repatriation Project Kyrie Greece."

A bunch of links to Kyrie came up, but none of them mentioned the fund that Athena said had awarded her money to restore her great-grandparents' house. Given that Athena had said she'd found the project while doing research about Kyrie, it seemed peculiar the fund didn't appear in a search. Not exactly proof of anything, though. And the fund might be buried somewhere on the Internet.

Then Maddie did multiple searches on "Athena Kyriakos, Kyrie, Greece," looking for Athena's grandmother but only came across dozens of articles written by Athena Kyriakos of *Wealthy* magazine.

She sat tapping her finger on her lower lip, then began absently twisting it, a habit she had when she was deep in thought, one that Jesse used to point out to her.

Before that, she hadn't even been aware of it. Now that she was, she tried to stop, but her fingers would lift up as if they had their own little minds and start mauling her lip again.

Was there any way that an entire island—population 24,000, according to a search—could be in league with a billionaire pedophile? Maddie spat out a laugh that was more like a cackle, then shook her head.

But what if none of them had any idea what was going on next door? The most the boaters on the southern tip of the island knew was that Hunt liked to ferry over young, pretty women. If lusting after youth and beauty was illegal, then most of the men in the world would be in prison.

From what Maddie could piece together, girls arrived from the mainland by ferry, then were picked up by private boat from various places in Kyrie, including Kalaria beach, an extremely remote area. Not only were people not standing around watching the girls get on Hunt's boat (or boats) but even if they were, they, such as Elias' friend Yiannis, couldn't tell the age of the girls. Dress them a little older, put a little makeup on them—it would be easy to make a 12-year-old look 15 or 16. Even Maddie had thought Ruby was older than her actual age.

All Hunt had to do to guarantee the locals didn't nose around was start a slush fund for Kyrie—one that bankrolled everything from home renovations to small businesses.

Even Athena had said it: *A guy who's rich enough to own*

the island next door and who must know every single important person around here and has paid them off to boot.

But there was one thing Hunt hadn't been able to control.

Gossip.

Loose lips sink ships.

If Maddie had her way, loose local lips were going to sink Dexter Hunt.

Chapter Nineteen

*A*bout an hour later, Maddie's brain was exhausted from Internet sleuthing and theorizing. She sat on the bed, reading a memoir of a British couple who'd tried to move to another Greek island, Skiathos.

A year and almost a hundred thousand dollars later, they were still trying to get permanent residency, trying to cut through red tape (they couldn't seem to get WiFi no matter how many people they paid), and were on the verge of returning home defeated.

Maddie hadn't asked Athena much about how she managed to live here full-time legally, but supposed her friend's ancestry worked in her favor. She picked up her phone and tapped out on WhatsApp: "Hey girl, I'm trying to find if that repatriation project has anything similar in Portugal. But I can't find any info. How'd you learn about it?"

Suddenly, there was an urgent knocking on the door that made her startle on the bed and nearly drop her phone. Wearing nothing but her bedtime attire of loose cotton shorts that said "Coney" on one butt cheek and "Island" on the other, and her yoga t-shirt that was so worn it was basically transparent, she grabbed her hoodie off the back of a chair and pulled it around her chest. Her first thought was that the knocker must be Logan. He'd probably found out something about Dexter Hunt.

But when she opened the door, Elias was standing there. Despite her misgivings about him, her heart sped up in a pleasantly excited rhythm. He had that effect on her—purely biological.

"Elias, what—"

He put his finger to his mouth, and stage-whispered, "Can I come in?"

"Uh, sure."

She closed the door behind him, and ushered him into the larger bedroom area, irrationally wishing to jet into the bathroom to run a brush through her gnarled hair and put on some lip gloss. He looked so anxious that she didn't bother to ask him to sit, he was giving off too much standing energy.

"Maddie," he said. "I know how we can get on Volinos."

"How?"

"I talk to my brother. I not say what you suspect, but I ask about Volinos and the man there. Anything I don't know, my brother and father do. Well, little did I know, my brother often bring Yastika to the island. Many cases for the guests. He bring it over on his boat. Maddie," he said, looking wild-eyed.

"Alexander go tomorrow. But I ask him if I can go instead. Tell him I want to start getting more involved in the business. This is very short trip, right next door. So, easy for me to do. I know my brother, he can be lazy. So, he say, fine, you go. I ask him, Alexander, do you meet the man there, the rich man? He say no, but one time he was inside the man's house. He say it is biggest house he's ever seen, and it all glass. It sit on a tall hill and overlook the island and a bunch of other little buildings.

Alexander say he go in because one day he forget the purchasing papers. He need that to get paid. So, another man, secure guard, bring him to rich man's glass house. My brother go to an office to get copy of the papers. There, he deal with purchasing agent.

While he there, he have to go to the bathroom. The man point down the hall and Alexander say that no one watch him. He wander through the house for long time before he find the bathroom. He see all kinds of rooms."

Maddie stared at Elias with her mouth half-open, arms crossed tightly in front of her chest. Her mind couldn't catch up with what he was suggesting. And as she'd suspected, the Doukas family did have dealings with the billionaire next door.

"You never knew your family delivered to Volinos?"

"No. I live in Athens. When I come here, I work on homes. Sometimes I see my father and brother, but we don't discuss the business much."

He stepped closer to her and took both of her hands in his, causing her hoodie to fall open. Her t-shirt was so worn that she might as well have been naked in front of him, but he didn't seem to notice, his electric blues boring into hers.

"So, Maddie. We go tomorrow. You and me. When we get there, if anyone ask, I say you're my fiancée, that you are learning business. And I am Alexander's brother, also learning business. Then I say I forget the purchasing papers. When they offer to bring us to the glass house, we go. There, you say you have to go to the bathroom. I will keep the purchasing agent busy, and you go look around."

"You—you don't think that will seem suspicious?" she asked, not daring to hope that this simple plan could work.

"I don't think so. Alexander say if anyone have problem, they call him. He explain I come instead."

"What if they mention me?"

He shrugged. "It's okay. I already tell Alexander I may bring girl on boat. He understand, yeah? He my brother. He will say what I ask."

His edgy energy transformed into one of his winning smiles. He appeared pleased with himself and was waiting for Maddie to express some pleasure with him, his grip on her hands tightening. She had to admit it did sound like a decent plan. Or at least better than anything she'd come up with. She wasn't sure that she'd see anything in the main house that would clear up what was happening over there, but it couldn't hurt to get inside.

Of course, if she happened to run into Ruby, the girl could easily blow the lid on her and Elias' story, but it would be worth it to see if Ruby was safe. Many things could go wrong, but many things could go right.

"When would we leave?" she asked.

"About nine. You meet me at the main port in Kyrie Town."

Her heart was thudding, her nerve endings tingling at the edge of fear. This was her last chance to stop all of this—to admit she'd let her imagination run wild, had let her experience with Daniel taint her perception.

She'd already told Athena she would give up this sleuthing and speculating. She could still luxuriate in what was left of her vacation, and perhaps even luxuriate in the handsome man in front of her who was still clutching onto her hands in that overly-demonstrative way he had.

Her phone dinged with an incoming message. Taking the opportunity to untangle her hands from Elias' grip, she reached for her phone on the bed and read the reply from Athena to her inquiry about The Repatriation Project.

"My grandmother's niece sent me the application," Athena wrote, "the woman I'm staying with. I think it's just a Kyrie thing! Are we meeting up tomorrow?"

Maddie put her finger up to Elias in a *hold on* gesture, then typed back, "Okay, thanks. Actually, I thought I'd head to Skelios. Been wanting to do a day trip. Should be back in the early evening."

A thumbs-up sign appeared next to her message.

It's just a Kyrie thing.

A chill came over her at the apparent confirmation that somewhere in the bowels of the island's local government was a slush fund seeded by none other than the billionaire next door. The money would keep coming to the island so long as it guaranteed Dexter Hunt a nice buffer for his activities—whatever they were. And there appeared to be only one way to even begin to figure them out.

Get on the island.

"Okay, Elias," she said. "Meet you at the port at nine."

Chapter Twenty

RUBY

*T*he day has come. The day I meet Mr. John's special friend.

Mom is so excited she can barely contain herself and I know I should be excited but I'm so nervous my hands keep shaking. Mom and I had breakfast very early on the terrace (blueberry pancakes) and stared out over the blue water. She could tell I wasn't acting like myself because I was so quiet.

Then we went inside and picked out a dress. Mom wanted me to wear the prettiest one—it was blue and red with all kinds of ruffles and glittery sequins, but I didn't want that. I picked out a long cotton dress that was plain black. Mom tried to talk me out of it, saying how I needed to look special for Mr. John's special friend, but I ignored her and put on the dress. She also wanted my hair hanging down loose like Max had wanted it when we first got here, but I put it in a ponytail.

The truth was, I didn't want Mr. John's special friend

staring too hard at me. I knew it was a fantasy, but I wanted to blend into the walls. Even though the walls were glass.

Outside, it was another crystal-clear day, with skies so incredibly solid blue, and everything was eerily quiet like it can be early in the morning. Max brought us in the golf cart over the hills but not to the glass house—to another building. This one was like a big box, plain, white, and square, but it had blue trim and looked more like the usual homes on Kyrie. It sat on top of a large hill, right at the edge of a cliff, overlooking the water, which was smashing on the rocks below.

A woman came out to meet us. It was Glenda, the same woman from the hotel in New York and who handed Mr. John the folder about me at dinner. She took us inside and had us sit on a long leather couch. She was smiling a lot, and like Mom, was acting like this was the most exciting thing that had ever happened to her.

"Now Ruby," she said. "Your mother and I will stay here for a few minutes while you and Mr. John's special friend get acquainted, but then I know he'd like some alone time with you. You're okay with that, right?"

My throat started hurting. I couldn't swallow. I stared at the floor. It was light blond wood with a criss-cross pattern.

"Ruby?"

"Yes, I'm okay with that," I said. But I know I didn't sound okay.

"She's just nervous," Mom said.

"Understandable," said Glenda.

She stood there smiling big at me and I wanted to run out of the place. Because I knew soon after I met Mr. John's special friend, it would have to happen. There would be no turning around, going back, changing my mind. Once he saw me, it was a done deal.

"Oh, here he is," Glenda said, hurrying to the glass doors.

I looked up and for a moment all I saw were two men in dark suits and sunglasses. I couldn't understand why they were wearing suits. No one on the island wore suits, not even the guards or people who worked here, like Max.

Then those men disappeared. There was a man behind Glenda, but she was blocking him. Mom looked at me and made a gesture that I should stand up, so I did, but I could hardly feel my legs. Then my knees started to shake. How embarrassing. There was no way he wouldn't see that.

"Come, she's right here," said Glenda, in that annoyingly excited way.

Then there he was. Behind her.

He was more handsome than I'd thought he'd be. And looked younger. He had chestnut hair that was sort of puffy, and his face was kind. His eyes were crinkly, and he was smiling at me. When he got closer, he put his hand out.

I reached my hand out and we shook hands, and then he looked at Mom and shook hands with her, too.

"Isn't she perfect?" Glenda asked him.

"Indeed. Indeed, she is perfect," the man said. He was wearing tan pants, and a light blue tennis shirt. He looked casual, relaxed, and so relatable and human. Maybe I could go through with this after all.

"Ruby," Glenda said. "I'd like you to meet Mr. John's special friend."

"Oh, is that what he's calling me?" the man said, and chuckled. I liked his laugh.

"What would you prefer she call you?" Glenda asked.

"My first name is fine."

Glenda laughed—it sounded stupid and fake. But I could tell the man liked her. She seemed like the kind of person everyone liked. Except me.

"I'll leave that to you," she said. "You two will have some time alone so you can get to know each other a little."

"I'm truly humbled that Dex—*Mr. John* thought of me for this honor," he said in a way that made it sound like he wasn't humbled at all. "The first to get to meet Ruby."

Glenda looked about ready to eat herself up she was so happy.

"You would be the first, you know that. But for formal introduction, let me say…" She looked from me to him, and then back again. "Ruby, I'd like to introduce you to…"

She giggled, gesturing in the man's direction, and nodding her head a little.

"Mr. John's special friend. Otherwise known as the President of the United States."

Chapter Twenty-One

*T*he small motorboat pulled up to a long dock around 10 a.m. Before they reached it, Maddie could see that it was patrolled by several large male security guards, all of them wearing dark clothing, looking like police.

She also spotted a German Shepherd, prowling unleashed. There were several large NO TRES-PASSING signs posted at various points along the shoreline.

It seemed unlikely there was any kind of major event —wedding, investment opportunity, science fair—going on as Maddie hadn't spotted one person on the island except the ones she currently saw, the guards.

As the motorboat came to a stop up against the dock, Elias began tying it off on a steel peg while looking up at the two men who'd strode over. They both wore sunglasses and stoic expressions.

"*Kalimera,*" Elias said. "*Écho to Doukas Yastika dianomi.*"

One of the men, arms crossed, began speaking back

in Greek as Elias gestured at the boat and its five cases of Yastika, tucked on the floor behind the seats. The boat couldn't have been more than 20 feet in length but it was what Elias told her his brother used to regularly ferry Yastika to Volinos.

Maddie eyed the security guard's beltline and saw what looked like a pepper spray can hanging from it. She didn't see a gun but wasn't convinced the guards didn't have them. Either way, the spray can was intimidating enough. The long, gangly German Shepherd sat panting on the dock and Maddie really wished they'd leash it.

Elias put his hand out for her to clamber onto the dock. She'd dressed in billowy, wide-legged, gray cotton pants, a black, sleeveless t-shirt, and worn a light gray nylon jacket over on the windy ride, but took it off as the they pulled up to the island, deciding to leave it on the boat.

"*Aftí einaí i arravoniastikiá mou,*" Elias said, gesturing towards her. The security guards gave her the once over and the dog continued to pant. One of the security guards spoke laconically while gesturing towards the Yastika cases in the boat, and then he and Elias were bringing them out and placing them on the dock. The other security guard spoke into a walkie talkie.

At this point, as they had rehearsed on the trip over, Elias climbed back into the boat and made a show of looking around in distress. Then he came out, speaking apologetically and shrugging.

Maddie knew he'd told the guards that he'd forgotten the purchasing papers. There was more back and forth with the most intimidating-appearing security guard, who was top-heavy and unnaturally muscular. He didn't look too happy and pulled out his walkie talkie, speaking into it.

This went on for several minutes, and Maddie was growing more and more anxious, wondering if their plan was working or not. The guards didn't seem inclined to invite them into the main house. Elias began gesturing towards the wooden cases sitting on the dock, and Maddie got the impression he was explaining that he couldn't leave them here.

Then one of the guards waved that Elias should follow him up the dock, and Elias gestured at Maddie, indicating that he wanted her to come as well. The guard seemed irritated but nodded. Then he spoke, pointing authoritatively to a small folding table on the dock. Elias looked warily at the table, then said to Maddie, "We have to leave our phones."

"Um, okay," Maddie said, reluctantly retrieving her phone from her pocket. She supposed it didn't matter anyway, as she had no active signal. But the idea of leaving it with strangers made her nervous. And the idea of Elias leaving behind his phone, which did have an active signal, made her even more nervous.

Relieved of their phones, the pair followed the security guard up the stone staircase of a large, long hill.

* * *

THE GLASS HOUSE was all squares and sharp edges. The inside was diamond-bright and all around them was the unimpeded beauty of the island, beauty so audacious that Maddie wondered how she'd ever move back to the muted, garbage-strewn streets of Hell's Kitchen.

Once you've seen *this*, how can you unsee it, not have it always in the back of your brain, always beckoning, *Come back, come back… this is what the world is meant to look like.*

A few of the walls were solid white, retractable, and cluttered with paintings and framed photographs. Maddie's eye fell on a cotton-candy blonde, naked, her profile peeking over her bare shoulder, eyes flirty but fragile. Marilyn Monroe.

Marilyn always gave her uncomfortable feelings. A pretty, very talented and troubled woman who seemed to perpetually and silently scream out, *Please love me!*

Although Maddie was slightly slick with sweat from the walk up the steep hill in the already-smoldering late morning sun, her skin felt cool with nerves from being where Dexter Hunt lived. Being where he may be bringing young, scared girls. *Ruby might be here somewhere.*

She was acutely aware that her eyes were darting around, trying to memorize her surroundings in case she needed to write about the house, and at the same time worried the guard they were following might notice her inordinate attention. She tried to make her expression appear as if she was only curious, as one would naturally be in such an overpowering house.

Maddie and Elias followed the guard up a staircase and into a small office, with all white furniture. Sitting at a desk was another man, who appeared to be somewhere in his sixties. Elias began speaking to him in

Greek but the man stood, saying, "Yes, you came with the Yastika?" in an unidentifiable European accent.

"I'm so sorry," Elias said, managing to sound deferential. "This my first delivery. I forget purchasing papers. I take over for my brother, Alexander, today."

"What happened to Alexander?" the man asked, giving off a distinct *I have better things to be doing* vibe.

"He not feeling well. And I learning business."

"And..." the man trailed off, turning his attention to Maddie.

"This my fiancée. She learning business, too."

"Hi," Maddie said, giving an awkward wave and not having a clue what to say. In fact, she was debating whether or not she should even risk slipping away and snooping around. Not only had she not seen anyone on the island from the perspective of the boat, but she hadn't seen anyone on the long walk up the hill either.

Logan's tips about "something big" happening on the island this week appeared to be wrong. Short of stumbling into a more recreational area filled with young girls and older men, she had no idea what she could see that might confirm her suspicions.

But they'd come this far and she wouldn't get another chance. At the very least, she should try to have a quick look around as the opportunity was right here within her grasp.

The older man handed Elias a clipboard and he began filling out whatever papers were on it. He glanced up quickly at Maddie, and the look seemed to say, *If you're going to do this, now is the time.*

"I'm so sorry," Maddie blurted, fretfully. The man

turned his jaded gaze on her. "I had some coffee before leaving Kyrie and I could really use a bathroom. Is there any way…?"

The man only stared at her. She thought for sure he was about to tell her no. But then he said, flatly, "Take a left down the hallway, there's a staircase. At the bottom, take another left. Follow that all the way down the hall, bathroom on your right."

"Thank you so much. I'll hurry."

She glanced once more at Elias and their eyes met. It seemed to her as if he was as nervous for her as she was for herself.

In the hallway, she realized she'd already forgotten the man's instructions. She'd been concentrating so hard on sounding natural that she hadn't actually been listening closely to him. But she did remember he mentioned a staircase. So when she saw a circular one, she went down it, uncertain if this was the staircase he'd directed her to.

At the bottom was a long hallway, and the walls were solid drywall, not glass, and there were no windows. She got the feeling she had descended into an underground area. Just the kind of place that, if Dexter Hunt was keeping secrets, would serve to better hide them.

The hallway walls were dark wood and every ten feet or so hung a painting. Abstract art seemed to be his thing; she felt as if she were browsing a museum. Soon, she came to an open door and glanced inside.

The room wasn't furnished in the sleek, chrome and glass way the rest of the house was—the walls were papered crimson, the furniture was wood, vintage, heavy, and ornate. An enormous antique roll-top desk dominated the space. Unless it was her imagination, there was a whiff of sweet cigar smoke in the air.

This room was definitely used—and frequently. Her heart rate kicked up with the certainty that Dexter Hunt spent significant amounts of time in this room.

She glanced behind her, back down the hallway from the direction she came, and saw no one. So consumed with nerves she felt she might throw up, she swiftly entered the room, placing her sandals down with deliberate strides, trying to keep quiet. She thought about closing the door but worried it might creak. And if someone passed who knew that the door was normally open, having it shut would draw attention. Instead, if interrupted, she planned to plead ignorance.

The walls were glutted with framed photographs, and she stared open-mouthed at row upon row of them. She had only been able to find a couple of pictures of Dexter Hunt online—and they were old photos—but he had a very distinctive face. Square-jawed, flinty-eyed, a head full of silver-flecked hair.

She walked slowly down the rows of framed photos. Hunt was in all of them, and under each photo was a small, brass plate engraved with the name of whomever Hunt was standing or sitting with.

She recognized a surprisingly large number of the names and even a lot of the faces. Movie stars. Musicians. Authors. A queen. A king. A prince. A princess. A sultan. A famous scientist who had a series of bestsellers.

She came to the end of one wall and, awestruck, moved on to another. This wall was taken up with three large framed photos hung side-by-side. The photos were much larger than the others—at least six feet tall.

In each, Hunt stood on a rolling parcel of land that could be Volinos. In the first photo, he stood next to a president that Maddie barely remembered, because she'd been a child when he was in office. The next president she remembered much better.

And the third, she remembered perfectly, because he was currently the President of the United States.

Chapter Twenty-Two

"*H*ave you lost something?"

Maddie's heart lurched into her throat as she whirled around. A man stood in the doorway—tall, with thick, wavy hair that was mostly silver, and a sturdy, square jaw. Handsome yet robotic-looking. He was in beige chinos with a white polo shirt tucked into his beltline.

Dexter Hunt. Absolutely, positively Dexter Hunt.

Fuck!

Her brain didn't quite register his words—she only knew she had to talk herself out of this one and fast.

"I'm so sorry," she said, fluttering her hands up to her chest. It was easy to pretend to be flustered because she truly was. "I'm looking for a bathroom."

"Does there appear to be a bathroom here?" he asked, craning his neck from side to side in an exaggerated fashion. "I don't see one."

Intuition was already telling her that Hunt's slightly hostile tone meant that she wasn't going to easily talk her way out of this, but she kept plowing ahead as if she might.

"If you can direct me to it, I'd appreciate it."

"May I ask who you are?"

"I came with the Yastika delivery. Elias Doukas. He's my fiancé."

Goddamn it, her voice was quaking. She sounded too scared to have been innocently searching for a bathroom.

"Is he now?" Hunt crossed his arms and smirked at her in that same slightly contentious way. "Related to Alexander?"

"Yes," Maddie said, relieved. "Yes, that's his brother."

Now her connection to the Greeks that Hunt did business with would win him over and he'd allow her to move on. "Elias is upstairs with the purchasing agent. I —I had to go to the bathroom, so…" She trailed off with an apologetic shrug.

"So you came into a private room."

"Like I said, I'm sorry. I got confused. And then, well, I admit I was looking at your photos." She gestured around, instinctively switching from damsel-in-bladder-distress to ego pumper. "It's really impressive. I guess… I got carried away looking at everything. I'm so sorry. I'll leave."

She started towards the door, wondering if he was even going to move, as he was blocking it. His stance gave her the impression he wasn't going to and panic began to steadily rise. The only thing keeping her some-what calm was the idea of Elias being right upstairs.

She was halfway across the room now and he hadn't moved, as if he had no intention of getting out of the way.

"You say you and Elias are engaged?" he asked.

At this point, her throat was too swollen with nerves to allow her to speak, so she stopped and nodded slightly, biting down inside her lower lip.

"Interesting. Where did you meet?"

"Kyrie," she said, quietly.

"I don't see a ring."

Maddie self-consciously rubbed her ring finger. "I don't have one," she said, unable to quell the slight tremor in her voice. "Not yet."

Then some kind of survival instinct gave her a surge of courage, and she added, rather imperiously, "Though I'm not sure that's your business." If she didn't start acting more confident with him, she felt she was doomed.

"Everything on this island is my business," he clipped out. "Including who is brought on it. Last I knew, Elias had nothing to do with his family's business, lived in Athens, and when he *was* here for the summers, was busy keeping all the ladies happy." He gave another contemptuous smirk. "But now he's *engaged*. I suppose congratulations are in order."

Realizing he wasn't going to move, Maddie said, calmly as she could manage, "Yes, and you're going to have to let me out of this room or I'll have to call him. He's a Greek citizen. This is still Greece last I knew."

"Is that a threat?"

"Not at all, I just don't understand why you seem to think you're going to keep me here."

"Maybe someone can explain it to you." He turned and backed partially out of the door and made a gesture. Maddie watched with her heart hammering in her ribcage, a nauseating intuition telling her what was going to happen next.

Elias appeared at Dexter Hunt's side.

"Tell her why she's here," Hunt said.

For a moment, Maddie's brain refused to correctly interpret the scene and persisted in clinging to the hope that he'd come to search for her. But it was only for a moment. Then the terrible truth she'd been trying to bury ever since Dexter Hunt sauntered into the room wearing that look of disdain—the look that said he knew *exactly* who Maddie was—became too blatant to deny any longer.

"You fucking traitor!" she screamed.

Elias said nothing and wouldn't make eye contact with her.

"You can go now, Elias," Hunt said.

Elias shot her a quick look, his expression sheepish and shamed, before he disappeared.

"Asshole!" she yelled, loud enough that she knew he could still hear her.

Hunt walked a little farther into the room, arms still crossed, expression still steeped in antipathy, as if he could barely stand having Maddie so close to him. "I try to plan for all contingencies but this isn't one I saw coming," he said. "A reporter for one of the biggest magazines in the world thinks I'm running a sex trafficking operation."

"Where's Ruby?"

"She's fine."

Maddie swallowed hard. She'd said that without knowing 100 percent that Ruby was on Volinos. She'd still nursed the hope that this was all a mix-up and that Ruby was really with her "uncle"—a benign expat on a nearby island.

"I want to see her."

He sighed dramatically, rolling his eyes up to the ceiling. "She's fine and I'm too busy to deal with all of this right now. You'll be escorted to a private cabin, one with a *bathroom*, and tonight at dinner, we'll have a mature talk."

"I'll go to Kyrie and come back later. *Then* we'll have a talk."

Although she had no idea how she would get back to Kyrie—she wasn't getting on a boat with that traitor, Elias—she desperately wanted to alert Logan to everything. Why hadn't she done that before? Sure, she'd been concerned he might alienate island security with a bossy attitude.

But the truth was, she'd been far more concerned that he'd elbow his way to the front of any story she might uncover. For once, *she* wanted to be the star reporter. *She* wanted the promotion and the accolades. And she didn't trust that would happen if she was working with Logan.

Now she was paying for her ambition, because Logan seemed the only person she could trust, someone who had no ties to Kyrie. It gutted her to think that Athena might have been sucked into Dexter Hunt's orbit, like Elias had, but Maddie couldn't dismiss the possibility. Both of them lived on Kyrie and therefore could be financially beholden to the billionaire.

The hideous reality was that Maddie was completely at Hunt's mercy. The one person who knew where she was—Elias—was working with him. And her phone had been taken by one of his goons.

"If you want to go now, you can go," Hunt said as if doing her a grand favor. "In fact, I'll have Elias ferry you back. But you're in no danger. Not only am I not a murderer by nature, I don't have any desire to start an international incident. Between your nationality, your profession, and being white, female, and relatively attractive, if you disappeared, it would be on a 24-hour news cycle. All I'm asking for is one night. As a journalist, I'd think you'd be curious enough to stay."

The horrific case of Kim Wall popped into Maddie's head. A young Swedish journalist who'd disappeared after boarding a homemade submarine to interview a brilliant inventor and rocket scientist by the name of Peter Madsen. Madsen—like Hunt—was obsessed with space. While Madsen tried to claim the submarine had sunk, dooming Wall, in reality, he had tortured, raped, and dismembered her before scuttling the submarine.

Maddie knew her somewhat high-profile magazine job was no guarantee that Dexter Hunt wouldn't get rid of her if he wanted to. He might be brilliant, stupendously well-connected, and obscenely rich—but he could also, like Peter Madsen, be pure evil. And if he *was* running a pedophile ring, he could be willing to do *anything* to keep her from spreading her suspicions.

However, another part of her—the reporter part— wanted to know what was happening on Volinos, and this was very likely her only chance to find out. But she figured she better try to ensure her safety, if possible.

"I want you to know there are people who know I'm here on Volinos," she said, embarrassed that the slight fearful tremor in her voice refused to go away. "People in the States, people at *Wealthy*." She didn't sound particularly convincing. More like a child insisting that she hadn't taken the last cookie.

As he stared at her with that unnervingly arrogant way he had, Maddie couldn't tell if he believed her or not. Probably not.

"Then you have nothing to worry about, do you?" he said.

* * *

ELIAS. Elias!

Why had she trusted him? She'd already pieced together that there was a chance every single person in Kyrie was sucking from the teet of the billionaire. But it was such a vast plan that her brain couldn't accept it. She'd also convinced herself that while perhaps a core group of insiders knew the real purpose of Volinos, the vast majority of the locals, like Elias, his family, and Athena, did not.

While there was no doubt Elias was working with Hunt in some capacity—given that he'd hand-delivered

Maddie to him—it didn't make much sense. If Elias was one of Hunt's lackeys, why had he fanned her suspicions?

He was the one who'd passed along that locals called Volinos "orgy island." He was the one who'd told her girls could be brought to the Kalaria beach house, then easily shuttled to Hunt's playground without any record of it. He was the one who'd brought her to his friend, the boatman Yiannis, who'd also solidified her hunch.

Why would he have done all that if he was helping to shield Hunt's activities? Why didn't he do what Athena had done—tell her she was imagining things?

A man had taken her on a black, military-looking golf cart up and down long, winding, paved paths to this cabin, which sat on the edge of a bluff, overlooking the water. He'd told her his name was Max, and he'd be right outside if she needed anything. She took this as a warning not to try to go anywhere.

Besides, where was there to go? There was no way she would make it to a nearby island. Greece may not have many sharks but it had plenty of turbulent water. And the neighboring islands weren't that close—it had taken almost an hour to get here from Kyrie. Standing on the cabin's small balcony, she could barely make out a dark mass huddled on the horizon. It could be Skelios, it could be one of the numerous small, uninhabited islands that she and Elias had passed on the trip here.

She was a decent swimmer but hardly an Olympic-caliber one. And even Olympic swimmers only swam the length of the pool.

She could kick herself for not telling Logan where

she was going. But he would have then wanted to accompany her, and he'd be in the same position she was in right now. When exactly did Hunt plan on letting her leave? *Did* he plan on letting her leave?

If he didn't, Logan would be the first one to notice that she wasn't around. Would he do anything about it or only assume she'd taken off with "Prince Charming" and was extending her vacation? He didn't know where Athena lived, so he couldn't alert her that Maddie was missing. And for all Maddie knew, Athena was in on this, too.

Dexter Hunt. Was he going to tell her truthfully what was happening on the island? He hadn't exactly confirmed her suspicions, but nor had he denied them. Why else would a grown man be ferrying young girls over from a nearby island? Why else would they all be attractive?

Why else would Ruby have given a false name, called Hunt her "uncle," and said that he was going to pay for her schooling? Why else would Ruby have—Maddie was sure she hadn't been mistaken—seemed uncomfortable and even scared at the idea of coming to Volinos?

Turning from the bright blue sea, Maddie went back into the cabin. It was maybe 200-square-feet, furnished simply with a large four-poster bed piled high with white bedding, a desk and chair, and a light-grained, wooden wardrobe.

Inside hung various dresses appropriate for island wear—short-sleeved, sleeveless, knee or ankle length, a couple of them basically miniskirts.

The color scheme that dominated, like the islands in

general, was white and blue. She glanced at a few of the tags along the collars and saw "S" and "M." Small and medium. She got the feeling the clothes were beckoning her, that they'd been bought for her. Then she went to the clean, modern bathroom.

Small porcelain sink, gray and white marbled countertop lined with travel-sized bottles—shampoo, conditioner, face cleanser, mouthwash. There was a wrapped toothbrush sitting inside of a cup. A wicker shelf to the left contained a small basket with a wrapped comb and hairbrush. Underneath the sink were two large, fluffy white towels, a compact hairdryer, and a curling iron.

Dexter Hunt clearly expected Maddie to make herself at home. As he'd expected of the girls who'd been in this cabin before her.

Maddie came back into the bedroom area and her gaze cast all around the ceiling and its corners, looking for cameras. If they were in the room, they were well-hidden.

She stood in front of the room's one mirror—full-length. She looked like what she was—a woman who'd taken a motorboat from a nearby island and was currently trapped with a potential predator and his goonish security guards.

Hair that had escaped from her ponytail due to the windy ride over was snarled around her face. Her skin had tanned, and every freckle normally in hibernation had bloomed darkly across her nose and cheeks. Her brown eyes were glassy and wild.

As much as the idea of showering, changing into a dress, and doing her hair seemed creepy to her—it also strongly appealed. Anything she could do that would help equalize the power imbalance between her and Hunt was a good thing. Showing up at dinner looking unkempt and frightened would only put her at a distinct disadvantage.

She had to remind him that she was a journalist for a very well-known magazine. The type of magazine that people in his circles had been on the cover of. She had to remind him that while she may not hang out with presidents and kings, she wasn't a nobody either—she'd met a lot of powerful people and a lot of them liked her because they liked being in *Wealthy*. She'd interviewed billionaires, celebrities, investors, entrepreneurs. She was in her thirties. She'd gone to the Columbia Journalism School. She was a New Yorker, for God's sake.

In other words, she wasn't one of his powerless young victims. She may not have his money or influence, but she had her pen. Hadn't he heard the expression *The pen is mightier than the sword?*

So, she'd shower, blow dry her hair, brush her teeth, and put on the most professional dress she could find in the wardrobe, or at least one whose skirt wasn't so short her ass would peek out of it.

Then she'd square her shoulders and head to dinner. She'd act as "untouchable" as he was acting. She'd make unwavering eye contact. She'd use every ounce of skill she'd learned to get people to open up.

And she'd interview Mr. Dexter Hunt.

Chapter Twenty-Three

"Champagne?" Dexter Hunt asked.

The pair were in an extremely large and impressive dining area with glass walls overlooking the Aegean as the sun began to melt into the water. The table was tucked inside of a small alcove and set for two —nearby was an impressively large wooden table that must have easily sat 15 or 20 people.

"No, thank you," Maddie said. She didn't want to drink anything that might blunt her senses.

Next to them stood a bald man in what she began to recognize as the island-employees' uniform—a white polo shirt with a "DH" logo embossed in gold on the left shirt pocket, and black work slacks.

The man, like Max, appeared the very picture of competence and discretion, barely making eye contact, yet somehow anticipating every need and getting everything done quickly and quietly. She imagined Hunt's employees were being paid fabulously for their well-oiled servitude—as well as their silence.

Maddie had both sparkling and tap water in front of her, so she took a sip of the sparkling while the bald server poured Hunt a half-flute of champagne and placed the bottle in a nearby ice bucket. Maddie noticed the label on the all-black bottle read "Dom Pérignon."

"Or," Hunt said, and Maddie caught a mischievous glint in his eyes. "We have plenty of Yastika. Doukas only, of course."

"No, thank you," Maddie said again, smiling politely. If he thought bringing up Elias was going to rattle her, he was mistaken. "I'm fine with water."

Hunt barely glanced at the waiter, who knew enough to make a little bow before retreating through the high-ceilinged, gargantuan dining space, then a back door.

"*Yamas*," said Hunt, tipping his flute towards her. Maddie said nothing and watched him take a long sip, eyes closed. He sighed satisfactorily.

"I have a vineyard in Reims, but even I can't resist Dom Pérignon."

He opened his eyes and stared at her in that strangely direct way he had. Maddie couldn't tell if his eyes were blue or gray—they were an indeterminate slate color she'd never seen before, and they gave his eyes a flat, difficult-to-read expression. His jaw was over-sized and square, like a cartoon drawing of Batman. He wasn't her type by any stretch—too steely and robotic—but she imagined many people would find him attractive.

"I want you to know," he said, "that I've read dozens of your articles. You're a good writer."

"Thank you."

"Every six months or so someone from *Wealthy* tries to contact me through various avenues. There is one young man... particularly persistent... Bernman, I believe the name is. It's somewhere in my notes, but my memory is a reliable one."

"Yes, I know him."

"You know him rather well I should think."

"What... what do you mean?" she stammered.

"Well, the two of you prowled all up and down the port looking to hire a boat, did you not?" he asked. "So, he's working with you?"

Maddie relaxed a bit as it became clear Hunt hadn't been referring to her and Logan once having had sex. Still, it was disconcerting to realize he had eyes and ears all over Kyrie. What a fool she'd been to not surmise that sooner. "No," she said. "I came here without telling him."

Maddie could scarcely believe she'd admitted that. It would be much more prudent to let Hunt think that a nearby *Wealthy* reporter was aware that she was on Volinos. But as she still didn't know what Hunt's plans for her were, she wanted to distance herself from Logan for his own protection.

"Why did you do that?" he asked, looking genuinely curious.

Maddie had the distinct impression that not much got by Dexter Hunt, so she decided to stick with the truth as a way of gaining his confidence.

"Because whatever is going on here, I want to be the one to report on it."

"I see," Hunt said.

His flinty slate eyes softened a little. He liked that answer. Not just that it was the truth, and that Maddie was admitting something rather embarrassing, but that he respected people who had ambition—and respected them even more if that ambition meant screwing someone else over. He was the type of man who'd out-maneuvered many smart people in his life, and he admired others who did it as well.

Soon the bald waiter was back and handed them hand-drawn menus on cream parchment paper.

"To your liking, ma'am, or anything you'd prefer to switch out?" the man asked.

Maddie greedily glanced over the menu, her stomach aching with hunger. Lobster bisque, half-shell oysters and shrimp cocktail, Greek salad, grilled branzino or seafood risotto, pot roasted vegetables, and chocolate baklava. Almost worth sitting across from a potential sociopath.

"I'll have the risotto and no need to bring the oysters for me," she said.

The waiter nodded solemnly and turned obsequiously to Hunt, who said, "The branzino, *parakalo*, and don't skimp on the oysters."

The waiter reclaimed the menus then disappeared again. Maddie was starving—she hadn't eaten since she'd left Kyrie in the morning, but was also worried about any somnolent effect so much food would have on her. She wanted to remain alert for this delicate show-down with Hunt.

"Mr. Hunt—"

"Dexter."

212

"Mr. Hunt, certainly you can understand why I'm concerned. You've admitted Ruby is here on the island. She's only 12 years old. At least, this is what she told me. I want to give you a chance to tell me your side of things."

"Isn't that generous of you," he said, lifting one brow in that imperious way he had. He was most definitely a man who wasn't accustomed to any kind of pushback—but she had the sneaking suspicion that, deep down, he admired her for having the guts to do it. "But we have a superb meal coming and I don't wish to spoil it. Let's discuss it after dinner."

"I don't think I'll be able to enjoy dinner until I know for certain that Ruby is safe."

"The girl is completely safe," he said, irritation grating his voice. "And I'll prove it to you. But first, let's talk about you."

Ugh, he was good. He knew exactly how to redirect conversation. Maddie decided to let him think he was getting his way for now.

"What do you want to know?"

"How long have you worked for *Wealthy*? I have some old issues here, and you're on the masthead. Far, far down the masthead, in the reporter section. Surely, a smart woman like you must be an editor by now."

"Still a reporter."

"Why is that?"

"I prefer writing to editing."

"Do you? I'd think you'd want a corner office with a higher salary. You're not satisfied to be in the lowly reporters' pool, are you?"

"It's fine for now."

The waiter returned, serving them their lobster bisque. A plate of oysters was put in the middle of the table.

"Are you certain you don't want any oysters?" Hunt asked. "Greeks love their cod, squid, and anchovies, but not so much their oysters. These were flown in from Cancale, France."

"I'm certain. Thank you."

The pair ate in silence for a good five minutes. The bisque was superb. Thick and creamy with plenty of large chunks of lobster. She watched as Hunt basically inhaled all of the oysters—one right after another, and poured himself another half-flute of champagne.

"You have the life here, Mr. Hunt," she said. "Your mother must be proud."

"She would be if she hadn't died of breast cancer when I was five."

"Oh, I'm sorry."

"Thank you. And you? Close to your parents?"

"My mother, yes. But my father died when I was 16. Prostate cancer."

"I'm sorry to hear. I almost think it was better that my mother died when I was so young, I hardly remember her. Only a few flashes here and there, ones I may have even imagined. You, on the other hand, knew your father well. It must have been devastating when he passed."

The inside of her nose and the backs of her eyelids began to tingle harshly, threatening tears, as often happened when she spoke of her father. Determined not to start crying, she took a deep breath, nodded tightly, and said, "It was."

"Imagine, Maddie… may I call you Maddie?"

"By all means."

"Imagine, Maddie, a world without cancer. Can you imagine that?"

"That would… that would be… incredible. Like heaven."

"Indeed it would."

Before she realized what was happening, the bowls and the plate littered with empty oyster shells were being lifted off the table and onto a trolley. She hadn't heard or even sensed the waiter's return. It was like he'd learned how to be invisible. Hunt didn't speak again until the waiter disappeared through the swinging door at the other end of the dining area.

"Now imagine—a world without war."

"Without war?" Maddie gave a cynical headshake. "That would be something. Probably never going to happen though."

"What makes you say that?"

"Humans have been fighting since day one. It's in our nature. Or at least man's nature, not so sure about the women. Women get each other in different ways."

For the first time, she saw a genuine smile on his face, transforming it into something a little less intimidating. For a moment, she felt as if the power balance was equal and she was merely interviewing a rich man for the magazine.

"Disease, war, famine. These are the three plights

that have plagued mankind since the beginning, you agree?" he asked.

"Sounds about right."

"We've invented all manner of ways of dealing with them—religion, medicine, politics, technology. And yet… we have the same issues we've always had. Perhaps not on the same level, there's been no black plague that has wiped out a third of the population for quite some time. Mass famine still exists, but it is relegated to certain pockets of the globe. War, we still have it, but statistically, we have much less of it, though it may not feel that way. On the whole, humankind progresses in the right direction. But this is hardly a utopia, is it?"

"Hardly." She found herself starting to fall into a sort of trance, started to question herself—a man concerned with such big issues couldn't be a child predator, could he?

But, of course, he could. She had to remain vigilant, not allow herself to get sucked into the charisma he was giving off. "For example, sex trafficking," she said. "Still a huge problem."

Not taking the bait, his expression grew startlingly intense, and he said, "What if we could solve these problems? In our lifetime?"

"I'd think that would be a very good thing," she said, for lack of anything better to say. He was starting to sound like the mad professor in a bad science fiction film.

The silent waiter was back and deposited their plates —risotto for her, branzino for him. Noticing that Maddie's sparkling water was almost finished, he topped it off without asking. Then did a slight bow and retreated.

"*Bon appetit,*" Hunt said.

* * *

THIS TIME THEY WERE ALONE, no waiter silently dipping in and out of the room, in a glass-enclosed terrace area a short walk from where they'd had dinner. The sun had set, leaving behind the amethyst glow she recognized as late evening in this part of the Aegean.

Hunt went to a sleek wet bar and poured himself a small glass of Yastika. Noting the blue eye of the Doukas label, she thought of Elias, torn between hoping he was safely back on Kyrie and hardening herself against him for his duplicity. The last look she'd seen on his face indicated he was ashamed at his behavior, but that made it even worse. He'd known what he was doing was wrong and had done it anyway.

Hunt, apparently realizing she was not going to accept any alcohol tonight, didn't bother to ask if she also wanted a glass of Yastika.

"Madison Ribeiro," Hunt said, contemplatively. It shouldn't have surprised her that he used her legal name —it was not on the *Wealthy* masthead—but it did. He clearly had been doing a deep dive on her. "You've put me in a very difficult position," he said.

"I didn't mean to."

"But you did. Young ladies coming to my island on a private boat, most of them looking like models, I can absolutely see why you're thinking what you're thinking."

"It's not only me," she said. "The Kyrie locals think it, too."

"Well, I figured they might gossip amongst themselves, but it didn't occur to me that they would spread that gossip to an American reporter. Nor that that reporter would happen to meet up with one of my girls —the most important girl. Ruby."

Maddie's stomach squirmed. The way he talked about "his girls" and "the most important girl" was so possessive.

"Mr. Hunt, Elias is clearly working for you, yet he was the one who told me the rumors about you and Volinos. Girls and wild parties. I'm puzzled why he would do that."

Hunt smirked, took a sip of Yastika, and stared into his glass for several moments.

"I assume he thought he was doing me a favor. Greeks don't have the particular brand of Puritanism that Americans do. Americans consume the most pornography of any country in the world, and are one of the biggest facilitators of child sex trafficking—yet you'd think America was a land of virgins and pious moralists. Americans are virgins and pious moralists in their minds only. Excessive piety has, throughout history, always been a scourge, leading to mass genocides and witch hunts, though those perpetrating it believe they're cleansing the world of evils."

"How would Elias have been doing you a favor?" she

asked, refusing to allow him to distract her with his speechifying.

"Because the locals know I want my privacy, but when you began asking questions, I assume he thought telling you I was merely a lecher who liked to party with pretty girls would assuage whatever concerns you had. It would have assuaged most anyone on Kyrie. Or perhaps he didn't know enough to keep his mouth shut. He doesn't live full time on Kyrie and maybe his family doesn't include him in business dealings for their own reasons."

"Is he working for you?"

"Not directly, no. But I'm almost single-handedly keeping his family's Yastika business afloat with large, regular orders. I've also opened up new customer bases for them; recommended them for important trade shows and the like."

"So you paid off everyone on Kyrie."

"That's a particularly crass way of putting it, but I suppose the truth. If any of the Kyrians need help, they know they can go to the municipality and tap a special fund. In return, they need to leave me alone, don't buzz my island with their boats or drones, and don't try to bring tourists here. I'm sure their minds couldn't conceive of what you—a pious American—were conceiving of. That I'm some sort of international pimp."

"If you're not, then what are young girls doing coming to your island? Why is Ruby here?"

"You saw she was with her mother."

"I have no proof that's her mother. And even if she is, plenty of mothers sell their children."

He settled his glass on a nearby chrome and seashell table, staring absently in front of him. She could tell he was deep in thought and internally wrestling with something.

"This…" he finally said, quietly. "*This* I can't have. This is exactly what I can't have. I can ignore a lot of innuendo. I know there's all kinds. I believe your friend Bernman thinks I'm evading taxes or running a Ponzi scheme or some such. But *this* I can't have."

"Then Mr. Hunt, I'm listening. Tell me what's happening."

"You've put me in a bad position, Maddie. A very bad position. I suppose I should have made the special fund contingent on not bringing reporter friends to Kyrie, and it pains me to know that I paid for the home renovation of the person who did. Athena Kyriakos? Your former coworker." He let out a mournful little sigh. "These are the types of snags it's almost impossible to predict."

"If it's any consolation, she tried very hard to talk me out of coming. In fact, the only reason I came here is because Elias brought me."

"Well, at that point, I knew I needed to do something. I told Alexander to bring you to me. Somehow Elias got the job."

Instinct told her to remain quiet. He was on the verge of revealing whatever was going on and anything she said might be the wrong thing, causing him to clam up.

"I've gone over and over in my mind what to do," he said. "I've even run computer models. The only thing I keep coming up with is to tell you the truth."

The truth will set you free, she wanted to say, but didn't. She still felt the best way to get him to open up was to say nothing. He looked as if the weight of the world was crushing in on him, his square-cut features softening, the haughtiness draining from his face. He looked older, frailer. For the first time, Maddie felt she'd gained the upper hand.

"Then that's what I will do," he said, more to himself, before making direct eye contact. "I'll tell you the truth."

Chapter Twenty-Four

RUBY

*M*om doesn't seem mad at me. Which I was really nervous about. She was kind of silent on the boat ride back from the island. And I felt really bad, *crushed* that we weren't going to get all the things Mr. John promised us. And I'm super embarrassed that my feelings came out just when we met the president. He seemed like a nice guy.

But I couldn't do it. I'm not even sure why. But I couldn't. I know I should have figured that out before Mom and I came all the way here. Before we wasted Mr. John's time. Before I met the president.

When we got back to Kyrie and came off the boat, Mom finally turned to look directly at me. She put her hands on my shoulders and looked me in the eye. I felt like crying.

"Ruby, I don't want you to worry about it," she said. "It's my fault for thinking you could handle something like this."

"I th-thought I could, Mom," I said.

"Let's go get you some of that gelato you like. Or anything you want."

Later, we came to the beach house. Mom told me that Mr. John had requested that we speak to someone on the phone. Since Mom didn't have service, Glenda, who came with us from Volinos, made the call.

Mom spoke into the phone for a little bit, saying things like, "Yes, she's fine. Thank you for asking," then handed the phone to me. I was really surprised to see Maddie on the screen.

"Ruby, you have a friend here who is concerned about you," Mr. John said in the background. "I know you two met on Kyrie, and she's been wanting to make sure you're okay ever since."

"Um, hi, Ruby," Maddie said, looking like she still wasn't sure if I was okay or not. It's crazy to me that she continued to wonder about this, and somehow even is sitting there with Mr. John in what looks like his glass house. I can't think of any other time a complete stranger has been so worried about me.

"Hi, Maddie," I said. "I'm fine."

"Where are you?" she asked.

"I'm on Kyrie, with Mom." I held the phone so Maddie could see her, even though she'd just seen her. "We were on the other island but came back."

I wasn't sure how much else I was supposed to say. Those papers Mom signed made it seem like we can never, ever say anything about anything. But it was weird that Maddie was sitting there with Mr. John. Did she know about everything?

"Ruby," Mr. John said. "Can you walk outside to the terrace and show Maddie the beach below? Kalaria?"

"Um, sure," I said. I walked outside, and Mom followed. I swept the phone all around so Maddie could see the beach and the rocks below the house. Then I put my face up to the phone again.

"Ruby, did anything bad happen to you here on Volinos?" Mr. John asked.

"Bad? No."

"Any other questions, Maddie?" Mr. John asked.

"Um." Maddie had her fingers up to her mouth, and she wasn't looking at the phone on her end. Like she was trying to decide what to say. "No, I guess that's it."

"Are you satisfied Ruby is safe?" Mr. John asked.

"Yes. Yes, I guess so," she said, quietly. Then she turned her eyes up to me and smiled. "I'm happy you're okay, Ruby. I won't bother you again."

"You didn't bother me," I said. "You just care."

Mom took the phone from me and said her good-byes to both Maddie and Mr. John. Then she hung up and handed the phone back to Glenda.

"Mom, I'm so tired," I said.

Mom said I must be. Glenda said she'd show me to my bedroom. She said the two of us could stay here as long as we liked, and she would get us a plane back to the States. Mom said a flight as soon as Glenda could get one would be fine.

Later, Mom came into my room and sat on the bed with me.

"I feel like I failed," I told her. "Now you'll never get to quit the bar."

"Honey," she said, stroking my hair. "I promise you I'll leave the bar. And get a good job. No matter what I have to do. In fact, I've been thinking very seriously about nursing school. I shouldn't have put the burden of improving my life on you."

"You didn't—"

"Yes, I did. I want you to know I'm sorry." She hugged me and kissed me on the forehead. I hope she's telling the truth about going back to school. Maybe then I won't have to worry about her so much. "Now let's chalk this up to a misguided adventure," she said. "We got to see a couple of great islands and have some amazing meals. So not a total loss."

"No. Actually, it was kind of fun."

So that's the end of Mom's and my adventure in Greece. I can't ever tell anyone about it. Sometimes I wonder if I hadn't met Maddie would I have gone through with it? Something about the way she was so concerned about me made me think maybe I shouldn't do it. I don't know.

Either way, I'm glad I didn't do it. Some things are too weird for me.

And that definitely was.

Good night.

Chapter Twenty-Five

"I don't understand, Mr. Hunt," Maddie said, handing a phone back to the expressionless man who'd walked into the room and silently handed it to her with Stella's somewhat bewildered face on the screen. Taking the phone, the man turned straight around and left.

"I'm happy to see that Ruby is safe, as you promised. But I still don't know what's happening here or what all the secrecy is about."

"How much do you know about me, Maddie?"

"Only what I could dig up online, which wasn't much. You've had a hedge fund since you were 21. Degrees from MIT and Harvard Business School. As I recall, you started MIT at 16. No children, at least that I could find, and divorced. That's about it."

"Space?"

"Oh, yes, you like space. You've been in high Earth orbit."

"And you saw that I own a space exploration company, Dex-X?"

"Yes."

Swirling his short glass of Yastika, he roamed around the glass-walled room. The light was exquisite, a gentle pinkish-purple, minutes after the sun had set.

"Every single thing you've heard about alien beings is utterly wrong," he said, unexpectedly. He stopped and looked at her. His expression was a bizarre mixture of awe and contempt. "Laughable, but for people believing it. Extraterrestrials can't enter our atmosphere any more than we can enter theirs. Biocontamination could very well destroy their ecosystem and theirs ours. They would have pathogens and bacteria to which we have no resistance and vice versa. The idea of them flying down and capturing us for experiments, or us holding them somewhere in Area 51, is inconceivable and impossible."

He looked out one wall. Maddie followed his line of sight. The sky. Her mind was tumultuous and blank at the same time. She couldn't imagine where his speech was going, but her intuition was crackling with the certainty that it was going somewhere unprecedented.

"But aliens do exist. A universe this big, how could they not? It's sheer human arrogance to imagine we're the only intelligent life in existence. Astronomers have been sending out radio waves and binary code into space since the sixties—ambient sounds, rudimentary messages and images. But no country—so far as I know, anyway—had ever intercepted communications from other solar systems."

He turned back to her. She couldn't move and realized her mouth was hanging half open. She closed it.

"Maddie, I'm going to have to insist that everything I tell you from here on out is off-the-record. Not on background. Completely off-record. Do you agree? Because if you do, I know you're good for it."

She internally squirmed. Agreeing that everything was off-the-record meant he could tell her pretty much anything and she'd be bound to keep silent. Journalists went to prison to keep off-the-record sources private. But she vowed if he was about to confess anything illegal, such as running a pedophile ring, she would have no problem breaking her reporter's confidentiality and turning him in.

"I agree. Off-the-record."

"As I said, no country had ever intercepted messages from another solar system." Pause. "Until it did. Eight years ago, Dex-X captured bio-data sent out from an area I'm not at liberty to reveal."

"Bio-data?"

"We have a genome, Maddie. Alien DNA."

Out of Maddie's mouth burst a sound that inappropriately resembled a laugh. But it wasn't a laugh. Or maybe it was. Because she'd never heard anything so strange and foreign before, and her mind couldn't decide if he was joking, bullshitting her, if he was crazy, or if this spectacularly bizarre announcement was true, and if it was, what that meant for the world.

She almost felt like she should apologize for the outburst, but couldn't speak, and stared at him, waiting to see if he smiled and clued her into his odd joke.

"I won't go into all of the scientific details, but suffice it to say that our next step is to combine alien DNA with human DNA. I'm sure, being an intelligent woman, you can infer why."

As fantastical as this news about aliens was, it was also, somehow, expected. The time before, when she hadn't known about aliens, seemed so far away, a life that no longer was relevant. Her life would be forever split into two sections—before she knew about this, and after.

"Oh my God," she said. "You... want a... you want... some kind of..." Her mind was fumbling, grasping, amassing. Everything she'd seen and heard in the past couple of weeks. All of her suspicions. This new information. All of it piecing together, but slowly, like a particularly frustrating puzzle. "...some kind of... alien baby. A human-alien baby."

"Correct. There's no telling if we'll get it. Much work needs to be done. But that is the goal."

"And... and you... you..." Fragments converging, parts linking. From this and that direction, migrating towards one inescapable conclusion. "... have these young girls coming to the island... to... to... harvest their DNA."

"Oh, we've already harvested it. They come here for the final leg of a rather long and involved application process. It's important that I meet the donor face-to-face, not the least in part to make absolutely certain the donor and the DNA match. In fact, they are tested again once they get here."

"You… you wanted Ruby to be… to be the mother of this alien baby."

"Technically. The embryo would have the extraterrestrial DNA combined with her DNA, just as a human has maternal and paternal DNA. She wouldn't gestate the embryo. Nor is she donating egg cells. We'll use an anonymous donor and do a maternal spindle transfer—empty the donor cell of its nucleus, and replace it with our combined extraterrestrial and human DNA for fertilization.

This is another reason I came to Greece, besides having plenty of remote and habitable islands for sale. This country allows maternal spindle transfers—the U.S. does not."

She could no longer stand and eyed the nearest surface, which she thought was a couch but wasn't sure as her brain could no longer take in her surroundings, could only take in Dexter Hunt, his words, his movements, and this new information. She somehow got to it and plopped down.

"Does this country allow for messing around with alien DNA?" she asked, surprised she had enough wits about her to formulate a complete sentence.

"There are no laws regarding alien DNA. It's hard to enforce something that doesn't exist."

Maddie stared at the dark wood floor for what seemed a minute or two. Then she looked out the glass walls for a while, out onto the sea and sky which were fused in one monochromatic shade of royal blue, as the moon, Venus, and the larger stars began to shine.

"I don't mean to be rude," she finally said. "But this

sounds utterly insane."

"Well, I don't know why." He sounded insulted. "It was only a matter of time before it happened. I have faith that a hybrid—if the embryo is viable and there's no guarantee of that—will have so much to teach us. The paternal DNA—for we believe the extraterrestrial DNA has paternal markers, not maternal—comes from an extremely ancient civilization, many more millions of years old than Earth, and very probably no longer in existence.

But knowledge is contained within a genome. If you have the genetic code of a being, then you have the entire history of the evolution of that being. Genetic mutations lead to behavioral and societal changes. A genetic mutation is what allowed modern man to digest starch with saliva, and dawned the agricultural revolution. This led to a population explosion and massively elongated the human lifespan. The hybrid could do everything from give us the cure for cancer to teach humans how to coexist peacefully with each other. Genetics are the code to everything."

Maddie made a few more guttural sounds that resembled laughs but weren't laughs—she didn't know what they were exactly—and scratched at her scalp. Then stared at him again, her eyes wider than she thought she'd ever felt them.

"Okay, let me…" She tried to organize her thoughts into something more rational, more probing. To pull her journalist side together. "Okay, why not ask a scientist to donate DNA, someone who would understand all of this? Instead of a random young girl?"

"This is a fair question," he said, heading to the nearest chair, a ruddy leather chair with a high back, and sinking into it. He placed his drink on the nearby glass table.

"The short answer is that I'm extremely concerned about the human reaction to a hybrid being. Humans don't do well with anything different from themselves. One need only read *Frankenstein* or *The Phantom of the Opera* to see that. Tribalism is powerfully ingrained in our reptilian brain. I'm afraid the hybrid will—to put it bluntly—be killed. Oh, not right away. At first, there will be a flurry of positive press, because if the embryo is viable, I'll go public. I'll really have no choice because too many people will know about it. But then will come the questions. Then the fear. Then the laws. Then the hunt. It's what human beings do."

Dexter Hunt was a man of supreme confidence who didn't have the nervous tics that most people did—or at least that Maddie did. But now he began to rub his knees with both hands, absently, as if unaware of what he was doing. She could tell the idea of his hybrid being hunted down and killed disturbed him greatly.

"I want to try to make the being... I suppose you could call it 'cute.'" His small pinkish mouth turned down distastefully at the word. "The more appealing-looking the hybrid is to humans, the less they'll want to wipe it out of existence. Essentially, I needed a female with the 'perfect face.' Or at least one that would hope-fully be passed down to the hybrid, triggering humans' collective instinct to protect and admire something that called to them on a genetic level. Not to mention that most scientists are well-versed in genetic ethics. It would be hard to find a scientist donor."

That last part didn't sit well with Maddie. The first part was batshit crazy enough, but the second part implied that ignorance was a trait he needed for his plan to succeed.

"So, you wanted a naïve kid and her naïve mother, and if they were in desperate need of money, all the better."

He sighed, and stopped kneading his knees, then took a quick sip of Yastika.

"I admit that the donor's circumstances were nearly as important as her DNA. I spent years running computer models, and a handful of young women stood out as their appearance being most likely to be accepted within a diverse array of ethnicities. Of those young women, Ruby was the best candidate for a multitude of reasons."

"Then why is she on Kyrie and not here?"

"To be frank, I gravely miscalculated. I'd been so focused on the perfect DNA that I didn't take into account the psychology of the donor as much as I should have. Primarily, her age. Young DNA is a wonderful thing to have, but a young mind—not so much.

In the end, she couldn't seem to reconcile having what she would think of as her child out there in the world. A child that was not hers, but belonged to science. Now, I own her DNA. I could go ahead and use it anyway. But that will lead nowhere good. I need a willing donor."

Maddie sat obsessively rubbing one bare shoulder, then dove full into her habitual nervous tic—twisting her lower lip. This all seemed too far-fetched to be real. And yet something deep down, something primal, told her it was.

Whether it was watching movies about aliens—she'd, of course, seen *E.T.* and *Close Encounters of the Third Kind*—or her own extremely limited encounter with a UFO—she'd always felt that humans couldn't be alone in the universe.

At the age of 13, she'd been riding in the passenger side of her family's car, her mother at the wheel, when she looked up into the night sky and saw what appeared to be an orange-hued, oddly-shaped flying craft. It was much lower and slower than a plane, and was completely silent. But when she tried to draw her mother's attention to it, it disappeared.

This was shortly after what had happened with Daniel, so her mind turned against her, telling her she must have merely seen a plane, or perhaps some kind of satellite, and the stress from "the Daniel incident" had warped her perception.

"I didn't think you could cross-pollinate species," she said, not certain she was using the correct terminology.

"That would be incorrect," he clipped out. "Hybridization is common in the animal world. Mules are the hybrid offspring of donkeys and horses. Yes, the animals are similar species. We don't see tigers mating with birds. Or humans mating with horses. Though I'm sure some have tried."

He grinned but Maddie was still too much in a state of shock to react to his little joke.

"Are human and extraterrestrial DNA similar enough that they can produce a viable hybrid? We believe so. At least, this alien DNA is. But we shall find out."

"Who is this 'we' you keep referring to?"

"A small amount of people who know about this. One island employee who coordinates the donor candidates, some astronomers at Dex-X, some geneticists at the DNA firm. And the handful of candidates who made it to the island. They're bound by very strict NDAs." Pause. "Oh, and a special friend of mine. He's rather influential and makes a lot of things easier for me."

On some level, Maddie still struggled with wondering if this was all an elaborate attempt to cover up something more simplistic—such as a fetish for young girls. If so, it was the most flamboyant cover story ever.

"Well, what's next?" she asked. "Ruby left. You say you won't use her DNA."

He stretched as if the conversation had gone on so long that it had become tedious for him. "It's been a long night, you agree? Why don't we continue this dialogue tomorrow?"

The idea of spending a night on Volinos sent her into a tiny riot of conflicting emotions. She'd interviewed lots of rich men who were, to put it mildly, eccentric. A man who thought he could create some kind of alien baby might be more eccentric than most, but she'd interviewed entrepreneurs with all kinds of nutty ideas. Some of those ideas not only came to fruition but became a normal part of the fabric of our lives.

She tried to imagine the first reporter to talk to Steve Jobs or Bill Gates, with their fantastical notions that one day everyone would have computers on their desks, would carry them around in their hands, would be able to slip them into a back pocket. Computers—the things that, only a few decades ago, took up football fields of space.

Imagine if that reporter had, upon being told of those excessively ambitious plans—had only expressed skepticism, burst out with inappropriate laughter, and then left the island—figuratively?

What of the people who were first told about germ theory? Or that the Earth revolved around the sun and not vice versa? Or any of the other inventions or discoveries that drastically altered human existence?

Once in a while, something came along that was so big, so extreme, that it changed everything. This could be one of those things.

So the reporter part of Maddie wanted to stay the night and hear what else Dexter Hunt was going to regale her with. If all of this was true—and not some elaborately outlandish attempt to cover up sex crimes— then this was the story of the century. Maybe of the millennium. She didn't want to be on the wrong side of history.

But the woman part of Maddie was persistently whispering that Dexter Hunt—ruler of his own fiefdom and giving off a distinct mad scientist vibe—could be dangerous. She was surrounded by water and security guards who had nothing but loyalty to Hunt, and she could end up one of the thousands of women a year who vanish off the face of the planet.

The reporter side won out but the woman side wanted a compromise.

"Fine, I'll stay," she said. "But I'd like my phone back. I'd really feel more comfortable with it."

"I'll have it returned to your cabin. But you should know your phone has been blocked from our satellite. I can't risk that you might tell anyone about my plans here. As I said, I won't ask you to sign an NDA but I must insist that you keep our conversation off-the-record, as promised."

She didn't bother to ask him who exactly he expected her to tell. She wasn't about to go spreading his alien hybrid story. For one, there was still a chance this was all bullshit and she didn't need to look like a fool.

"I'd prefer that the phone work so I can at least check in with people," she said.

"It's only for the night."

He smiled and she felt it was pointless to continue to press it. Besides, the adrenaline she'd been running on since he'd cornered her in the downstairs study was nothing but fumes. It was better to act unperturbed, continue to let him believe she had nothing to worry about, that plenty of people cared about her and knew where she was.

"Alright," she said. "Let's finish this tomorrow."

Chapter Twenty-Six

"*M*addie."

At first, she thought she was hearing only the wind rustling the palm trees Dexter Hunt told her he'd had planted on the island. Or the sea, which could be heard crashing and rumbling below the bluffs.

"Maddie!"

Louder now, she turned to look all around her, expecting to see one of Dexter Hunt's lackeys. But the shadow that came out from behind a dark stone wall and crystallized into a man was Elias.

"Elias, leave me alone," she said, tersely, continuing along the path that Dexter Hunt had told her would lead directly to her cabin. She didn't know what had happened to Max but apparently Hunt was satisfied that she wasn't going anywhere.

Before she could say more, Elias was keeping pace alongside her. Now she had a good idea why Max wasn't around—Hunt must have sent Elias to keep an eye on her instead.

"I know where I'm going," she snapped at him.

"Maddie, *please*," he said, quietly. "I only did what I did because if I did not, then Alexander would. I thought better if I here with you on the island, not him."

She stopped and turned. There were only a few tiki torches scattered along the path for light, but she hoped he could see the furious look in her eyes. "You've proven you can't be trusted. I told you something very private that happened to me, that went a long way towards making it difficult for me to trust people, and yet you did this."

Then she bounded off down the path, certain he would keep following.

"Please, listen," he begged, keeping his voice low, getting slightly ahead of her and walking backwards. "I didn't know how much Kyrie need this man. How much my family need this man."

He got in front of her and she had no choice but to stop.

"We in business for hundreds of years and we close to—how you say it—bank—bank—" Giving up on striving for the word that stayed out of reach, he continued, "—having nothing. No way to make living on our little island. We survive plagues, pirates, and Turks. We can't die off because of money. My father, he in his seventies now. He know no other way. He, my mother, my brother, they will never leave Kyrie. You are American, how you understand 700 years in one place?"

If she was irritated with him before, now she was full-on angry. Not only had he betrayed her by hand delivering her to Hunt, but she was supposed to feel sorry for him.

"Elias," she hissed out. "You have no idea what that man has planned for me and I'm stuck here. I'd thought you were my backup. I wouldn't have agreed to come otherwise. Just because my ancestors moved around more than yours doesn't give you the right to put me in danger."

She pushed by him and continued along the path, but he refused to give up, keeping alongside her.

"Alexander promise me the man want only speak with you. Nothing more. That he want to tell to you he not doing anything wrong, not doing this thing with the young girls you think he's doing. Two Americans talking, that is all."

She stopped and glared at him more. They happened to be under a tiki torch, and between that and the swollen full moon and plentiful stars, she could see his face was contorted in an expression of beseeching. She tried to keep her voice as low as his, not knowing who might be lurking around listening in or even if Hunt had bugged the trees with surveillance devices.

"And you *believed* that," she hissed. "I have no way of getting off this damn island. Did you get your phone back?"

She didn't like the way Hunt was so concerned she might tell someone about his plans that he'd blocked her phone—eventually, she'd have to leave and then what? He either trusted her to keep her word about everything being off-the-record, or he didn't. And it seemed he didn't.

"No," Elias said, sheepishly. "But Maddie, if you think you in danger, I come soon as it light and take you away. The boat at the dock. No one will stop me."

The machismo in him that had formerly amused her now filled her with contempt. As if the pair of them could fight off a horde of pepper-spray wielding security guards and a formidable-looking German Shepherd.

"And then what?" she asked. "Hunt cuts off your family? They starve because of me?"

"Then… then *yes*. So be it. They get into business with this rich man. I won't have you hurt for them."

Maddie charged around him and quickened her pace. She wasn't sure she could trust anything coming out of Elias' mouth. He might have been sent to her by Hunt to test whether she'd reveal what she knew about the alien hybrid plan. She couldn't forget how convincing Elias had been in her studio on Kyrie, making her believe they were going to sneak onto Volinos for a look around and that he was on her side.

"You should have thought about that before, Elias," she tossed back.

Spotting her cabin, she ran the hundred or so feet to it and shoved open the door. Closing it, she saw no way to lock it, so she stood staring at the door for several minutes, breath coming quickly, wondering if he was going to try to enter.

She cast around for something heavy to blockade the door but all she saw were the large wardrobe and the bed, neither of which she'd be able to move. A desk in the corner appeared too light to act as an adequate barricade.

She decided that if he came in, she'd scream her head off in hopes that one of Dexter Hunt's henchmen would take care of him.

But he didn't come.

Chapter Twenty-Seven

*T*he next day, a different waiter, though it was another man with an equally as simultaneously stony and obsequious manner, served Maddie and Dexter Hunt lunch. They sat on a terrace at the back of the glass house, overlooking a spectacular view of the Aegean.

No matter how many times she looked at it, the impact never dulled. The sea stretched endlessly blue before them, the sun sparkling off the calm water, the sky just as blue and endless, without a wisp of cloud.

To her surprise, she'd slept wonderfully, the *shush shush* sound of the waves below her cabin lulling her into the deep sleep she seemed to only have in warmer climes.

Luckily, she had not dreamed of Daniel and Chelsea —and no alien babies made appearances either. But she did wake up with the remnants of a dream about Logan still floating in her mind. He was probably wondering where she was. Even if he assumed she was spending time with Athena or Elias, she would have at least come back to her studio occasionally.

Despite her resentment of Logan, she had to admit he was a decent reporter. Perhaps he'd sniffed out that something was wrong. Perhaps he was asking around, or on social media, trying to track down Athena.

Or she could be delusional and he was merrily drinking Ouzo, sunning his pale, freckly self, and picking up girls.

"Mr. Hunt, I need to ask you something," she said, putting down the sparkling water the waiter had poured. "Can you please tell me how much the people of Kyrie know about all of this? People like my friend Athena? You said you paid for her house."

Hunt eyed the waiter until he retreated back into the double glass doors of the house.

"They certainly don't know what I told you last night," he said. "All they know is that they can get help if they need it, and most of them do. I'm putting locals through European universities and helping lovers get visas. I bought the hospital an MRI machine, the police department new scanners. I was told the island desperately needed more full-time residents, so I started a fund for repatriation." His expression turned a little sour. "I imagine once you informed your friend Athena what you suspected was happening over here, she became conflicted as to whether she should continue to redirect your attentions away from me."

Maddie thought about the things Athena had said to

her—on the one hand, almost guilting Maddie into giving up trying to get on Volinos. On the other, encouraging her to continue reporting when she returned to New York.

Athena must have figured this was the perfect compromise. She'd been relying on The Repatriation Project, not only for funds to restore her house but to stay on the island legally. At some point, the relative who was hosting Athena must have informed her that continuing to get money meant leaving Hunt to his own devices. She probably also told Athena that a lot of the locals, even perhaps Athena's relative herself, were dependent on Hunt's *largesse*.

What must it have felt like for Athena to know that it was her own guest who was putting all the Kyrians in jeopardy by poking around?

The locals can be very welcoming on the surface but, underneath, they can be really hard to crack. I've got to live with them, you know?

"It puts the locals in an awkward position, owing so much to you," Maddie said.

"Do you think that's so different from anywhere else? I suspect you know it isn't. I didn't count on the fact that many of them gossip more than a ladies' sewing circle and some of the boat captains were keeping keen eyes on the comings and goings to the island."

"Yes, Volinos has a nickname: 'orgy island.'"

For the first time, he looked shocked, widening his blue-gray eyes, then he chuckled under his breath. "That's the thanks I get for supporting them. I suppose it's in their nature to bite the hand that feeds them given their centuries of oppression."

"Well, you can see how I got the wrong impression."

The waiter returned with their Greek salads and side dishes of olive oil-braised calamari and potatoes, and uncorked a bottle of white wine. Maddie decided she might as well have a few sips. Last night, she'd been determined to remain completely clear-headed, but now she had a sense that the danger had waned, or if Hunt planned on doing her any harm, it at least wasn't going to be at lunch.

"*Yamas*," he said, holding up his glass.

For a while, they ate in silence while admiring the eye-popping view. The surroundings were so dazzling, the food and wine so exquisite, that she felt herself starting to slip into a kind of trance. Dexter Hunt may be privileged beyond belief, but he was also using that privilege for the betterment of the world, to advance science, or so said her mood in the moment.

He may indeed find the cure for the thing that had killed Maddie's father and Hunt's mother. He may indeed discover how to ensure world peace. Perhaps this alien-human baby held the key to it all. Sitting before her could be a genius on the level of Edison, Aristotle, Newton.

No wonder she'd thought the worst of him—she wasn't capable of thinking on those exalted levels. Her mind dwelled in the gutter, crawled around with the worst of humanity.

"Mr. Hunt, the idea of a hybrid baby… it brings up a lot of ethical questions. Are you going to raise it here? Will it have a mother? Friends? Will it only know you?"

"I'm afraid those aren't questions I'm inclined to answer at the moment," he said. "I appreciate your interest. But I told you what I told you because I knew you wouldn't stop with this pedophile ring nonsense otherwise. The island and I don't need that kind of scrutiny."

"Okay, then back to Ruby. You selected her to be the donor. I gather that's no longer the case, and that's where the conversation ended last night."

"Correct, she's no longer the donor. A great disappointment but it's too risky to have a donor who isn't on board. And I do have ethics. Despite your theory about me, it's not my intention to traumatize a young girl. If she doesn't want to do it, then she shouldn't. This is a high honor, not a punishment."

"Why didn't you take anonymous DNA?"

"There's no such thing. If you mean, why didn't I use the DNA without telling the donors what it was being used for, that would be at the risk of negating the contract. It would be fraudulent. I couldn't risk that the donor, pleading complete ignorance when signing the contract, would then gain legal control of the hybrid."

"Of the *child*."

"Yes, the child."

"So, what will you do without Ruby?"

He gave a little disconsolate sigh, glanced out over the water for such a long time she thought he might not answer, then returned his attention to her.

"Any good plan has backups. We have second, third,

and fourth choices. I've now eliminated anyone under 21. These candidates don't have all of the attributes Ruby does, but they'll undergo further psychological testing, and hopefully they'll have one of the most important attributes—they'll be certain this is what they want."

After lunch, Hunt offered to drive her to a nearby beach cove that had pink sand and emerald water, a combination, he assured her, that was exceedingly rare. They hopped in one of the military-style golf carts—this one bright red—and zipped up and down long, winding hills. The vehicle was electric and whizzed along silently. Hunt drove rather fast, and Maddie clung to the curved handlebar attached to her seat.

Ten minutes later, they pulled up to the top of a bluff, then made their way down steep stone steps to a small cove whose sand was, as promised, gorgeously pink. The water was clear as glass but tinted distinctly emerald as opposed to blue. She wished she had her phone so she could take a picture but supposed Hunt wouldn't allow her to do that anyway.

"It's absolutely stunning," she said, speaking loudly over gusts of wind. "Why is the sand pink?"

"Foraminifera—otherwise known as tiny sea creatures with pink shells. They wash up on the shoreline. I didn't even know this cove was here until after I'd bought the island. It was quite a bonus."

The pair flipped off their sandals, dug their toes into the colorful sand, and then waded into the water. Maddie knew on a deep level that Dexter Hunt was—quite masterfully—seducing her. Not in the way men normally seduced her, but in a way that was making her brain soft, making her certain that she would and *should* keep his secret, and trust that he only had the best in mind for humanity.

At the Columbia Journalism School, an ethics class professor had sternly exhorted the students not to take *anything*, not even a cup of coffee, from a source. Not only did that put you in a position of owing something to the source, but you could quickly start to lose your edge, push aside your skepticism.

And Maddie had been treated to far more than a cup of coffee. Only yesterday, she'd been worried Hunt might try to kill her for poking around in his business, but with her feet in the delectably warm, emerald water, her toes curled in the technicolor sand, she felt like any moment she might ask him if she could come to work for him. After all, she was a writer. She could draft public relations pieces. She could act as an emissary with Kyrie—tamp down those rumors about "orgy island." Hell, she could scrub toilets.

Feeling her reporter's neutrality going to mush, she turned from the water and glanced up at the limestone bluff, trying to fight off the spongy, sucking sensation that was pulling her down into full complacency.

"Maddie, I want to ask you something," he said. "This seems like the perfect place to do it."

She turned to him. The sun glazed his skin, making him appear more supple, younger, and had smoothed out his robotic features. He was wearing all white—a button-down cotton shirt, and long, loose pants rolled up around his ankles.

In that moment, her brain did something very odd. It clicked into a space where the pair of them were soulmates, and yes, they had met under bizarre circumstances, but this is sometimes how soulmates met. Now it only remained for them to kiss.

With that thought, she felt herself moving through the water towards him, or rather being pulled towards him by some invisible, magnetic force.

She got a foot or two from him, and shielded her face with one hand, not saying anything, half-aware that something terrible and outlandish was happening. It even occurred to her that her wine had been drugged. She'd only taken a few sips of it, but it had been enough to strip her of clarity, to make her compliant—and even attracted to him.

"Maddie," he continued, his honeyed voice barely audible over the wind. "Do you remember a year ago, you took a DNA test with your friend Athena? When she was applying to come here to Kyrie?"

"Yes?"

"Maddie," he said, his slow, masculine voice continually drawing her in. "I own that genealogy company. I had a look at your DNA. It's quite lovely."

Maddie knew she should be angry and horrified that Dexter Hunt had scrounged around in her DNA without her permission. But the breathtaking beauty of the island—the salmon-colored sand and emerald water, and the radiant, white sun—had infiltrated her senses so thoroughly that she kept docilely staring at him.

"You also filled out our psychological questionnaire. I liked your answers."

She grinned foolishly, as if he'd paid her a compliment on her hair or clothes. *There was something in that wine*, she thought, but the thought was coming to her from far away, a radio signal barely intercepted.

"You're attractive, you have a diverse ethnicity profile," he continued. "In your thirties, you're a full-fledged adult." Pause. "What would you think, Maddie, about being my donor?"

Her legs went rubbery, and she buckled slightly, sinking deeper into the sand. He reached out and held one of her arms.

"I'm okay," she said, but the world seemed to be happening in slow motion. The tender waves licking at her calves were coming in more languidly, and the wind caressing her cheeks had thinned, the sun had paled.

There was something in that wine!

"You don't have to answer right away," he said.

She pulled herself from his grip, made her way up the sand, and then plopped down. She was wearing one of the cotton dresses she'd found in the cabin's wardrobe. It was a royal blue tank dress, very casual. She pushed her feet deep into the sand, and stared at its pink luster.

"You want *me* to be the mother?"

He came and sat down on the sand beside her. He was so close she could smell his cologne—it was light and a little spicy, traces of smoke and wood. Not as nice as Elias' cologne. Speaking of which, was Elias still on the island?

She pulled her gaze up to Hunt's face. Looked him

directly in his slate eyes. They seemed much kinder and gentler, free of the metallic hardness they used to have.

He's human after all, she thought. *He does love. But what he loves is this idea of the hybrid. That is his great love.*

"I'm not any of the things you said you wanted," she said. "I thought you wanted some great beauty. The perfect face, all that."

He gave a derisive snort and stared out over the water. "I had my reasons for that, and it's all based in science and evolution. But I was wrong." He looked back at her. "I need someone more like you, Maddie. On your questionnaire, you said you wanted children."

"Well, yes, but… human ones."

They began laughing, staring out into the long sea, cackling that half-pained laugh that humans use to cope.

When they stopped, he said, "I assure you the hybrid… the *child*… will be at least half you."

She grew quiet, staring at the area between her knees and thighs, below the hemline of her tank dress. She hadn't put on any sunscreen before meeting Hunt for lunch and her thighs had a pinkish cast, one she knew could turn to sunburn if she didn't get inside fairly soon. She realized she was focusing on such a mundane matter because the previous few minutes were too much for her psyche. In fact, maybe the past 12 hours were too much for her psyche.

Not only did she find out there was irrefutable proof that intelligent life existed out there in the universe— intelligent life that had the technological ability to send its DNA through space—but there was a good chance that this intelligent life would soon take the form of an alien baby on Earth.

And he wanted her to be its mother!

"Mr. Hunt, this is all very overwhelming," she said breathily, not even certain he could hear her over the wind and droning *swish-swish* of the waves.

Maddie realized if *she* was this thrown into an emotional maelstrom by the idea of being mother to an alien baby, what must Ruby, who was only a child, have felt? Then again, perhaps Dexter Hunt had known what he was doing.

Surely, a 12-year-old wouldn't have been bombarded with as many questions as Maddie was being bombarded with?

Such as, how much mothering would she do to this being? Would it be a normal human baby that would cry and breastfeed? Given that Maddie wouldn't ever be pregnant or give birth to it, she wouldn't produce milk, so what would feed this being? Formula? Would it require something else?

Would Maddie love it or would something in her reject it? Would the being love Maddie? Would the being love in the way that humans loved or in an entirely different way unknown to humans? How much would it belong to her, and how much to science and to humanity in general?

"Mr. Hunt." The wind had died down so her voice was louder than anticipated. "I—I have so many questions. I mean, how does this thing—I mean, this child—how does it eat?"

That wasn't exactly what she wanted to ask and

wasn't sure why that was the first question out of her mouth, but it was an example of the dozens of questions that were whirling in her brain.

"In most ways, this will be a typical human derivation. I promise you," he said.

Child, she thought. She hated the way he avoided the word. It proved he wasn't thinking this through. He may *love* the hybrid, the *child*, but he truly only loved it for himself, how it would serve him and his goals. He wouldn't love it as any sentient being deserved to be loved—just because it existed.

"As I said," he continued, "you have time to think about it. Not all the time in the world, but time. I want to inform you as soon as I began entertaining this idea, I did more background on you. I know you had a miscarriage approximately three years ago. That was not due to any genetic mutations on your part that I could find."

She wondered if she'd misheard him. But a few moments later, the shock of hearing such personal information coming from this relative stranger's mouth was enough to begin to lift the mental fog that had encircled her.

"You *know* about that?"

The only people aware of her miscarriage were her mother and Athena. No way in hell would her mother have shared that information with anyone. She was sickened at the idea that Athena would betray her, share such personal information with this man because he was paying for her fucking house renovation.

"I can't believe Athena told you that," she snapped. "She's my friend. I'd *thought* she was my friend."

"I'm sure you can understand needing to protect sources," he said, "but I want to assure you it wasn't Athena."

"Okay," she growled, completely shoving off her moony trance. "Then who was—oh my God." She put her hand up to her mouth, stared wide-eyed at him. "It was Jesse. My ex-boyfriend."

"As I said, I can't—"

"That shithead. How much did you pay him?"

"I'm afraid we're getting off track. I regret I mentioned it."

"Who did you send to search around my room? Elias? Alexander? Athena?"

"I sent no one to search your room."

She pushed her hands into the hot sand, and wobbled upright. Something was definitely wrong with her. "And you drugged me. Put something in my wine that you thought would make me say yes. But I didn't drink enough of it."

He stood as well, brushing sand off his white pants in short, abrupt strokes that were more like slaps. When he stopped, his expression was hardened; whatever bonding that had occurred between them in the past ten minutes had evaporated.

"I did not drug you," he said. "I understand why you don't trust me, but you're accusing me of things I did not do."

"Well, I feel very strange!"

"The wine is made on Volinos, fermented in wooden caskets." His voice was clipped and monotonous; he was clearly struggling to hold down irritation. "It's possible some bacterium formed that you're allergic to. I'll have my staff look into it."

"A likely story!"

Snatching her sandals from the sand, she stomped barefooted up the small pink slope towards the stone stairs with the intention of trying to find her way back to the cabin. She had to lie down.

When she got to the top of the bluff and saw the golf cart, she decided to sit in it. She was too disoriented to know how to get back to the cabin, and it was probably a long walk. Slipping into the passenger seat, she felt betrayed and demoralized. How could Jesse have told Hunt's people about her miscarriage? And what else did he tell them?

A minute later, Hunt slid in the driver's seat but didn't push the vehicle's start button.

"I'm sorry I mentioned that," he said. "But I wanted to be honest that we researched you. We had to. What would it do to make an offer like this, only to find out later there's a major skeleton in your closet? I can't say where or how I got this information but I would urge you not to jump to conclusions."

"Can you bring me to my cabin?"

"Of course. Forgive me for disturbing you."

* * *

WHEN THE CART pulled up to the cabin and stopped, Maddie carefully climbed out, still a little woozy, though on the short ride over, with the strong sea-breeze on her face, she'd regained much more of her equilibrium.

She couldn't get Jesse's betrayal out of her mind. For if it hadn't been Athena who'd blabbed, nor her mother (and there was no way it was her mother), then there was only one other person it could have been.

Hunt could have bribed records out of medical staff; they could have broken HIPAA law. She'd read of cases where that very thing had happened to celebrities. But given the short amount of time between Ruby leaving and Hunt's offer, Jesse was the most plausible suspect. It would take less time to track him down and interview him than to find the hospital where Maddie had her D&C and bribe staff. Besides, she knew money was Jesse's weakness.

There had been times when she'd wondered if she'd done the right thing breaking up with him. Perhaps her expectations for men were too high. But now she knew unquestionably that she'd made the right decision.

"Should I send someone to see to you?" Hunt asked. "We have a nurse on staff. You also have pharmaceuticals in your bathroom cabinet—aspirin, antacids, and the like."

"No, it's fine. I feel better now." She grinned sheepishly. "Sorry for accusing you of drugging me. Oh, and being a pedophile. But I'm still pissed you dug up personal medical information."

"You see, Maddie," he said, wagging one finger. "I'd love for the hybrid to inherit your way with words."

"The first thing I'd do is ask you to stop calling my child 'the hybrid.' The kid will have enough problems."

He laughed. At least, she thought it was a laugh. He bared his very straight white teeth and made a small chest rumble. "Will you have dinner with me tonight?" he asked. "We can discuss this more."

"I guess." She shrugged. "It's not like I have other plans."

He smiled, said, "See you at eight o'clock," and zipped down the hill on his golf cart.

Chapter Twenty-Eight

*I*nside the cabin, she first went to the bathroom and found some aloe gel inside of the wicker basket that contained pharmacy products and rubbed it on her legs and shoulders, hoping it would ward off the sting of a mild burn she could feel forming.

She stared at herself in the mirror. Her cheeks were flushed bright through her tan, freckles were dark on her nose. She applied some face SPF she found, brushed her teeth, and decided to take a nap. He may not have drugged her, but the sun and their bizarro conversation had fatigued her, though it was that brand of fatigue that was accompanied by the fizz of adrenaline, so she didn't know if she'd be able to sleep. She'd try.

On the bed was her phone. Someone had returned it while she was out. She grabbed it and saw that the signal bar was grayed out. Just in case, she opened her email app and tried to send a test email to herself but it didn't go through. He had indeed blocked her phone from whatever satellite he used to get service on the island.

It occurred to her that perhaps there was a long shot that she could pick up a signal from a nearby island, so she walked to the edge of the balcony and held her phone aloft. The signal bar was still gray but determined to test it again, she opened her social media app and began scrolling. She'd try to post something.

In her feed were a bunch of posts she hadn't seen before, and she realized that while her phone had been with Hunt's security, they must have hooked it up to satellite service to search it. That had made her social media feed update.

And then she saw it. A post from Chelsea Pewter. She had no idea why Chelsea's post would show up in her feed as she had no memory of following her. But there it was. Unmistakable.

A wedding photo. It was a medium range shot. Chelsea was in a sleek, white silk dress with a low-cut V-neck. Daniel was in a tuxedo but his tie was bright red instead of black, a nod to nonconformity.

The couple stared into each other's eyes, smiling and ecstatic. They'd been married not long after "the incident," so he looked exactly as Maddie held him in her memory. She also remembered that the couple had run off and eloped somewhere. Her father had been miffed about not being invited.

As an adult, it seemed obvious to her—he'd gotten married so shortly after what had happened between them as a kind of penance. Not that he didn't love Chelsea, he clearly did. But Maddie felt in her bones that he'd jumped quickly into marriage and family life as a way of putting what had happened behind him.

And he'd done so. Swiftly moved on, leaving teenage Maddie alone to struggle with all her emotions, unable to share them with anyone, and unequipped to navigate them.

How dare he do that?

Looking at the photo, felt sick to her stomach and began shaking, heart racing. He was so handsome here. Daniel. As she'd known him. As she'd loved him, in her naïve, childish way.

Inside, she sank onto the four-poster bed, staring at the photo.

And now she knew what she wanted to say to him. It was all she wanted to say to him. She would pass the message to Chelsea. Ask her to please give the message to Daniel. Maddie would not explain herself. She would just say it.

The message. It was:

I see you.

That's what she wanted. She wanted him to know that she *saw* him. That the rest of the world may know him as a perfect husband and father. But she knew him better than anyone, even his own wife. She saw him. The real him.

Sitting on the edge of the bed, thumb still twitching with nerves, she reached to click on the post so she could get to the message icon. But before she clicked away, she read Chelsea's text next to the picture, which said:

Happy anniversary, darling! Though I haven't heard your

voice in 15 years, my love has never dimmed. You are my angel, my rock, my man! My husband! Forever and always, your loving wife.

Maddie went cold. She hadn't absorbed the words but knew something was wrong with them. Slowly, her eyes backtracked through the text.

Though I haven't heard your voice in 15 years…

No. No. Hadn't heard his voice in 15 years? She began trembling so badly that she thought she might lose control of her bladder. She groaned, placing the phone on her lap. Holding her stomach for several moments, the words began to truly, truly sink in.

Daniel was… dead?

Dead?

She would never get to confront him. Never get to say, *I see you.* Never get validation, and be seen as well as see. Everything in her mind that she'd fantasized about saying to him (*Why did you take advantage of that situation, Daniel? I was a child. Would you want a friend of yours doing the same to Amity?*), she would never get to say now.

Beyond a feeling of being robbed was the simple wrecked feeling of a man she'd once cared so much for being gone, forever. She also remembered so many great things about him. Times they'd talked and talked. Times that he'd joked with her and listened to her prattle about school, friends, TV shows, books, whatever was on her mind. Times he'd come over while her father was dying, bringing food, bringing Dad's favorite DVDs and magazines, sitting with him for hours in Dad's bedroom.

No, he wasn't all bad. He wasn't. This was what made everything so terrible.

How had he died? He was so young. Had he gotten

sick like her father had? How come her mother had never mentioned Daniel dying? Maddie thought that Chelsea would have at least invited them to a funeral. Then she realized in the corner of the wedding photo was an icon that read "1/3."

There were other photos behind this one. With much trepidation, she placed her trembling thumb on the photo and slid it to the left.

The picture was of a man in a white bed. It reminded her of her father's last weeks—spent propped up in bed, a husk, a shell of himself.

The man was unrecognizable to her. Extremely pale and gaunt, hair shorn to his scalp, one hand curled into a claw.

Oh my God. Oh my God.

It was Daniel. She was sure of it. The eyes were large, empty, and staring off into nothing, staring, it seemed, in two opposing directions.

What was wrong with him?

She slowly slid her thumb to the left. This time Daniel's face was young and smiling again. He was back to himself, arms crossed, grin carefree and boastful, wearing the black leather jacket she'd seen in a previous photo, and astride his motorcycle. But the photo was faded. And over it scrolled red text.

Daniel,

November 16 was a day I and the children will never forget. It was on that day that you were taken from us in so many ways. Loss of the husband you were. Loss of the father Amity and Amos, still so young, needed. But in other ways, you have given us so much: the profound ability to love unconditionally.

On that day, you were doing the thing you cherished, which you felt gave you a freedom and vitality you couldn't get anywhere else. The thing I'd been so worried about, that we had arguments over. And on that day, my worst fears were realized. You hit a wet patch, helmet crushed, and sustained a massive brain injury.

Gone were our hopes for the future we'd envisioned, but not gone was our love for you. You will always remain my husband, father of my children. Love you more each day. Chelsea

* * *

MADDIE HUNCHED over on the edge of the bed, phone limp in her hand. She was caved in with a feeling of sadness, of devastation. What a loss. Vital, athletic, adventurous husband and father Daniel Pewter. Living in a bed. Apparently, he didn't speak anymore. Did he hear? See? Understand?

Fifteen years. Not long after Chelsea had given birth to the twins. She'd been left to raise them from toddler-hood on her own.

Is this why Amos and Amity were always toddlers in Maddie's dreams? Did she somehow sense that this is when their lives irrevocably changed? When their father went from playing with them, caring for them, talking to them, laughing with them, to… what he was now?

All of the bristly indignation Maddie felt when she'd first seen Chelsea's message lifted from her. Seeing Daniel propped in that white bed, his body skeletal and lopsided, his eyes vacant and staring in opposite directions, only induced overwhelming sorrow.

Anything she felt he'd taken from her had been taken from him, tenfold. Now when she thought, *I see you*, it had a different connotation. It no longer meant *I see the worst of you*. Now it meant *I see your humanity. I see your mistakes. You have paid for them.*

And I forgive you.

Chapter Twenty-Nine

*W*alking over the hill to the glass house, Maddie noticed a crumbling stone wall to her left. Volinos, like all the Greek islands, was blessed with these types of ancient archeological artifacts everywhere. The wall was no doubt hundreds of years old, and had once served to protect from all types of invaders, yet she'd barely noticed it before.

There was a gap in the wall and Elias stepped out from it, startling her so much that she instantly stopped in her tracks, one hand on her heart, the other straight out in a defensive posture.

"Jesus, Elias!" she gasped. "Will you stop sneaking up on me?"

"Sorry, Maddie. I try not scare you."

"Well, you're not trying very hard. Why are you still here, anyway?"

"I thought I was taking you back to Kyrie tonight, but then a guard, he tell me you stay and I can go. Soon as he walk away, I come up. I want to see if you're alright, and if what he said is true."

"I guess it's true," she sighed, staring off towards the long pathway that led to Hunt's house. "I mean, yes, it's true. I'm just not sure how I feel about it."

"Why you stay, Maddie? Because you *want* to stay?"

"I'd *thought* so. I *guess*." She walked closer to him and lowered her voice. "Do you know anything about what goes on here?"

"No." He looked stricken. "My family say it nothing bad, that they been here many times. Maddie, did you find something bad?"

"I don't *know*."

Rubbing her arms to ward off a cool breeze off the water, she wished she'd taken her jacket with her from the boat. She'd had no idea she would get stuck here, and the wardrobe contained only summer dresses.

She wondered if she and Elias were being surveilled. She'd spotted no cameras on the island but that didn't mean they didn't exist. "It could be bad or good," she told him. "I'm not equipped to fully assess it."

Elias wore an expression of befuddlement and she could tell her English had gotten away from him—not that she was making much sense, anyway.

"Maddie, I leave now before it get dark. Why not you come with me?" he asked.

"For one, who knows where you'd even take me. You have a rather loose relationship with the truth."

"I… don't understand. My English." He looked apologetic.

She needed to make a decision. Trust Dexter Hunt… or trust Elias? One may never want her to leave the island given the information he'd told her. And the other may simply be doing the first man's bidding. But given the reluctance she felt in continuing on her walk to the glass house —her legs barely moving her forward, making her feel as if she were wading through sticky, knee-high mud—she knew she wanted to leave. Her body had decided for her.

Yes, Hunt's alien hybrid experiment might be the greatest story of the century. And yes, if she became the donor, she could become one of the most famous people on the planet.

But there was no way she could ever think of any offspring that carried her DNA as a "hybrid," as anything other than her *child*. It didn't matter if the child was gestated in a tube or whatever he was planning. Whether it looked like her or did not. Whether it even looked human. It would be her *child*. And she couldn't think of having a child in any other way than the old-fashioned way—with someone she loved.

Not to mention that it rankled that, in a short period of time, Dexter Hunt had managed to dredge up extremely personal information about her. Anyone who had that ability wasn't someone she wanted to be involved with on any level, and especially not on a level that involved a child—*her* child.

It was clear that this being would belong to Hunt and only to Hunt, and he was not someone Maddie wanted to wrangle with on a frequent basis. She knew she would lose.

Of course, she could walk to the glass house and

simply tell Dexter Hunt she was leaving. But she still had the uneasy intuition that he then might do something to make sure she didn't tell anyone what she knew. Perhaps she was being paranoid, but she didn't want to risk it.

"Elias," she said. "Let's go to the boat. Right now. Take me back to Kyrie."

"Are you sure?"

"Yes. There's nothing in the cabin that I need. Oh wait! My phone."

"Maddie, we should go. Now."

Elias was right. Her cabin was a good five-minute walk away. That might be enough time for someone to see them together, get suspicious, and alert Hunt. She'd have to use her laptop to contact people and forget about the phone.

"Okay, let's go," she said.

Elias grabbed her hand and began briskly walking her down the long path towards the dock. She worried their breakneck pace and the fact that they were holding hands would draw the wrong kind of attention, but Elias seemed fearsomely determined and instinct told her to let him take charge.

When they got to the bottom of the hill, he instantly dropped her hand and slowed his pace to a casual stroll. Maddie followed suit. Her heart began hammering when she saw two men standing idly on the dock: security guards.

"*Kaló apógevma,*" Elias said to them, and began speaking at length, gesturing and looking at Maddie a couple of times. One of the men eyed her suspiciously while the other stood listening to Elias with an inscrutable expression. Then the suspicious-eyed man unhooked a walkie talkie from his belt and said a few Greek words into it.

Maddie felt she knew exactly what was happening—the man was verifying that it was okay for her to leave the island. Fear clutched at her even though she felt she had the right to leave. It's not as if Hunt had kidnapped her. But he'd subtly and not-so-subtly controlled her every move since she'd arrived.

"Come on, Elias." She glared at the man who wasn't talking into the walkie talkie. "Let's go," she said in a *don't-even-try-to-mess-with-me* tone.

Elias grabbed her hand again and ushered her to the motorboat they'd come in on. He stood aside as she clambered aboard. Then he followed, leaned over, and swiftly began untying the boat from the steel peg on the dock.

The two security guards stood looking at them but didn't make a move to stop them. The boat floated off a bit, then Elias slid into the driver's side and turned the key. Maddie looked up at the main hill in time to see a man—almost definitely Dexter Hunt—standing on the terrace of the glass house, the very place where she'd had lunch with him.

"What did you tell him?" she asked Elias, speaking loudly over the slushing of the water and the low roar of the boat's motor.

"That we need to return to Kyrie to get your passport. That you need it for trip with Dexter Hunt and we be back soon."

"Good thinking!" Though even as she said it, she

was staring back at the receding Volinos, fearful that any moment she'd see security giving chase in their own boat. But the sea remained wide, blue, and empty, with only a churned-up, frothy, white wave-trail behind them.

* * *

"WELL, *EFHARISTO*, ELIAS," she said. "I'm still not thrilled at that little trick you pulled, but you got me out of there."

"Maddie," he said, leaning towards her in the tight space of his Fiat. "I'm sorry. I mess up. Again."

"Yeah, a little bit, you did." But she smiled at him to blunt her words because his expression was laden with regret. And he had gotten her off the island. If Hunt was the type who was going to come after her, Elias put himself in danger, as well.

"What you do now?" he asked.

"I'm getting the hell out of Dodge—that's Greece. No offense to your country, I love it, but I have no idea if Dexter Hunt may try to find me."

"Why he try, Maddie?" His hand was on hers. "Tell me what happen."

"I can't. Not now. When does the first ferry leave tomorrow, do you know?"

"It always leave nine-fifty."

"I'm going to be on it."

She pulled her hand out from under his. "*Adio*, Elias."

"Wait, Maddie…" He peered up at her from his side as she stood with the door open. "I see you again?"

"Not on this island, I'm afraid. It's a bit too risky right now." His face fell, so she said, though she didn't quite mean it, "Maybe in Athens. One day."

"Or Nyew York, yes?"

"Sure. Oh, and Elias? You know those genealogy places?" At his interested but clearly baffled expression, she went on, "The ones where you test your DNA?"

"Ah, I think so?" he said, still appearing good-naturedly confused.

"Yeah, avoid those. *Gia sou*, Elias."

"*Gia*," he called as she raced down the little hill to her rental, trying to swallow the sadness that unexpectedly rushed forth at the idea she'd never see Elias again.

Chapter Thirty

"Splash!"

"Can I come in?"

"Sure, sure. I'm packing."

Logan stood to the side and Maddie hurried into his studio, rubbing her hands, feeling wired with adrenaline and exhaustion.

Logan was staring at her wide-eyed, he had on black shorts and a white t-shirt, his hair was half-wet, and he smelled of soap as if he'd recently come from the shower. She strolled quickly into the bedroom area and noticed his roll suitcase was open on the bed, with clothes folded inside.

"You're leaving?"

"Well, yeah, you kind of disappeared and, honestly, I can't get anything going with Hunt. So, I decided to go back a little early. How's Prince Charming?" He avoided eye contact as he said this, scrounging around in his top drawer, bringing out t-shirts and folding them into his suitcase. She sat on the edge of his bed, numbly watching him, then said, "Do you have any booze?"

"Are you kidding? Of course. Ouzo? Yastika? Beer?"

"You stocked up."

"Hey, I'm on vacation." He grinned and she felt like hugging him. Right now, she couldn't remember why he used to annoy her so much. Right now, he was good and familiar, the only person she felt didn't have some kind of hidden agenda.

"Yastika is fine."

"You okay? You look kind of…"

"I really need a drink, Logan."

"Sure, sure, okay."

Logan poured them a couple of glasses of Yastika, then waved at her, indicating they should drink it on the terrace. Outside, she settled into the short, flat couch— the same type she had on her own terrace—and took several long sips of the familiar sweet liqueur until she could feel her mind beginning to unknot and relax.

"This tastes like Elias' family's brand. Doukas."

"It is. When I first got here, I asked the owners which brand they recommended since everything I read said I had to try the Yastika while I was here. They said it was owned by an old Kyrian family. I looked it up and seems like they've been producing the longest. Sold. I didn't know it was your guy's family though."

"He's not my guy. Listen, Logan, I'm going to try to get a flight back with you. If I can't get one, I'm going to go to the airport anyway. I'll sit there until I can get one."

"I—I don't understand," he said. "Did something happen? You two get into a fight?"

"I wasn't with Elias," she said, closing her eyes for a moment, trying to decide how much she should tell him. It felt inevitable that she would tell him, because she couldn't stand being completely alone in her knowledge, and the alcohol had already eroded her critical thinking.

"I was with Dexter Hunt. On Volinos."

"Get out of here," he said, his mouth half open. "How'd you manage that?"

"It's a long story."

"So, what's happening over there? Is there a pedo ring like you thought?"

She shook her head and sank back into the couch, breathing in the fresh night air, listening to the waves lapping along the shoreline.

"Logan, do you mind if I sleep out here tonight? I— I can't sleep alone." The couch wouldn't fit her, but she'd curl up on it. Better a stiff back and neck than wondering all night whether someone would break into her studio and try to drag her back to Volinos.

"Sure, um, no problem. But, ah, I mean, the bed is a king... I won't, um, I promise I won't... Maddie, what the hell happened?"

"I'll pack my stuff and come right back here, okay?"

"Maddie." He leaned forward on his knees, lightly swirling the liquid in his glass as if it was an expensive wine. "You want me to not ask questions?"

Putting down her glass on the nearby side table, she drew in a deep breath, and held her hands in a prayer gesture. Then she began nervously flexing them, her body unable to be still. She could feel it gurgling up from her chest, the irrepressible need to tell him.

"Logan, he's got some crazy shit going on over there."

Logan was utterly still, staring at her. Damn, she wished she smoked. She was craving a cigarette but had no idea why.

"It's—it's—Logan, he says he has alien DNA."

"Alien?" Logan said, quietly, as if he didn't understand what the word meant.

"Extraterrestrial. Like E fucking T. That Dex-X retrieved it from space. And he wants to combine it with human DNA and make some kind of hybrid baby. An alien-human hybrid."

"What?" Logan said with a staccato burst of edgy laughter. Then he went silent and only stared at her again.

"I'm not kidding. This is not a joke. I don't know what to do. He even asked if I'd donate my DNA and be, like, the mother of this thing."

Logan kept staring at her for several moments, then he sighed and began slowly sipping his Yastika. He stared into the glass as if bewildered as to where most of it had gone.

"Maddie," he said in a slightly disappointed tone. "He's fed you some bullshit story to get rid of you."

"No, no!" she cried, then lowered her voice in case Hunt had already sent someone to spy on her and the person was crouched somewhere in the darkness beyond the terrace. "I thought about that but he went into elaborate detail over two days. And it all adds up. He owns a genealogy firm and knew that Athena and I had sent in DNA last year. When he decided to ask if I'd be the alien baby's mother, he began investigating me and found out something incredibly private. He wouldn't have gone to all that trouble for a bullshit story. I actually escaped with Elias because I was worried since I know about his plans, he wouldn't let me go."

Logan rubbed his forehead, still looking skeptical. "Did he show you any proof of alien DNA?"

"Show me DNA? Of course not. But he owns a genealogy company. He owns a space exploration company. He knows all about spindle transfers or whatever the hell it's called. It's all plausible."

"Orrrr…" he drawled. "It's an elaborate hoax to get you off his back."

"What are you saying? You think he really does run a pedo ring?"

"Nope. I think he's running a big shell game, hiding assets and evading taxes for the ultra-rich. That's it."

"Then why'd you come all the way over here if you think that? You could have reported that from New York." She couldn't disguise the flaming irritation in her voice.

"I hoped I'd get on the island. Get some color. Maybe even talk to him."

"Alright, well, believe what you want. But I still feel I can't stay alone tonight. I want to be on the first ferry out of here in the morning."

"Me too." He paused, then said, "You going to write about this, Splash?"

"I can't. I'd told him everything would be off-the-record. I feel like I should do something, but what, I don't know. It's not like what he's doing is illegal. It's just kind of immoral, in my opinion. But I'm sure if I knew everything science does, I wouldn't like a lot of it." She crossed her arms. "The other thing is that he's got this slush fund. Pretty much everyone on Kyrie is dipping into it, including Elias' family. If I write about Hunt, he might pull it and leave most of the island destitute."

She put her glass to the side and stood, the booze making her a little wobbly. She stuck her hand out to brace herself. Let Logan not believe her. Actually, it was better that he didn't. She shouldn't have told him anyway. It could put him in danger knowing, and it could put her in even more danger that she's blabbing.

This was a great lesson for her. Even Logan—supposedly a bloodhound reporter—didn't believe it. That meant no one else would. If she went back to *Wealthy* and pitched it to any editors, they'd laugh her out of the room. Then maybe fire her for inventing stories. Dexter Hunt would, of course, deny it to anyone else who asked about it. Ruby and Stella, as well as all the other donor candidates, were bound by an NDA.

It's as if the story didn't exist.

There was no way he'd been lying. If he'd wanted to "get her off" his back, coming up with such a juicy story was no way to go about it—that was more like throwing red meat in front of a dog. He could have come up with something much more boring if he wanted to make a reporter go away. Besides, she doubted he was a brilliant actor as well as businessman. And only a brilliant actor could have seemed so convincing in this outrageous tale of his hope for an alien hybrid baby. That look in his eyes while they sat in the pink beach cove—there was no way he could have faked that. It was the look of love.

"I'll pack and be back in 15 minutes," she said. "If I don't return, come look for me, okay?"

"Jesus, Splash. Why don't I come with you if you're that nervous?"

"Can you sit on the patio and keep an eye on my door?"

"Of course."

The pair returned to the studio, put their glasses in the sink, then left.

Chapter Thirty-One

*A*t almost midnight, Maddie and Logan returned to his rental, Maddie rolling her suitcase into his closet and placing a small bag of essentials—toothbrush and toothpaste, face cleanser, floss—on his sink.

As he went to the terrace with another glass of Yastika, she set up her laptop on his desk and logged into her desktop WhatsApp, seeing several messages from Athena.

Hey, girl, you up for going out tonight?

Maddie?

Okay, you must be out with Elias, I can't reach him either.

Morning, you back yet, slut?

Hello?

Hey, I dropped by the studio but Karen said she hadn't seen you in a couple of days. I saw Logan (He looks good, btw! A little sun becomes him!) but he hadn't seen you either. You and Elias didn't go to Volinos, did you? Ugh, Mad. Get in touch as soon as you can.

Maddie typed back: *Hi, I'm so sorry, hope you weren't too worried. My phone died and I didn't have any way to charge it. Did not go to Volinos, but Skelios. Just a day trip. I'm totally fine. Exhausted, will be in touch tomorrow.*

She felt it best not to say she was leaving. Once she was safe on the mainland, she'd reveal that. About five minutes later, her message got a thumbs up sign.

Returning from the terrace, Logan shuffled along to the kitchen, then came back out rubbing his mouth and looking tired.

"Splash, I think I'm going to turn in. Ferry leaves at nine-fifty so I'm setting my alarm for seven-thirty. Too early for you?"

"No, no, that's fine."

"You okay?" he asked, tilting his head at her. "Anything I can do?"

"Logan," she said. "Can you hug me?" Then, realizing how pathetic and boundary-busting that sounded, gave a long shudder. "No. Sorry. I didn't mean that. I'm tired and—"

But instantly he closed the space between them and had her in his arms. He folded his bulk around her, big and easy. He smelled so clean, so simple, like home.

"It's okay, Splash," he said, softly. "You don't have to tell me everything. I'm sorry I was harsh with that alien-baby story. I just think that asshole is trying to play you. But we can talk about it more tomorrow."

"No, you're right," she murmured, burying her face deeper into his soft cotton shirt. He smelled so good. "I guess I fell for it."

She felt him gently rubbing her back, and instead of

281

putting her off, the gesture comforted her. More than comforted her; she was tingling in a way that distinctly signaled arousal.

"And if you said no to being the mother of an alien critter, that's good. More fun the old-fashioned way, right?"

She chuckled, still savoring his succoring bulk. They stood like that for a good minute or two before things started to get a little awkward—a little heated, and she felt his groin starting to expand. She laughed nervously and pulled back. "Thank you, I really needed a hug. And you hug extremely well."

"Everyone needs a hug sometimes. Now listen. Don't worry about being in the same bed with me, alright? For one, I'm too tired to make a move. For two, I only have sex with ladies who want it, and want it bad. Who, like, *beg* me." His eyes glinted mischievously. "For three, I can't help what my body did right then, but it didn't do it with permission from my brain. So let's get a decent night's sleep and in the morning, we'll blow this popsicle stand. Know what I mean, jellybean?"

"I never begged you, Logan."

"Oh, you did. Begged so bad. You must have forgotten." He winked.

"By the way, I feel like I could peel off an extra skin." She scowled and shuddered. "All crusty. Do you mind if I take a quick shower?"

"Mind?" The hint of a lascivious grin slid across his mouth. "Of course not. If you need any help in there, be sure to let me know."

"I thought you were too tired to make a move," she laughed.

"I woke up at the thought of you in the shower," he said. "Kidding! Go. Take your shower. By the time you come out, I'll be asleep. Seriously."

Impulsively, she hugged him again, this time not lingering, and retreated to the bathroom.

* * *

SHE HAD STEPPED out of the shower and was busily drying herself when there was soft but urgent knocking on the bathroom door.

"Splash?" Logan said. "I hate to do this to you but we need to talk."

"Um, okay?" she called out, bewildered.

"It's important."

She slipped on her black leggings—reluctant to wear her too-short "Coney Island" shorts to bed with him, and a sleeveless black t-shirt, and opened the door. Steam gushed forth so that for a couple of moments, she could barely see his face.

"You didn't hear any of that?" he asked.

"Hear what?" Her heart pumped forebodingly. Perhaps Logan had heard someone outside calling her name—someone sent by Hunt.

"Your friend, Elias. He was just here."

"What?"

"I went outside because I left my phone on the patio and saw him at your door. I told him you were show-ering at my place. He definitely looked a bit disappointed at that and I was about to explain, but then he started talking."

"What—what did he want?"

"Splash, come out for a minute."

Maddie slowly strode into the bedroom area, getting more nervous. Logan put his big hands on her shoulders.

"I don't want you to be scared, okay? I'm not going to let anything happen to you."

"Fuck, Logan, what's going on?"

"He said we should both leave. That we're not safe here. He said he'd talked to someone who said that—well, that Hunt is out for you."

She started to tremble with nerves and grasped Logan's forearms.

"He said we should take off, right now. Grab our passports and credit cards and go. He said he'd meet us in a couple of hours and keep us safe. Then tomorrow he'd make certain we get to the ferry."

"Oh my God. Where are we supposed to go?"

"He said there's some kind of abandoned village, Krem... something."

"Kremos!" she gasped. "Why—why go there?"

"He said no one will think to look there. That we shouldn't trust anyone on the island, not even Karen and Kostas, not even Athena, that they're all in on it with Hunt."

Even Athena? her mind cried out, but she only said, "Yeah, I—I figured as much."

"Do you trust him, Maddie?" he asked. "Do you trust Elias?"

She paused for a long time, considering, then said, "Yes, I do. Without him I'd still be on Volinos. He's the one who handed me over to Hunt, but I know he regrets it. Kremos is where one of his ancestors died, she jumped off the cliff before she could be captured by Turks."

"Well, that's where he wants us to go. Should we?"

"Oh my God, Logan. I can't believe I got you involved in this."

"Let's not worry about that right now. Should we go to this place and wait for him or not?"

"Fuck." She let go of his arms and began furiously biting one thumbnail. Then she said, "If Elias says it, then yes. Let's go."

Chapter Thirty-Two

It was a rather long drive to Kremos, which was on the northern end of the island. They were in Logan's rental car. Maddie had only rented a scooter, and she'd left it back at Sideratos. When she saw Elias, she'd ask him to return it for her.

As both she and Logan had already packed their suitcases, they'd simply grabbed them, their passports, some cash Logan had in his safe, and they were out of the rental in minutes. Both had prepaid for their studios, so they didn't have to worry about that.

His phone was perched on the cup holder, a navigation application open, and every ten minutes or so, a female voice emanated from it giving them directions. The roads were essentially empty until they got to a small glut of traffic around the town center, mostly people on scooters. Then they veered off, following signs for the north. She kept darting her eyes around the nearby cars, wondering if any of them were following, if any of them contained someone sent by Hunt.

What did he want with her? Would he really kill her so she couldn't spread his alien baby secret? She'd vowed it was off-the-record, did he not believe her?

Soon all other cars peeled away and they were utterly alone, snaking up into winding, blind-curving roads, up, up, up, into the mountains. There were no streetlights, no guardrails, only light-reflecting signs that warned drivers of the 180-degree bends that happened every hundred feet or so. If you miscalculated, you'd dive off a cliff. This wasn't an uncommon occurrence, and the roads were plentifully dotted with small, sad shrines to drivers who'd plunged to their deaths. They were often in the shape of a miniature church, and contained candles and pictures of the late loved ones.

She anxiously glanced at Logan, who was staring hard ahead of him. She didn't dare speak, not wanting to distract him for even a moment. The headlights only went out so far before being swallowed into pitch black. They might have been safer barricading themselves inside Logan's studio and waiting for morning. But she hadn't been to Kremos and had no idea how dangerous the trip would be. Elias, accustomed to these killer roads, probably hadn't given one thought to their harrowing drive.

Not to mention that apparently even Karen and Kostas weren't trustworthy, and they had keys to the studio. They could have let anyone inside.

Finally, the road flattened and Logan slowed the car to a near crawl. "Your destination is on the left," said the automated voice from the phone.

"Left where?" Logan asked. "I don't see anything, do you?"

Maddie stretched towards Logan's side of the car, trying to stare up into the darkness out of the window. They drove past what appeared to be a high wall and a long crop of trees, and then she saw it.

High atop a bluff, with the dark purple sky glutted with bright stars, appeared a stone village. The village perched perilously at the peak of the mountain and there were three lights spread out towards its bottom. There were hundreds of rudimentary, boxy homes clustered together and tumbling down the side of the bluff. Built out of the surrounding granite of the mountain, the homes blended perfectly into the environs, like anthills in the sand.

Logan kept driving until they reached a small parking lot. He pulled into it and they sat gaping up through the windshield, the engine still running.

"I don't know about this," he mumbled.

"Turn off the car and the headlights," she said, not wanting them to draw attention to themselves. It seemed highly unlikely anyone would find them here, but she was crawling with paranoia. "Did Elias say what to do when we got here?"

"No. Just said he'd be here in a couple of hours and would keep us safe. Splash, I hate to say this, but I'm not sure we should listen to this guy. Maybe we need to find another hotel."

"I'm telling you, he's right. We don't know who we can trust on Kyrie. And that includes Athena."

"Okay, but if this dude doesn't show soon, let's get out of here. It's fucking creepy."

Maddie felt herself opening the car door. She stood staring up at the cliff-top town, in awe. Imagining all of the people who used to live here, living so high up with the hope of avoiding invaders. She had no idea how they managed to routinely get food, water, and other supplies way up here. The sheer tenacity and skill it must have taken to not only build these far remote dwellings but then exist in them.

Their perch atop the high point of the mountain meant relative safety from assailants but it also meant if the invaders were intrepid enough to make it up the mountainside, there was nowhere for the residents to run. They were trapped.

She imagined the women lining up along the five-hundred-foot drop on the sides of the village and plummeting to their deaths rather than falling into the hands of pillaging Turks. Would she have been brave enough to jump with them?

"Come on," she said to Logan, who had also exited the car and was staring up silently. "Let's go take a look." First, she grabbed her nylon jacket off the top of her travel bag, anticipating that the mountain would be cold and windy.

Logan didn't seem thrilled with this idea, but he turned on his phone flashlight and followed her. The stone pathway started at the end of the parking lot. Maddie kept her eyes down at her sneakers for most of the trek, wanting to make sure she didn't trip over the squat, crumbling stone steps.

When they hit the first plateau, she saw the three streetlights illuminating the path and realized electrical wires were strung all the way up here for a small taverna with many tables out front that was obviously for the tourists who made the climb to the abandoned village.

The taverna was closed but two cats came running and meowing up to them, apparently thinking the humans had food. Maddie wished she had something to give them but she didn't. She stopped to pet them, and as they seemed plump enough, concluded they must be getting regular feedings. Logan bent down next to her. The calico sauntered over to him, circling all around him with loud purrs as he stroked her.

"This guy better show," he muttered.

"If he doesn't, we get back in the car and sleep here. Then drive to the terminal for the first ferry."

"I need to return the car."

"Leave it at the terminal and email them. Tell them you had an emergency. I'm sorry but if Elias says we're in trouble, then we are, and we need to avoid people until we get out of here."

They stood and watched as the cats sashayed away, accepting that the visitors didn't have food for them. Then Maddie and Logan climbed their way higher into the medieval village.

Chapter Thirty-Three

The village was a warren of den-like homes on either side of a narrow path packed with stone and dirt and flanked by stubby grass. They passed the shells of homes that were nothing but a few feet of crumbling walls, and then homes that seemed as intact as they must have been hundreds of years ago, when the village was teeming and bustling with life.

Logan used his cell phone flashlight to guide their way up the steep cobbled path which curved in and around the empty dwellings, broken up by sets of flagstone stairs. As they passed open doorways, Maddie saw lambent light within some of the homes. Drawing Logan's attention, he pointed his beam into one of them. A tall votive candle flickered on a small memorial. Maddie realized that people still came to this ghost town, still lit tribute candles for the ones who'd died here.

"Elias' great-great-great... I forget how many greats," Maddie said, somewhat breathless from the climb. "Four or five or six. She jumped off the cliff here with her baby in her arms to get away from invaders. The baby survived. A boy."

"Terrible," Logan murmured. "Where did she jump, I wonder."

High up as they were, the moon glowed brilliantly above them. Between that and Logan's flashlight, there was a decent view of the surroundings. The interior of the homes were black as pitch, but the pathways and exteriors could be dimly seen.

"I don't know but be careful," she said. "A wrong step and we might find out."

The pang of regret that she hadn't taken the extra few minutes to run back to her cabin on Volinos and grab her phone was sharper than ever. It hadn't occurred to her that she might need its flashlight.

Eventually, the pair came to what felt like the summit of the mountain, the ground leveled out beneath her feet, the tension in her legs decreased, and the unimpeded wind kicked up sharp and strong. Hair flying around her face, Maddie took an elastic band from where she always kept a couple wrapped around her wrist and pulled her hair into a tight ponytail.

"This must be the top," Logan said. "Whatever you do, be careful. Don't walk out too far."

He pointed the beam at the ground, and in between a large gap in the stone homes they saw that the ground vanished about 30 feet in front of them. Maddie shuddered, for beyond it, she knew must be a drop-off. One of the points where despairing women fled with their children. It had happened right here, where she was standing, and yet she had a difficult time bringing her mind to that level of desperation and panic.

"I can't imagine it," she said loudly over the wind. "They must have been so terrified."

"They must have," Logan said solemnly. The beam from his flashlight disappeared and she realized he'd put his phone in his back pocket. He stood next to her, then came close behind her. His voice was low and somber. "It would be best to go quickly, not think about it. Don't give yourself time to feel fear."

His big bear arms wrapped around her and for a moment she thought he was hugging her again, and he was going to turn her into him and kiss her. Her brain had only enough time to wonder how she should respond to his overture when his embrace tightened in such a way that her body knew this wasn't a seduction. She stiffened and her heart rate accelerated. He began to push her forward.

One side of her brain thought, *He's joking around.* But the other put everything together—and put it together instantly. The long drive here. The empty roads. The remoteness. It made no sense that Elias would ask them to come here. Now she saw it so clearly, how little sense it made.

But it was too late, and she was in perilous danger with a man she'd known from the beginning was trouble, but whom she'd fooled herself into misjudging because they came from the same place, the same types of people, and she'd wanted to believe she had a protector, a friend. She did not.

Instinctively, she went dead weight on him as he

continued pushing her forward through the dirt and stones. She stuck both legs out rigidly, heels digging furiously into the ground, desperately trying to brake the propulsive and relentless force hurtling her forward.

He stopped for a moment to get a better grip on her, and made the mistake of moving his hands from her shoulders to her forearms. She pulled herself forward and bit into his wrist as hard as she could—like a dog she bit, rabid and unmerciful.

He emitted a pained gasp-groan that turned into a "Arrghh!" and then a "Fuck!"

She didn't know how she got away from him but found herself running in the opposite direction, back into the ghost village, back down the crumbling path.

"Maddie!" he groaned. "What the fuck!"

She kept running and yet trying not to run so fast that she would trip and fall. She only had the moon for light. Her breathing was rapid and loud and she tried to quiet it, knowing he could follow the sound of her.

"Jesus Christ! I was kidding around! Maddie!"

The path ended at a house and she became disoriented in the dark. Sticking her hands out and feeling the rough shell of the house, she found the path curving around it and continued forward but had the sickening sensation she would never find her way back down to the parking area. Not without more light. And what was she supposed to do if she managed to get there? She'd be out in the open and he'd have an easier time finding her.

The fear that attacked her body when he began pushing her through the dirt assured her that he hadn't been playing around. He'd tried to toss her over the cliff. He'd made up a story to get her out here. He knew Elias' family owned the Doukas brand of Yastika. He'd been to the website and seen the section about Sofia throwing herself off the cliff at Kremos.

I looked it up and seems like they've been producing the longest. Sold. I didn't know it was your guy's family though.

He knew the ancient mountaintop village would make the perfect place to kill someone. A five-hundred-foot drop. Utterly remote. He could say the pair of them had come up at night to look around and Maddie had walked too far and slipped.

The people of Kyrie weren't after her. *He* was after her.

But why, why? Why did he want her dead?

"Maddie! I swear to God, I was joking around! Please!"

His voice was louder, closer now. He was going to catch up with her.

Instinctively, she ducked into the doorway of one of the homes, ran to the opposite side of a large room, and crouched down. It was so dark she couldn't see her own body. Her chest was heaving with adrenaline and she did her best to control the raspy sound of her shallow breathing, stuffing her fists over her mouth.

She heard nothing for what felt like forever and wondered if he'd gone all the way down to the parking area. If so, she could stay in this hiding spot all night. But she had no idea what time the taverna workers and tourists began arriving. Probably not until late morning. He could easily come looking for her, and find her, when it got light. She had to figure a way out of here.

"Splash, please!" he called again. She could tell by the acoustics of his voice that he'd passed the home she was in and was farther down the mountain. "I'm so sorry! It was a really dumb joke!"

He hadn't seen or heard her but unfortunately now she was trapped. There was no way for her to get down past him. She had a sudden chilling insight to what the women of Kremos must have felt as they knew they couldn't head down the mountain but heading farther up only meant a precipice over which they'd be forced to throw themselves.

A small side of her brain began to poke her with doubts—had he really been joking around? She knew he could be clumsy and inappropriate. Was he capable of a *joke* that he must have known would scare her to death? But she was trembling too badly with fear, the kind of fear that kicks in for survival.

"Alright, Splash," he called out. "I'm going to leave you here. I'm not staying here all night and that guy Elias should be here soon. Maybe he'll talk you down. I had no idea a bad joke like that would affect you so much!"

There was something tinny in his voice, the kind of flat awkwardness you hear with bad actors. He was lying. Every fiber of her knew it. She buried her face in her flat palms, trying to further muffle her breathing, trying to wrap her head around why Logan wanted her dead.

And then it dropped into her brain. Fully formed.

You going to write about this, Splash?

Oh my God, she thought. *Oh my God.*

He wants the Dexter Hunt story!

Logan sure as hell did believe her about Hunt having alien DNA, about his plan to make an alien-human hybrid. Not for a moment did he think that Hunt had been spinning a hoax. He believed every word and he wanted the story for himself. Unlike Maddie, he had no qualms about publishing off-the-record material. He had no qualms about the people of Kyrie and their dependence on the billionaire. All he cared about was the story.

He'd been the one coming into her studio, trying to get into her computer. Trying to see what kind of story she might have dug up. How had she thought for a second anyone else would have done it? He had the prime motive and the perfect opportunity. Right next door, he knew precisely when she wasn't around.

For several minutes she heard nothing but the thick pumping of her blood in her ears, so loud she was certain Logan would trace it right to her hiding spot. Then she heard the soft stomping of footfalls over the stone steps. He was coming back up the mountain. He must have deduced she couldn't have gone very far and would have done exactly what she did—duck inside one of the homes.

Trembling uncontrollably, she watched a beam of light hit the pathway right outside the home's open doorway. She was torn between moving deeper into the home in case he directed the beam into the room and scoured its corners, and not wanting to move in case she hit something hidden in the dark and made noise.

"Maddie," he called out again. The way he didn't loudly project his voice let her know that he'd concluded she was nearby. "I am telling you that was a bad joke. I'm scared and I fucked up. You're the last person I'd want to hurt. Listen, you might as well know I'm in love with you. I have been for a long time."

White light from his cell phone briefly flashed inside of the doorway of the home. She froze, crouched and rigid in the dark, hands flat up against her face trying to suppress any sound that might escape her nose or mouth.

"I don't know what I was thinking back there. I thought you'd get a laugh out of it but of course you wouldn't. I'm so stupid." There was silence but she could sense him, he was right on the path outside of the home. "You don't have to love me back or anything like that. But I feel like I should tell you because I need you to know that I would *never* hurt you, okay? Never."

The last part of his appeal sounded farther away than the beginning of it, leading her to believe he had slowly moved back up the mountainside. Should she slip out and down the pathway? How quietly could she run? What if one of those fucking cats came to a hiding spot farther down and gave away her location?

She tried to remember whether he'd taken the car keys with him or had left them in the car but didn't know. If only he wasn't so damn hefty and muscular. She felt she would have a fighting chance otherwise.

Prying her hands from her face, she looked around

trying to see if there was any weapon she could grab but the room was so dark all she could distinguish were shadow forms that could be anything.

She purposely clawed on the dirt floor, feeling around for a rock. It wasn't long before her right hand curved around one about the size of a large apple. She clutched it, weaponized it in her palm.

"Maddie?!" he called. She could tell that he was even farther up the mountain. Far enough that she could slip out and he wouldn't see her. Very slowly, she unfurled from her crouched position, fingers bowed so tightly over the rock they began to ache.

She was shaking with fear and adrenaline and wasn't certain she'd be capable of hitting him in the head. He was much taller than she was, and her trembling hands would make it difficult to solidly land the rock. Her best bet was to keep away from him; she might be able to outrun him but she was never going to be able to out-fight him.

Worried she'd get trapped inside the room, she moved stealthily toward the opening, her heart hammering so hard against her chest that she worried she might pass out. She stopped at the wall near the opening and listened.

"Maddie, I don't know what else to say. I deserved to be bit. If you come out, you can punch me in the face. Please, I'm getting worried!"

She curved her hand around the stone wall then hurried out and fled down the path, trying to keep control of her raspy, shallow breathing. Suddenly, she was flying through the air and she landed hard on the stone stairs. The back of her skull hit solid rock and for several moments everything was gone. All hope. The pain seared through her skull as she stared at the starry sky.

She'd cried out when she landed, and was now sprawled in the middle of the pathway. The rock was gone from her hand. She didn't think she could even stand. He was going to be looming over her any moment, and could easily drag her up the mountain and fling her over the cliff. Or maybe he'd strangle her. It was over, over.

The fight was over. Life was over. Why hadn't she stayed in the home where she was safe? Why had she taken this chance? Why hadn't she run slower, more carefully?

Something touched her hand, flesh on her flesh. Unable to control herself, she made a small scream of fear. Logan. He'd come back and had knelt down beside her. It occurred to her to play dead so she tightly shut her eyes but her chest was still rising and falling with her panting, rapid breaths. He would know she wasn't dead.

"Come quick," the voice said. "Hurry. Follow me."

It was a woman's voice. Maddie tried to open her eyes but the pain stabbing inside her skull like a hot poker made it difficult.

The hand was pulling at her, pulling hard.

"Hurry, Miss. Hurry. He's coming back."

Maddie woozily sat up and looked at the source of the voice, the source of the hand on her hand. A young woman was standing next to her.

In the dark, and with Maddie's head blaring with

pain, she couldn't tell what the woman looked like—only registered that she was young, maybe in her late teens, and her dress was white.

"Follow me," the young woman whispered loudly and urgently. "Hurry. He's coming."

Maddie nodded, which only made her head hurt more, and she managed to stand. The woman kept a tight hold on her hand and led her down the stone path. Then the woman abruptly veered into the open archway of a stone house. Inside, she grabbed a votive candle that was flickering brightly on a makeshift memorial.

"This way," she said. "Don't make a sound."

Maddie followed her, absolutely astonished that people lived here still. Or perhaps the woman owned the taverna, and had come back to do some work, heard Logan up in the village and had come to investigate. She saw what appeared to be a dark wooden door and as the woman opened it, it scraped and creaked.

"Careful," the young woman said. "Steps."

"Where are we going?" Maddie asked, her voice slightly slurry. She also felt her eyesight was blurred, but it was difficult to tell in the dark, and she was having trouble feeling balanced, staggering a little from side to side, not knowing if this meant the staircase was lopsided or if there was something really wrong with her.

"Ssh! Follow. Take care."

Maddie followed the strange woman down steep stone steps. All around them was a stone tunnel, dark and festering with damp, smelling of water, soil, and mildew. The passage was so narrow she could keep her hands on the walls for balance. The farther down they went, the more the wet cold seeped into Maddie's bones.

They came to an opening in the stone tunnel, where the ceiling rose up high above them. Maddie realized they hadn't descended into a basement, but into a cave.

The young woman turned and asked, "Do you have food?"

The candle illuminated her face. Maddie could see she was definitely in her late teens, perhaps early twenties. She had on a thick, white headband with wild, black curls spinning all around it. Her white dress—what Maddie could see of it—looked almost like a nightgown. Part of the charm of the island had been the elderly women in their black traditional Greek dress, a look from another time, but Maddie hadn't seen any of the young women in anything but modern clothes. Until now.

"No, I'm sorry," Maddie said, speaking slowly and quietly as every word drove a nail of pain through her skull. "No food."

The woman turned back around and moved deeper into the cave. Maddie stood watching as she bent to the floor. When she stood back up, she was holding a bundle of white cloth. "I gave him laudanum to keep him quiet," she said, whispering urgently. "But I've run out."

To her astonishment, Maddie realized inside of the white wrapping was a tiny baby. She could barely see its still little face peeking out of the folds of the swaddling.

"What—why do you…" She couldn't process what she was seeing. "Is that… ? Oh my God. That's a baby."

"Ssh! The barbarians are here," the woman hissed.

"They blasted down the walls of my village and took my husband out to sea to sell him at the slave markets. Oh, my poor dear husband. His fate is worse than mine. To be killed is far better than to be enslaved. I grabbed my son and got away. I ran to the monastery, but when I arrived—" She violently shook her head and covered her mouth with her hand. "—They'd killed all who'd sought sanctuary. The dead were piled on the grounds, slaughtered like goats. I ran and ran through the forest and found some who were coming here to Kremos to hide in the caves. I don't know where they are now. What is the news? What village are you from?"

Hell's Kitchen, Maddie almost said, but couldn't speak. She was obviously in some long, convoluted, spectacularly realistic hallucination and could only wonder if she was lying on the stone pathway, unconscious. Or perhaps the hallucination stretched back even farther, and even Logan trying to push her off the cliff had been part of it.

When did it start? What terrible nightmare was she in and how could she escape from it? She knew she had vivid dreams in the warm climate but not *this* vivid. The chill dampness shuddered along her neck, and she could smell the festering mold of the cave. She never recalled having smells in her dreams. Or feeling hot or cold.

"You dress rather like a pirate," the young woman said, taking in Maddie's black leggings, black t-shirt, and light gray nylon jacket. Then, suddenly nervous: "You cannot be a pirate, can you? A woman?"

"No, not a pirate," Maddie said. "I guarantee you that."

"That is good." She sighed, seemingly relieved at this news. "I found water in a cave pool but how long can we stay here without food?" She touched her bare throat, her white garment stretched flat across her chest. "How long can my child survive? I'm running out of sustenance for him. When he awakens, he'll cry and they'll find us. Good lady, should I smother him?" Her expression was a mask of torment.

Maddie had no idea what to say to this, so she asked, "What is your name?"

"Sofia Doukas from Yastichoria."

Maddie's mouth slowly dropped open. Of course, of course! She was dreaming about Sofia, Elias' ancestor. Because Maddie was at Kremos, where Sofia had died. When she'd fallen against the stone pathway, she must have cracked her head and was currently unconscious.

"And you, good lady? Do I know your kin?"

"I don't think so," she said. "I'm Maddie."

The strangeness of the circumstances made her forget about the pain in her head. She walked closer to Sofia, and put out her arms for the baby, thinking the young mother might need a break from holding him. She now knew the baby must be a boy—must be Constantine Doukas.

Gently, Sofia handed the baby over and Maddie stared into his small, sleeping face. His eyes were puffy slits, his long thatch of hair jet black. He was perfectly still and Maddie wondered if he'd been drugged to the point of death.

Placing her palm under the swaddling, she felt the tiny rise and fall of his chest. He appeared no more than a few months old, maybe less. She couldn't imagine giving birth and all that entailed and then somehow finding the physical strength to flee up a mountain.

The baby made a small sighing sound, letting Maddie know for certain he was alive. She stood very gingerly bouncing the baby, who weighed almost nothing at all.

"You have a child?" Sofia whispered, moving closer.

"No."

"You are fortunate. One less thing to worry about."

Sofia began pacing again, gnawing on one finger. Maddie couldn't believe all that this girl had been through. Having her husband taken away to who knows where, and now here in this cold, dark cave with no way to survive and a baby that might wake up any moment and start screaming.

What an unspeakable thing to have to contemplate —killing your own child so that he wouldn't cry. Or killing yourself and him so that you wouldn't be taken captive. Maddie was full of contempt for every moment she'd ever wasted being gloomy over things that were nothing compared to this, nothing compared to the hell that Sofia was in.

"Sofia," she said. "We can stay here for the night but in the morning the workers will come to the taverna. Then we can sneak out and run down and ask for help."

"My lady, they spared some workers in Yastichoria but not the nobles. My father was dragged out by his hair and hanged in the square. My mother was beheaded right in front of me. These are heathens of the most atrocious order. They are not human. There is nothing to do but wait and hope they leave once they've stripped every house of worship down to the floorboards and slaked their thirst for blood. Why always the endless killing? A year or two will pass in peace and then again more will come and kill. When does it ever end? Why do men only want to kill and kill and keep killing? I would have jumped long ago but for my son."

She began softly weeping. Trying to comfort her, Maddie carefully handed over the bundle.

"Is his name Constantine?"

"Yes," she sniffed. "Do you know us?"

"I do. Listen. He'll survive. He'll go on to have children, and those children will have children."

"Are you a prophetess?" Sofia asked, choking down tears. "Can you for-foretell the-the future?"

"Yes. I want you to know that your baby will survive, okay? You can be sure of that."

The candle on the ground was flickering feebly, giving barely enough light for Maddie to see what Sofia looked like—a strong nose and wide, thin mouth, and large, dark eyes that were glistening with fear, exhaustion, and resignation.

Maddie had read that the women of Kyrie were renowned for their extraordinary beauty—something in the water or the altitude that gave them clear, glowing skin; bold features; and statuesque shapes. Sofia had all that but her expression was too stricken with horror to be beautiful.

"Will I survive, dear Maddie?" she choked out.

Maddie said nothing, unable to bring herself to tell

306

Sofia that she would not. Sofia seemed to understand what the silence meant.

"Who will take care of him? Will he know of me?"

Maddie only stared at the young woman's agonized face. Maddie had no answer for her, and she didn't want to lie.

"Does the killing ever end? Does peace ever reign?"

"Yes, it does," Maddie said. "At least in this land."

"Oh, how I wish I could see it. I can't imagine it. It seems like heaven to exist without killing."

This news seemed to calm her and she stared at her sleeping baby while gently swaying him, then said, very softly, "Will you survive, dear Maddie?"

Maddie paused for a long time, watching the baby too, before she said, "I don't know."

* * *

MADDIE WASN'T sure how much time had passed—maybe an hour—but she felt as if she was in a timeless place. It seemed odd that a dream could last so long and have such eternal stretches of not doing anything. She was scrunched down on the cold, hard floor as Sofia stood staring out over the cave's opening onto the deep violet, starry sky beyond.

Perhaps this was not a dream at all, but a loop in time. Or Sofia was a spirit, doomed to haunt the scene of her horrific last days. If so, why was the baby Constantine here? According to Elias, the baby had survived. And why would Sofia be speaking English? Perhaps she wasn't. Perhaps the pair of them understood each other because, in this time-loop, they were the same—both women being hunted by men.

"I'm so hungry," Sofia moaned. "I'll have no choice but to go out at daybreak and search for fruit and olives."

"In the morning, we'll get food, definitely," Maddie said.

The idea of staying in the cave all night was dreadful but she had no choice. Whatever was happening, real or not, she couldn't bring herself to go out and risk running into Logan. When he'd tried to push her off the cliff—that had been stunningly real.

She would never forget how sudden and unexpected his movement had been, with what swift and cruel power he'd aimed her toward the sheer drop of the mountain as her feet had scraped impotently against the dirt and gravel.

It hadn't been any kind of joke. Every hair on her body prickled with the too-clear memory of it. Yet on another level, it was almost impossible to reconcile the man who would do that with the man who'd so tenderly hugged her back at his studio. The man she'd been convinced was the only person she could trust on Kyrie. The man she'd worked with for years. The man she'd once spent an intimate night with.

Sure, he'd always been annoying, but in truth, she'd found his brassy, provoking ways kind of attractive. She couldn't have ever guessed he was capable of what she knew on a bone-deep level he'd tried to do. Her heart rate wouldn't have exploded if it had only been a joke. She wouldn't have found the animal determination to sink her teeth into his flesh. Her mind may have been slow to catch on, but her body knew she was only several feet away from death, and it had instinctually reacted.

"Will you do me a favor, dear Maddie?" Sofia asked, making her way over to the side of the cave where Maddie crouched down trying to conserve body heat, her light jacket failing to keep out the cold damp. She was so thankful she'd worn long leggings. "If it is true that my son survives, will you... protect him?" Sofia continued. "If possible, will you raise him as your own so that he's not raised by the heathens?"

How could Maddie express to a young woman doomed to die that the person she was currently speaking with didn't live in the same century that Sofia did? That, in fact, all of this was in Maddie's imagination?

But none of that mattered because everything was perfectly real—the relentless cave chill, the surreal darkness broken only by the weakening light of the votive candle, the earthy smell of the cave, and Sofia's primal urgency to save her child.

"Yes," Maddie said. "I'll protect him."

Sofia was fiddling with something on her neck. The next thing Maddie knew, the young mother was handing her a cross pendant. It was about five inches in length, hanging on a thin loop.

"Take this," she said. "My mother gave it to me for protection but I no longer need it. Everyone I love is dead or gone except my son."

Maddie caressed the cross. It was heavy in her palm. In the dark, she could see it was silver and as her thumb traced its surface, she felt it was carved with intricate details. Although not actively religious, Maddie had been raised Christian, and even briefly attended Sunday school as a child. She felt the unmistakable shape of the Christ hanging on the cross. She wanted to tell Sofia that she couldn't possibly take such a personal effect but knew it comforted the young woman to hand it over, so she said, "Thank you. I'll take care of it."

"Now dear Maddie," Sofia said, peering down into the swaddling. "Constantine is stirring. Within moments, he'll begin crying and alert the barbarians to our hiding place. I don't wish to put you in danger, and refuse to allow him to be taken and raised as one of their own, where he'll be trained to despise and slaughter his own people."

Maddie didn't like the sound of this, it had the ring of a goodbye speech.

"I trust your prediction that he'll go on to have children of his own, and their children will have children, and in time our beautiful Kyrie will be free of carnage. To have that future, I know what I must do."

"Listen," Maddie said, struggling to stand on the uneven, craggy floor. "Just stay here until morning. Then other people will come. People who work at the taverna. And tourists."

Why was she trying to talk a dead woman out of her death? It made no sense. But Maddie clung to the hope that somehow their two worlds would continue to unite, and Sofia would survive, giving birth to a future that was similar in outcome but different in its journey to that outcome.

A wailing cry pierced the silence of the cave. Constantine had awakened. His cry was louder than Maddie had anticipated, given he was apparently drugged. She had the strong urge to reach over and clasp her hand over his mouth.

She and Sofia made terrified eye contact for one long moment before Sofia drew away and was moving inexorably towards the cave's opening. Beyond that was a black abyss that was only a slightly darker shade of black than the cave, on which Maddie could see the fabric of the sky pin-pricked with millions of white stars.

"Wait!" she yelled, but Sofia's white gown was nowhere to be seen and the cry of the baby had quickly faded. Maddie's gut was nauseous with the certainty that Sofia had jumped out of the cave, which must be on the edge of a cliff. But she didn't dare move towards the opening as it was so dark, she feared she might step into it by mistake.

She shivered down to the cold, hard floor, wilted flat onto it, prostrated with heavy grief, feeling as Sofia must have felt as she plunged to her death, free-falling through the black night.

"Maddie?"

She froze, listening.

"You okay? What happened?"

She recognized the voice. Logan.

Her first instinct was to open her eyes but instantly followed a second instinct.

Play dead.

Play dead.

He was silent but she could sense him standing above her.

Don't open your eyes. Try not to breathe. Let him think you're unconscious.

Then she felt his hands slide underneath her and she was being lifted off the ground. Her heart hammered loudly in her ears; he drew her body against him as she remained limp.

He's taking me to the edge. He's going to throw me over.

Maddie's fingers curled around Sofia's cross pendant. She was careful not to move her hand in case Logan felt it, just her fingers. The cross was secure in her palm. It was hard, solid, metallic, with sharp edges.

"Maddie," he sighed. "What kind of reporter are you that you'd let the biggest story in the world go? It makes no sense. None at all."

Up, up, up, they were moving up the mountain. Her face was squashed against his barrel-chest, one arm draped over her stomach, the other spread behind his arm. She had to time it precisely. She had to wait until they were close to the drop-off, until he was about to hurl her over. But if she waited too long, she was doomed. And there was no way to open her eyes, turn her face, to see exactly where she was.

Her breath was coursing in and out of her lungs fast and shallow, hyperventilating. He must know she was conscious—yet it was so dark and he was lost in his own world. She bounced slightly with the movement of his legs up the stone pathway. She would have to pay careful attention to his legs, to when they were no longer climbing.

Soon, the ground leveled out and she stopped being shuffled up and down. They'd come to the top of the mountain. He was moving forward, towards the edge. She had to do it at the exact right moment. One moment too soon and he'd gain control of her. One moment too late and she'd be free-falling through the black night like Sofia.

Her fingers tightened on the cross.

"This is a terrible thing you're making me do, Splash," he said.

She felt him slow as if he was approaching the edge; his arms pulled her forward as if preparing to roll her down them, down into the abyss.

Now, she thought. *NOW!*

She came awake, pushing one hand on his chest and the other pulling back, aiming for his eye but unable to see much of anything, plunging her arm down with all of her might, drawing from every moment she'd ever spent doing push-ups or pulling weights in the gym. She could never out-muscle him, but she had the element of surprise and was level with his most vulnerable areas. Cross gripped in her hand, she launched both arms down with as much power as she had, slamming the base of the cross into his eye.

He screamed and she instantly was dropped to the ground. The fall stunned her into paralysis. Nauseatingly, she felt she'd hit the end of her spine in such a way that she was permanently paralyzed. The pain flared up her spine and snapped like fire at the base of her neck.

He continued to scream agonizingly, not sounding anything like the man she knew. She must have been more successful than she could have hoped, must have stabbed him directly in the eye.

There was no more time to wonder how or where she might have damaged herself, so she tried to pull forward and was able to half-stand. She staggered toward his silhouette, threw herself at his bulk, collided with it, and leapt backwards to the ground.

His tortured scream faded as she scrambled away from the edge while the dirt loosened its spread under her feet and she heard the sound of rock hitting rock echoing far below.

Chapter Thirty-Four

"*M*addie. It *is* you."

Elias crossed the hospital room, his expression one of shock and confusion. There were other patients in the room, blocked off by curtains. At the side of her bed, he looked down, speechless.

Maddie had been in the hospital for several hours, and any time a female under forty approached her—whether it was to help get her into the X-ray machine (the same one Dexter Hunt had paid for, no doubt), to take her blood, or to give her pills that mercifully floated her above the sizzling pain in her spine—she would say, "Do you know Elias Doukas?"

Eventually, the eyes of one of the women—the prettiest one—widened in recognition. Maddie asked her to please get in touch with Elias. To tell him that his friend Maddie was in the hospital.

"What happened?" he asked.

"It's such a long story," she sighed out, slightly slurry

from the pain tablets. "The short version is that my friend from New York tried to kill me."

"Athena?!" he gasped.

"No, no. Not her. A different friend."

"I don't understand," he said.

A nurse entered with a small stool, said something in Greek to him, and set it down behind him. The hospital was a series of lemon-yellow squat buildings along the water in the *chora*. Maddie had lain all night on the craggy peak of Kremos, in too much pain to walk back down the mountain and to see if Logan had left the keys in the rental car.

She was sure she had shattered her spine, though she could still move her toes so she was fairly certain she wasn't paralyzed. Still, she was tortured all night by the idea of what the fall from Logan's arms had done to her.

As for Logan, at first, all she could think when she heard him go over the side of the cliff was, *Serves you right, motherfucker.* But throughout the course of the excruciating night, guilt began to fester—deep, sharp, and inexplicable.

He'd tried to kill her, twice. Yet the guilt was so profound, so thick and physical, she felt it eating away inside her veins like poison. All night it gnawed at her, the guilt and pain, until a couple of tourists stumbled upon her in the morning and called for help.

She didn't know if she would ever get over it. Was there anything else she could have done? Could she have stabbed him, then run away? No, after she fell from his arms, she could barely move. If she hadn't found the strength to push him over, he would have merely picked her up again and this time finished the job.

But the vision of his parents came to her mind. She'd never met them but assumed that, like most parents, they not only loved their son but would not see him capable of being a killer. They would not believe her version of events. Neither would his friends. She wondered if anyone at *Wealthy* would either. He'd been popular at work. Her, not so much.

An X-ray at the hospital showed she hadn't broken her spine. She had severely bruised it, something that could be as painful, even more painful, as a break. She also had a concussion. She could only hope these injuries would prove there had been a struggle on the mountain—and that she'd been in his arms and he'd dropped her when she stabbed him. Why else would she have stabbed him in the eye unless she'd been in imminent danger and how else could she have reached his eye unless he was holding her in his arms? And why else would he be holding her in his arms unless he'd intended to throw her over?

She realized she would have to tell police everything, including Dexter Hunt's alien baby plan. She'd have to give them one hell of a great motive for Logan to want to kill her.

Having no phone and no one's phone number memorized, she'd hit on her plan of asking every youngish female if they knew Elias. He'd lived on the island his entire life, and he certainly got around in terms of dating. Eventually, she figured, she'd find a girl who knew him. And she did.

"He tried to throw me off the cliff at Kremos," she told him.

"Kremos?" Elias gasped again.

"Yes, like I said, it's a long story. But he convinced me you wanted to meet us there."

Elias sank onto the little metal stool, his hand dramatically at his chest. "Me?" he breathed. "Why me?"

"Elias, I don't have it in me to tell this whole story. Please do me a favor. You see those lockers over there?" She weakly pointed to the far wall. "I'm locker number ten."

She slipped off her key ring wrist coil and handed it to him. Inside the locker were her clothes, which hospital staff had locked up after undressing her and slipping on her nightgown.

"Please open the bag in there and get out my black leggings. Go into the right pocket. There's something in there I need you to see."

"Alright, yes, Maddie," he said, dazedly, doing as he was told. A minute later, he was back, bearing the silver cross pendant in his hand.

"I have no idea how criminal investigations work on Kyrie," she said. "But I killed a man last night. He gave me no choice in the matter. But the only reason I was able to do it is because I was given that cross pendant."

"Yes, Maddie," he said, still looking stunned.

"Come here, I need to be quiet."

He sat and pulled the little stool closer to her.

"Elias, do you recognize that cross? Have you ever seen it?"

"Yes, Maddie. It belong to my family. I found it in my grandmother's jewel box after she died and my mother said I could have it."

"Oh my God," Maddie groaned, sinking back and staring at the white fluorescent-lighted ceiling. So it was true. Everything was true. Everything *had* happened. She hadn't imagined any of it. It hadn't been a hallucination induced by her concussion.

She'd *met* Sofia Doukas and baby Constantine in a cave at Kremos. Sofia had really handed her the cross pendant—had saved her life.

It had not been a hallucination but a kink in time.

Unable to speak, she kept staring at the ceiling until Elias said, "Maddie?"

"She gave it to me," she said.

"Who gave it to you?"

"Sofia Doukas. I was in a cave with her and Constantine. I watched her jump."

"Oh, dear Maddie," Elias said, reaching out to fold one hand over hers.

"That's what she kept calling me. 'Dear Maddie.'" She smiled, dragging her gaze from the ceiling to glance at Elias. "She was so young, so scared. She loved her baby so much. I told her he'd survive. And then—then she handed me the cross, and went over when he began to cry. She was worried the barbarians—that's what she called them—would hear him and find us. I used the cross to stab Logan in the eye."

"Loh-gawn?"

"The man who tried to kill me. Elias, I was on the ground all night long and in the morning a couple who were sightseeing found me. I put the cross in my pocket. Two policemen came here earlier but they went to find an interpreter. I assume when they return that they'll take the cross. It's evidence."

"Should I take the cross with me?" he asked.

"No, no. I don't want to do anything that will get me into more trouble than I'm already in."

"My friend Tomazos is lawyer. Best on island. I'll call him."

"Good. Thank you." She reached out for the pendant and he handed it to her. She clutched it tightly to her chest, caressing it.

"I held on to it all night," she said. "Squeezing it tight. Praying… praying to Sofia, not to God. Asking her to help me get through the night. If I did, I promised her I would do everything she asked of me. I'd make sure Constantine was protected—but I assume he's long dead."

"Constantine? That is my great-great-great-great-grandfather. Maddie, I named after him. Constantine Elias. That my name."

"Oh, wow," Maddie breathed. "Of course it is." She melted into a smile, the drugs had thankfully kicked in a while ago and she was riding their peak of soothing bliss.

"I'm so happy I give you cross," he said. "I was not sure you would want it, so I secretly put it inside your pocket when you on the boat back from Volinos."

Maddie's blissful smile slowly deteriorated; she could feel it slipping back down into a puzzled line. "Sorry?" she asked.

"On the boat, you have your jacket on the seat. When you look away, I take off my cross—" He made a motion of unlooping the pendant from around his neck. "—and put it in your pocket. I feel you need protection. Something strong tell me, she need protection. So I do it."

"Are—are you sure this is the same cross?"

"Oh, yes." He leaned over. "You see there?" He pointed at a string of Greek letters etched across the top of the cross. "That say St. Demetrios. The saint of protection. It definitely my cross." He smiled patiently, as if talking to someone who wasn't all there.

"Did your grandmother get this from her mother? It was passed down through the family?"

He shrugged. "I don't know. St. Demetrios crosses in shops all over the island."

Holding the pendant, she stared and stared at the ceiling, then giggled in shocked embarrassment.

"You gave this to me. You put it in my jacket."

"Yes, but you not mad, no? It did protect you, yes?"

"That's true, it did."

"And you dream of Sofia Doukas."

"Yes, I guess I did. Elias, do you know how her parents died?"

"I know they were killed. That all I know."

Maddie sighed. It wasn't right to burden Elias with the details of the gruesome murders of his ancestors. She could do more research later; see if there was any way of verifying what Sofia had said about how her parents had died. If she could crosscheck what Sofia had told her in the dream with real life, that would go a long way towards proving this profound vision hadn't been merely in her imagination, but had been something unexplainable, something mystical.

"Elias," she croaked.

"Yes, my dear Maddie?"

"Come closer," she said.

She was getting sleepy, the drugs deepening their hold, and she didn't have the strength to speak loudly. Plus, she knew other people were in the room. Behind the curtains on either side of her were other patients.

One was quiet, only occasional clearing of the throat or murmuring to a nurse. But the other one was suffering something badly and had cried out many times over the past few hours.

At first, before Maddie had become certain that the voice belonged to an older woman, she'd begun to wonder, in her drug-induced half-sleep, if the curtained-off patient was Logan. Logan who'd survived the drop from the mountain. She couldn't decide how she felt about that.

On the one hand, it would let her off the hook. She would no longer be a criminal and could simply slip back into her old life.

On the other, she felt that Logan would never give up trying to kill her. That when the lights went out, he'd lurch up from his hospital bed, stagger over, and strangle her.

Maddie didn't want either patient to hear her, so she gestured to Elias, who leaned even more over her bed. It was time to be honest. With everything that had happened, there was no way to keep it secret any longer, no point in it.

"Closer," she said. His cheek was almost on hers; his hand wrapped around her right hand, the one still holding the cross pendant.

The familiar, calming, sensuous scent of him. How happy she was that he'd come for her when she'd asked, it made things so much easier. She had to say it all before the police came back and perhaps ordered him to leave.

She'd been released from so much since she came to this magical island, released from the painful parts of her past. Now she could say what she wanted to say, could live the life she wanted to live.

"I need to tell you something," she said.

"Tell me, Maddie."

"Elias," she whispered, brushing her mouth against his ear. "Find the number for *Wealthy* magazine. In New York." She gripped his hand tighter and smiled. "I have one hell of a story for them."

Chapter Thirty-Five

GLENDA

*N*aturally, it's up to me to fix everything. What was he thinking with this 12-year-old business? How would that have looked?

I admit, I fell under the sway of her. I'd never seen a 12-year-old who looked like that. Face of an angel. Stopped your breath. A miracle coming out looking like that. A genetic miracle. But did you see the mother? Nothing to write home about. What does that tell you? Genes are no guarantee.

Then what does he do? Drinks and dinner with a reporter. Inviting her to sleep over. Bringing her down to the pink cove and losing his mind.

No doubt the story will be all over the news within days. Maybe less than days. Then what? The backers pull out. We're swarmed with media.

All of the things we feared would happen—too much attention, scrutiny, rivals bribing the government, public whipped into their usual frenzied, pseudo-moralistic outrage, and the laws enacted to stop everything.

What is wrong with him? And the bigger question, why am I working for him and not vice versa?

"Dex," I said, sitting across from his desk. He looks exhausted, pained, his square jaw seeming like it could cut glass.

Normally, he's so inscrutable that I'm the only one who can tell what he's thinking but this time it's obvious for all to see. He knows he screwed up. A man like Dex isn't used to screwing up.

"We need to push aside these setbacks and forge ahead," I said. "I've already received a call from a backer this morning wondering what was going on over here. He's heard we're having issues."

"There is no issue," he said, obviously disinclined to face reality. "We simply move to the next candidate."

"The 21-year-old? I must disagree. You're obsessed with youth and beauty. Has this disaster not taught you anything?"

"I'm hardly obsessed with youth and beauty, Glenda. The world is."

I leaned over to my briefcase on the floor and pulled out the folder. I placed it in front of him on the desk. He glanced at it warily.

"I'd like you to reconsider," I said.

He barely looked down at the folder, kind of sniffed at it, as if it was something he didn't want to eat. The candidate's number was bold as could be on the top.

"I've considered this profile," he said. I knew he'd say that.

"I said *reconsider*."

He sighed, picked it up and stared apathetically at the printouts inside.

"A lack of divers——"

"Oh, forget your diversity." That came out more scornful than intended, but I was losing patience. "The more diverse a profile, the better the odds that enormous swaths of humanity will hate the hybrid."

"This is incorrect. The models——"

"The models! Did the models tell you that the girl would change her mind? Did the models tell you there's a reporter out there who knows everything?"

"It's off-the-record."

"Are you kidding?" It's my job to remain cool at all times, and it's something I'm good at. But he was beginning to enrage me with this obtuseness. "She's a mediocre reporter whose own magazine won't even promote her. Now she's got the story of the century. She'll run with it. Mark my words." I pointed at the folder that he barely still had open. "This candidate is perfect. Healthy, no mutations. Intelligent, articulate, resilient, emotionally stable, and knows what she wants. It used to be called *good breeding.*"

Dexter put the folder down, and stared stoically at it. It's a shame I can't move ahead without him, but much as I know about people, their DNA is a bit of a mystery.

You see, I dropped out of secondary school—high school for you Americans. It was a waste of time. I wasn't a good student. Hated sitting there listening to people who hadn't gotten anywhere in life telling me what to do. My father wasn't happy, but he understood. After all, he'd never gone to school past the eighth grade, because that's when the war came. He managed to start over, a child all alone in a foreign country, and make something of himself. I did get his genes, at least.

"I tell you what," Dex said. "Circumstances have obviously changed. We're in a different position than even a day ago. If she comes here, I'll spend a little time with her. Make no promises, Glenda. Hear me? *No* promises. But if she comes, we'll get to know each other better, and I'll make a decision."

"The backers are getting restless. That reporter is out there."

"This is bad movie dialogue." He waved his hand dismissively. By God, he was a toad sometimes.

"Dex, you need to figure this out fast. She's perfect. She's willing. She's nearby. And importantly, she knows how to keep her mouth shut. She knows how to take direction."

"I've said my piece. You should know I don't repeat myself."

With that, he leaned over, holding out the folder with two fingers as if to say, *Take this thing off my hands.*

As I said, I know him. Better than anyone. He's usually incapable of admitting he's wrong. So I'll take this victory. One small step for mankind, one giant leap for Glenda. I also know when to back off and let him think he's in charge. I didn't get into this position by regularly challenging him.

"Understood, Dexter. Thank you for reconsidering. I'll arrange everything."

I went outside on the main terrace to call her. Signals are always better outside. I had already let her know I was going to try again because I didn't want her going anywhere.

Bad movie dialogue. More like saving the movie from being a get-up-and-flee-from-the-cinema flop. Personally, I'd never want some alien spawn with a face that's half mine. Talk about a movie. A *horror* movie, darling! *Invasion of the Body Snatchers.* But apparently some people don't mind it.

"Darling," I said when she picked up, which she did quickly. "It's a go. He's willing to meet with you. I can arrange to pick you up on Kyrie." I stopped to listen to her reaction. At first, she was silent. I knew she hadn't changed her mind; she was just overwhelmed. Then came a small, breathy sound, almost like a giggle. She said how honored she was and to please thank Dexter for her.

Thank Dexter? How about thanking *me*?

"Listen, darling," I said. "It's not definite. But once you get here, you'll enchant him. Tell him everything I told you to say, and use your own considerable charm. Once you're here, face-to-face with him, he'll come around."

Her tone was measured but immensely pleased, I could tell.

"Can you come tonight? Let's get to him before he changes his mind. I'll arrange for his favorite meal and we've got some new cases of Dom, so hopefully that will put him in a good mood."

She could come. Excellent.

"Then I'll let you get ready. I'm excited as well. This will work, I know it will. Oh, no need to thank me."

Damn straight there was a need to thank me. At least she finally got around to it.

"Yes, me too. See you soon. And you may want to dress casual, but *pretty*. Feminine. A summer dress, sweet and coquettish. Perhaps something pink or with flowers."

I stopped so we could both laugh a little. What else can you do? It's laugh or cry.

"You know these men, darling. They get so intimidated by an accomplished woman." I paused so I could phrase it with utmost diplomacy but decided to just come out with it. She didn't get where she was by being thin-skinned.

"Try to look a little more like a college student," I told her. "A little less like the First Lady."

* * *

For more thrillers by C.G. Twiles, please sign up for her newsletter at CGTwiles.com or keep reading.

If you enjoyed this book, it would be much appreciated if you leave a review at your favorite retailer.

Thank you for reading *The Perfect Face*.

More Thrillers by C.G. Twiles

Please request my books at your **local library** or **bookstore**. See CGTwiles.com or my Instagram page for all retailers.

Brooklyn Gothic: *A Modern Gothic Romantic Thriller*

While working in a Gothic mansion, an idealistic young reporter begins to suspect her multimillionaire boss—and lover—is keeping dark secrets.

The Neighbors in Apartment 3D: *A Domestic Suspense Novel*

Cintra suspects her new neighbors have kidnapped a child. But who will believe a compulsive liar?

The Last Star Standing: *A Psychological Thriller*

A forgotten talent show winner has a second chance at success. But first, she'll have to murder the runner-up. How far will Piper go to save her family and reclaim her former glory?

The Little Girl in the Window*: A Psychological Thriller*

At 14, Romy accidentally killed the town's beloved prom queen. Years later, a crisis forces her to return to her rural hometown. Now it seems someone knows her secret—and is determined to make her pay.

The Ghost Wife*: A short tale of suspense*

All Tabitha wants is for her family to accept reality. And the reality is… she's dead. So why are they acting like she's alive?

Neighbors and Other Dangers*: A Psychological Thriller Box Set*

Contains three full-length psychological thrillers at an economical price: *The Neighbors in Apartment 3D*, *The Last Star Standing*, and *The Little Girl in the Window*.

About the Author

C.G. Twiles is the pseudonym for a longtime writer and reporter who has written for some of the world's largest magazines and newspapers.

She enjoys traveling, animals, old houses, ancient history, and cemeteries. She lives in Brooklyn.

Please find her on social media, she'd love to connect!

facebook.com/cgtwiles

instagram.com/cgtwiles

goodreads.com/cgtwiles

bookbub.com/profile/c-g-twiles

Acknowledgments

As always, sincere gratitude to my readers, for without you, there are no books.

Efharisto poli to the people of Greece, especially the island of Chios, for being my muse. I'm no historian, and the historical details in this book, while drawing inspiration from that island's brave and tragic history, shouldn't be taken for rigorous fact.

I would be remiss if I didn't acknowledge the journalists who diligently battled for justice in the Jeffrey Epstein case.

To my friend Liz Alterman, comrade in publishing, and my astute beta reader, Megan Easley-Walsh. To JS Designs for her creativity and patience.

Gratitude to my online support network, especially those at Wide for the Win and Bookstagram.

Made in the USA
Las Vegas, NV
09 February 2024

85495439R00187